# RECLAIMING YANCY

*RECLAIMING YANCY*

JB MARSDEN

SAPPHIRE BOOKS

SALINAS, CALIFORNIA

*Reclaiming Yancy*
Copyright © 2018 by JB Marsden. All rights reserved.

ISBN - 978-1-948232-04-3

This is a work of fiction - names, characters, places, and incidents are the product of the author's imagination or are used fictitiously. Any resemblance to actual persons living or dead, business, events or locales is entirely coincidental.

Editor - Heather Flournoy
Book Design - LJ Reynolds
Cover Design - Treehouse Studio
Cover photo: Joyce Beaulieu

**Sapphire Books Publishing, LLC**
P.O. Box 8142
Salinas, CA 93912
www.sapphirebooks.com

Printed in the United States of America
First Edition – March 2018

This and other Sapphire Books titles can be found at
www.sapphirebooks.com

# Dedication

To my wife, Molly, whose love and encouragement make
my life sing with joy.

# Acknowledgments

At age ten I wrote my first short story, but, because I needed to earn a living, I never became the writer I dreamed of being. Yes, I became an author, but no one read my academic treatises for fun—especially not me. So here I am now, finally publishing my first novel, only because of a small Sapphic army who produced the book you're holding. First, thanks to Chris Svendsen, the publisher at Sapphire Books, who made me giddy to hear that my manuscript had been accepted, leading to champagne toasts with my family, those wine-loving Franco-Americans. Next, Sapphire's editor Nikki Busch, with whom I have surprising things in common, took the time to recommend several constructive resources to improve my novel. Thank you so much for holding my hand and believing in my book. Because of her, I learned to write a novel worthy of publication. Many thanks to Sapphire editor Heather Flournoy. Her gentle and gracious comments, recommendations, and corrections created a safe environment for me to write a much better story. She aerated the writing into a meringue fit for human consumption. Also at Sapphire Books Publishing, thank you to graphic designer Ann McMan, who made my cover stand out from the crowd. To all the other staff at Sapphire who labor to make their authors shine, you are the best.

Next, a string of thank yous to my friends and family. To a long list of writing friends in my former home of Kentucky, where opportunities abounded to take myself seriously as a writer, thanks for your diverse voices, and for giving me the courage to use my voice. To my writing friends elsewhere around the country, thanks for your words, and blessings on our mutual labors. To my sisters, Bonnie, Peg, and Jill, who have always cheered me, even when they didn't understand me. I couldn't have a more loving and supportive family. To my wife, Molly, my love and my biggest fan, thank you for believing in me. She never ceased to be delighted that I was holed up, typing away, nor failed to laugh when her conversations with me went unheard.

# *Chapter One*

Roxie frowned at her best friend. "Why are you being so self-destructive? What the hell, Yancy?"

"You don't get it, do you?" Yancy blew out a big breath.

"Apparently not. I certainly don't understand why you do these Friday nights with people you don't intend to have relationships with, who are only a fling…play time."

"I need it," Yancy said. She paced in front of Roxie. "It's my only outlet. I work my ass off all week long. It's the least I can expect—a little time to blow off steam."

"There are plenty of healthier ways, and you know it, dorkhead," Roxie said in a louder, clipped tone. "I'm really tired of having this conversation with you. It's been nearly five years since Trisha died. You need to move on."

Yancy took two steps closer to Roxie, threatening with a pointed finger. "Don't tell me what I need! And don't tell me what to do." She turned abruptly and slammed out the door of Roxie and Kate's house, stomped to her Rover, and spun out of the drive in a shower of gravel.

"Hey, gal." A medium-height, brown-haired woman with plenty of eye makeup winked at Yancy from down the bar at Spanky's as she sidled up to her. Darkness and the smell of spilled beer enveloped them. "Where you been keeping your handsome self? I've been kind of lonesome without you the last couple weeks." The last was said in a petulant tone, with a pouting lower lip while her curvy body pressed into Yancy. Cheyenne draped an arm around Yancy's waist and kissed her seductively on the lips.

Yancy sighed and deepened the kiss. After pulling back, her eyes slowly followed Cheyenne's body up from the blue boots, past tight jeans covered with silvery bling, up to the frilly pink cowgirl shirt strangling large breasts. She stayed riveted on a great deal of creamy cleavage. "You look good enough to eat."

Yancy's hands pulled her closer, clasping the small of Cheyenne's back, and her lips nestled in her neck and caressed her smooth throat. She dipped lower between the cleavage for a light brush along the soft sides of cushiony breasts. The sight of the twin mounds and the skin she caressed sent Yancy's libido into hyper-drive. Cheyenne put her in a tailspin, got her juices flowing.

Cheyenne smiled crookedly, no doubt knowing the effect she was having on Yancy. Her eyes rested on Yancy's lips that lay a couple inches above hers, while she ground her hips into Yancy's. "Gonna buy me a drink, good looking?" she cooed.

Dressed in jeans and a new white Western shirt, Yancy was, indeed, looking good and ready to do whatever Cheyenne needed from her. She signaled to Carla, tonight's bartender, and received a cold bottle of

High Country Pale Ale for herself and a hard lemonade for Cheyenne. Carla uncapped them and placed them on the sticky bar surface in front of Yancy.

"What brings you to town?" Cheyenne murmured, clinking her bottle to Yancy's.

Yancy ran her left hand down to cup Cheyenne's ass, then took a long pull from her bottle, and whispered in her ear, "You, you sexy thing." She hoped this come-on would help her seduction, but, if truth be told, if Cheyenne acted anything like the last time she saw her, she didn't need much enticing.

Yancy's tongue flicked over Cheyenne's ear and created a groan she could hear even over the noise of the bar's chatter and the twang of guitars tuning up in the band. They drank in silence, with intermittent make-out moments, oblivious to the rest of the bar. Some women chatted in groups sitting at small round tables, others scanned the room for a hookup or just a dance. Spanky's was the place that drew Denver women for "Country Friday Night."

Guitars played the opening rift of a k.d. lang ballad. Yancy grabbed Cheyenne by the hand to drag her onto the small dance floor. They settled against each other. Cheyenne breathed along Yancy's right ear, licked above her collar. Yancy brought Cheyenne close by wedging her knee between Cheyenne's thighs. They swayed to the rhythm. Although Yancy loved to dance and had some smooth moves on the dance floor, dancing was not her chief aim tonight. So, only three dances later, they collected their drinks, drank the final dregs, and clunked the empty bottles on the bar. With a tacit understanding of Cheyenne's wish, Yancy led her out the bar's door. Her breath rasped with her impatience to leave the crowds of women swaying in sexy rhythms on the dance floor.

As soon as they were on the streets in Yancy's Land Rover, Cheyenne nuzzled Yancy's neck. Her hand found Yancy's thigh and began a teasing stroke up to her crotch, catapulting Yancy's center into a hot mess.

Yancy growled as she clutched Cheyenne's hand to break off her distracting touch. Yancy would drive up a tree otherwise. Cheyenne stuck her tongue in Yancy's ear, licking down her earlobe and lower into her neck above the collar of her crisp shirt, then whispered, "Don't worry, lover. We can pick up later where we left off," while she stroked along Yancy's arm.

In fifteen minutes, they arrived at Cheyenne's place. Before getting out of the Rover, Yancy unbuckled her seat belt so she could turn in her seat to face Cheyenne. She leaned over to put her hands on both sides of Cheyenne's head and kissed her hungrily, flicking her tongue deeply while she fondled down that chasm of cleavage. They both began to pant more heavily. Cheyenne pulled the back of Yancy's head to her lips for a crushing kiss.

"Let's get out of here," Cheyenne said as she broke contact and hopped out, slamming the door. Yancy felt burning all along her core, wet and hungry. They hurried to the door of Cheyenne's brick townhouse. Cheyenne fumbled in her purse for the keys, and as soon as she had them in her hand Yancy impatiently grabbed them, unlocked the door, and they tumbled into the foyer. After Yancy ripped it open, Cheyenne's blouse floated to the floor.

Yancy unhooked Cheyenne's lacy bra, then took control over Cheyenne's body, firmly clutching at her bulky breasts, licking and kissing all along her neck and cleavage, then sucking first the left, then the right nipple, in rapid succession. Yancy moaned loudly, eagerly, and needing so much more.

Cheyenne cried out when Yancy unzipped her jeans, pushed them down, ripping her lace panties to her knees. With a feathery touch down her torso and into her wetness, Yancy teased. Pink, fresh skin smelled like expensive lotion and felt like satin to her fingertips. Yancy gasped her need. She nudged Cheyenne into the wall next to the door. Her hand found Cheyenne's sweet, shaved V, its small mound soft and inviting. Still standing, Yancy swept fingers through the folds, found moisture. One finger, then two, entered Cheyenne and pumped rhythmically. Cheyenne growled out, "Oh, fuck me, baby. Yeah, fuck me! I'm so wet for you." She trembled, collapsing into Yancy, biting her neck and clutching at her waist. Both women panted and gasped in rhythm with the strokes.

Perspiration coated Yancy's body in her efforts, her breathing growing increasingly rapid and labored. Cheyenne grabbed at Yancy's shirt and bucked wildly against her. Yancy met her urgency with one of her own, feeling sweat drip between her breasts, her clit throbbing painfully. After some minutes of frenzied action, Cheyenne jerked and spasmed against Yancy, yelling, "Yes, yes. Oh, fuck, yes!"

Just as Cheyenne's jerks began to still, Yancy impulsively fell to her knees and ran her tongue over the wet folds, causing Cheyenne to clutch and moan again. Yancy felt the slightly sweet, post-orgasmic moisture coat her tongue, her chin, and it generated a groan deep within her. Cheyenne trembled and fell forward onto Yancy's mouth, moving her hips with the stroking, licking, and sucking, while pushing Yancy's head deeper. Cheyenne squeaked out high-pitched whimpers that matched the pace of licks and thrusts, her voice rising steadily in intensity.

☙❧❧☙❧

Two hours later, lying in Cheyenne's bed, they both stretched lazily. Yancy took in the sated look on Cheyenne's dreamy face and smirked about what she had been able to do. Cheyenne stroked Yancy's stomach with slow, lazy circles, her head lying on her shoulder, and she exhaled deeply and sleepily. Coming out of the near-coma post-coital fog, reality struck Yancy. She needed to get out of there. She was done for the night.

"I've got to get going." Yancy kissed Cheyenne's hair. Disengaging from her in one swift movement, she leapt from the bed in search of her jeans and shirt, both strewn on the floor of the entryway. She had only been with Cheyenne once before, but found her to be demanding. She couldn't get out fast enough.

Cheyenne hopped out of the bed, threw on a robe, and strode into the living room, watching as Yancy yanked up her jeans and zipped them. "Do you have to run, lover?" She sidled up to Yancy and ran her hands up her arms, around her neck.

Yancy took hold of both hands and tugged them down, pecking Cheyenne quickly on the lips. Her eyes squinted as they drilled into Cheyenne's gray ones. Her words sounded rehearsed and tinny. "You know the drill. This is what it is. I told you the first time, I don't do the staying-over thing. I don't do the girlfriend thing. I don't do the joined-at-the-hip thing." Her breath was quick and rapid, her pulse rising. She had to get away, because she had nothing more to give.

"No one is joining anyone at the hip. Hell, I hate that, too. I'm asking for a little consideration. Is breakfast too much to ask?" Cheyenne countered with her arms across her chest. Her mouth formed a tight line, and her gray eyes squinted back at Yancy.

Yancy sighed in exasperation. "Bye, Cheyenne." She turned away, grabbed her keys off the table in the foyer, and was out the door.

Cheyenne followed her onto the stoop, angrily grabbed at Yancy's arm, and hissed out, "How in the hell am I supposed to get my car from Spanky's?"

Turning to face Cheyenne, Yancy dug her billfold from her back pocket. She thrust a fifty-dollar bill into Cheyenne's fist, then about-faced to stride into the night.

"You son of a bitch!" Cheyenne screamed as Yancy's car door closed.

# Chapter Two

The Triple D Ranch woke early. Cows lowed in the distance, horses whinnied from the corral abutting the horse barn. Yancy tussled with her jeans and sighed loudly. She looked out her bedroom window toward the barn, where Victor, her head wrangler, tossed hay, flake by flake, into the north corral for three horses roaming its confines. She hadn't slept well, again. Her head ached and she felt lethargic. Like many nights, sleeplessness had dogged her. Her mind failed to shut down after she got into bed, so, most nights, she got up to read something boring, like *The Ranching Times*, until her eyes began to close on their own around three in the morning.

Groaning, Yancy tugged on her dusty boots and clomped down the stairs. As she strode through the kitchen to the back door, she called out, "I'm checking on the fence on the south pasture this morning. May not be home for lunch."

Connie, the Triple D's housekeeper and Victor's wife, looked up from cleaning the kitchen counter and placing dishes in the dishwasher. "You didn't have any breakfast either, Yancy. Let me get you some sandwiches or something," she said to Yancy's retreating back. The back door banged shut, and Yancy was already halfway to the horse barn.

Yancy mentally shook her head of its fuzziness to focus on the work at hand. In short order, she brought her Palomino gelding, Marquette, into the barn, and groomed, saddled, and bridled him. She led him out onto the ranch road and adjusted the girth, then mounted him and squeezed her thighs to speed him to the south pasture. After the barn chores, she knew that Victor had left with the truck loaded with fence-mending equipment, so Yancy could begin immediately on the repairs needed where the fence stood vulnerable to further damage from weather or cattle.

Putting Marquette at a relaxed lope, Yancy squinted in the heat of the morning, the sun unrelenting in the plains east of the Colorado Rockies. She noted the dry pasture. Her nose itched from the dust clouds stirred up by Marquette. After a forty-minute ride, she located the pasture fence she was seeking. Next to the most worn area of fence, Victor unloaded wire and other supplies from the ranch's green Ford truck. He looked up and nodded to Yancy as she slowed to a trot, then reined her horse to a halt. She dismounted smoothly and tethered Marquette to a fence post. Without needing to speak to Victor, she picked up the staple removers and started the repairs to a patch of fence just a few feet from the truck.

"I'm going into town to get the truck's new exhaust system installed. You be okay out here without it?" he asked.

Yancy took a moment, looking at him, then the truck. "Sure. I can leave anything I don't use right here for you to pick up later. I'm moving down the fence line for a couple of miles south. That's where the most gaps are. I should be back by early afternoon. Marlene Edwards's lesson today." Yancy winced at the name.

Victor looked at Yancy and smirked. "The boys will check the herd for new calves today and tomorrow. We'll get them all set up with microchips and vaccinations by the end of next week."

"How many so far?"

"Alan and Chuck counted about two dozen since they herded them up to Pine Bluff the last week of March. But they think there's maybe another ten or so about to calve. They didn't do an exact count."

"Sounds about right, by my count, too."

"See you later." Victor started the truck and sent a dust cloud rising in his wake.

Yancy finished the job on the south sections of fence in good time, glad she had brought plenty of water, because the temperature had to be getting into the unseasonable eighties, with a hot wind coming from the southwest. She was glad of the hard work to occupy her time and thoughts. After checking down the fence line to estimate the rest of the work needed, she rode back through the pasture, feeling happily spent and sweaty. As soon as she was in the barn, she groomed Marquette and let him into the paddock, leaving some oats and pumping more water into his trough. She let out a long exhale, wiped her forehead with her handkerchief, and headed into the kitchen.

The house was empty. Connie probably had ridden into town with Victor. The headache that had started that morning still pounded dully, so she got some ibuprofen from a kitchen cabinet and swallowed them down with water. The fridge held a tuna sandwich in a plastic container. She bit into it, standing at the kitchen island that separated it from the great room. She filled her water bottle, then leaving most of the sandwich, grabbed the bottle and sat on the back porch to cool off. She hated air conditioning, even though it had felt pretty good after being out for nearly six hours. She watched the horses swat flies lazily with their tails, then marked a couple of hawks riding the thermals toward the river. Her mind still felt mushy.

The hot air dried her sweaty shirt and arms, and she breathed deeply to prepare herself for her three o'clock Tuesday riding pupil. In this lazy mood, she mused about Marlene Edwards, who made her crazy. She unsuccessfully tried to put the married woman out of her mind, but her body had other ideas. Marlene was the sexiest woman going. She could turn Yancy on with one grin. Well, one grin and a well-placed grope. Yancy smiled at the memory, just as Marlene's BMW crunched the gravel into the yard of the ranch. Yancy rose from her perch and slowly walked to the driver's side with her hands in her pockets.

Marlene smiled widely as she got out of the car. "Hey," she said seductively, thrusting out her breasts as she pulled her expertly bleached-blond hair into a high ponytail. Her makeup was flawless, her lizard-skin riding boots and designer jeans spotless. She ran her hands over Yancy's chest and pecked her lightly with reddened lips. Yancy took in the smooth curves, the lithe body with a trim waist, and dark complexion that countered the hazel eyes, outlined in hints of blue liner. Marlene smelled of her usual perfumed self, her diamond tennis bracelets and large, gem-studded rings exuding suburban Denver wealth.

"Mrs. Edwards." Yancy nodded at her slightly, her lips in a small grin. "Ready for more cantering practice?"

Without replying, Marlene sashayed sexy hips into the horse barn, where the quarter horse she owned stood ready to be groomed and tacked up. After she saddled and bridled her mare, Marlene then proceeded for an hour to work on her cantering technique in the fenced corral used for lessons, with Yancy intermittently voicing observations and suggestions on keeping her back straight or her heels down in the stirrups. Marlene had a tendency to fight against the feel of the horse's body moving under her seat, which Yancy constantly harped on. Today, Marlene concentrated on her riding well enough. When the hour ended, she trotted over to the mounting block, slid off her mare, and turned to Yancy with a question in her eyes.

Marlene gripped the front of Yancy's shirt. Yancy leaned in for a kiss that Marlene returned with even greater fervor. She murmured in Yancy's ear, "James is gone till late tonight."

"And my house is empty."

Marlene ogled Yancy and grabbed her hand, pulling her toward the ranch house.

Marlene's BMW left the Triple D around 5:15 p.m. Yancy, still reclining lazily in bed, knew she should break off seeing Marlene, but, well...the sex rocked. What could a girl do? Marlene was sex on a stick, and free for the taking. What worried Yancy was that Marlene practically had forced her into this affair. And while she wouldn't say no, did she really have a choice when it came to her unruly libido? Yancy didn't like being pushed around, but Marlene presented a dilemma: either give in, or go wanting.

Rubbing her eyes, Yancy reluctantly rose from the bed to get cleaned up for supper, coming out of the shower just as Connie and Victor walked in the door.

"I'm putting supper in the oven," Connie yelled upstairs when the water stopped.

"Yeah, thanks," Yancy yelled back down. "See you tomorrow." She heard Connie and Victor close the front door, after which the house was deathly still. Another night alone on the ranch for Yancy.

༄ ༄ ༄ ༄

On Saturday morning, Yancy carefully dressed in new jeans and an ironed Western shirt. She drove into town and parked in the lot of the Ryan Delaney Clinic for her ten o'clock meeting, entered, and made her way to the board room, a nice but functionally appointed space. It held a shiny walnut table ringed by ten brown vinyl swivel chairs. Against a wall sat a credenza holding food and drinks. Pictures of scenic Babcock County hung on two walls, while on another wall hung a whiteboard for presentations. Large windows overlooked the scenic mountain valley on the fourth wall.

Yancy sat viewing the room with pride, although it didn't bring back her little brother, Ryan, she smiled, remembering his goofiness, still like a boy more than a young man. They played horseshoes a lot in the summer when they weren't racing their horses into the pastures. After he turned eighteen, they drank beer together and drove to Denver to catch the Colorado Rockies lose another game at the then-new Coors Field.

Interrupting Yancy's reverie, Jim McDonald, administrator of the clinic, entered. Jim exuded managerial confidence, his salt-and-pepper hair giving him that touch of handsome found in forty-something guys. He was followed by a stunning woman wearing a pastel-blue skirt suit. "Dr. Lambert, this is Mary Ann Delaney, President of the Valley View Board of Directors. As I explained over the phone when we set up your interview, Valley View manages both clinics as the umbrella nonprofit organization."

Yancy shook herself out of her focus on the doctor's auburn hair and winning smile, and stood. She grinned her approval of the gorgeous doctor, then took her hand and met her green eyes directly. "Very glad you are interested in working with us here, Doctor." Yancy eyed the doctor's healthy rose complexion, the buxom curves, and intelligent eyes. The woman's body rocked. Her face entranced her. Yancy breathed deeply, taking in her essence. *Be professional*, she admonished herself.

The doctor seemed a bit taken aback. Yancy couldn't imagine why. "Good to meet you, Ms. Delaney."

"I hope you enjoyed Jim's tour of the facilities. And call me Yancy, please." Yancy winked and kept holding the doctor's hand while she made firm eye contact with her.

"And I'm Gen," she replied, blushing a little while she extricated her hand.

Yancy was nudged back into the present when Jim announced, "I'll let y'all have some time to talk. We have refreshments on the credenza. Coffee, water, and tea. And blueberry scones, too." He smiled politely. "Come on down to my office after you finish." He glanced at Yancy before he backed out of the room and closed the door.

Yancy directed the doctor to a chair. "What can I get you, Doctor?"

Gen sat. "Coffee and a scone would be lovely, thank you."

Yancy poured two coffees and served Gen one, along with a scone. Gen's skirt had ridden up her thigh when she sat, luring Yancy's eyes to shapely legs, then up to the cream-colored blouse that draped tantalizing curves. Gen quirked her head and raised an eyebrow slightly. Yancy cleared her throat, only slightly embarrassed that her checking out the doctor had been noticed. *This is one classy woman, maybe a tad out of my league. But hell, it makes it more challenging.*

"You're not joining me for a scone?" Gen asked quietly.

"No, thanks. But you will find none better. Connie makes them from scratch. My mother taught her, and they can't be beat."

"Connie?"

"My cook-housekeeper. My mom employs her so I won't be a candidate for one of those 'worst housekeeper' reality shows. She also feeds me pretty well." Yancy used her most winning smile.

Gen smiled. "You don't cook?" she teased.

"I can hardly boil water. Not my thing. But if you like riding on the range, I'll be happy to set you up." Yancy sighed, having a hard time looking away from the doctor's piercing examination with those captivating eyes. Yancy crossed one booted foot over her knee and leaned back into the soft chair. She took a sip of the hot coffee while she got herself under control, cleared her throat, and said softly, "We should probably talk about the medical director job."

"Yes, right." Gen nibbled her scone and returned Yancy's dazzling grin.

For the next twenty-five minutes, Yancy regaled Gen with the history of her family's founding of the Valley View Medical Center and the construction of its two clinics, all stimulated by her brother's death at age twenty-one from leukemia. Yancy felt her sadness coming on again. She shifted in her chair to a more erect posture.

"And I understand you want someone who can develop a program here for family medicine residents from the university medical school? A rural preceptorship?" For Yancy, this was the meat of Gen's experience, and Valley View's reason for flying her to Colorado yesterday from Kentucky.

Yancy shook off her despondent moment, and beamed at Gen. "I know you've had the tour of both the Delaney and the Fielding clinics. The Delaney clinic is where you would have your office, and your practice. The Fielding center is a first-contact office for the outlying ranches. So, you know how well equipped we are. You know medical residents would get an outstanding rural experience. Your Kentucky skills would transfer seamlessly here, I think, even given the different environment. We believe you would be the perfect fit."

By the end of the interview, Yancy had efficiently cited all the arguments for coming to Colorado, and she hoped Gen couldn't think of any reason not to. Yancy's knowledge of rural medical care issues and her hard-won management skills made her a savvy board president, and the credentials of the staff, along with the clinic's good reputation, made her confident that they could lure Dr. Lambert from the University of Kentucky. In addition, the good-looking woman did not leave much not to like.

Yancy grazed Gen's back lightly, leading her to the door, and detected an underlying current between them as soon as her hand touched the doctor. Gen blinked at Yancy, looking a bit dazed. They smiled at each other as Yancy led her to the administrative offices in search of Jim.

Yancy shook Gen's hand, squeezing lightly. "I

have enjoyed meeting you, Doctor. Please let me know if you have any other questions." Yancy handed Gen a professional card. "And you should be hearing from us soon. I think we all would work together very well." Then Yancy gave Gen's body a good casing, grinning one of her come-on grins. Gen did not return the smile.

# Chapter Three

*Genevieve M. Lambert, M.D., M.P.H.*
*University of Kentucky Rural Health Center*
*Department of Family Medicine*
*115 Medical Center Way*
*Lexington, Kentucky 40503*

*Dear Dr. Lambert,*

*It is with great pleasure that the Board of Valley View Medical Center offers you the position of Medical Director for our clinics in Babcock County, Colorado. The contract we agreed upon is enclosed for your signature. Please sign in the marked areas and send it back to the Ryan Delaney Clinic within ten days.*

*Also, we invite you to join the Board in a barbecue to welcome you, shortly after your arrival, to be held at the Triple D Ranch. You will be introduced to the Board members, their spouses, the staff of both clinics, and a few of Valley View Medical Center's major community supporters. We promise the best of relaxed Western hospitality, with music and the best barbecue in Colorado.*

*We hope your remaining time in Kentucky and preparations for coming to Colorado go smoothly. Should you require any assistance with your move, please contact the administrator of Valley View, Jim McDonald, at the phone and email on the letterhead.*

*Sincerely,*
*Mary Anne Delaney, Valley View Medical Center*
*Board President*

Stacy rapped twice on the open door of Gen's office. "Got time for a quick consult?"

Gen looked up from filing her letter of offer and her copy of the completed contract from Colorado, and smiled her brightest at her best friend. "Sure, what've you got?" She signaled for Stacy to find a seat among the packed boxes piled in her office.

Stacy sat down across from Gen at her desk, opened the tablet she was grasping, and listed the symptoms of her patient: a post-hysterectomy, forty-two-year-old woman with stomach pain, lower left quadrant, especially acute at night. No sign of infection, blood work looked good, pelvic exam okay. "Of course, no health insurance, so I'm trying to be conservative with the tests. What do you think? Time for a scan, or should I start with an ultrasound?"

"Yeah, I'd go with the ultrasound to start with. Maybe something that can be followed up with some exploratory surgery, then we can get the folks in insurance to get her on Medicaid at that point. Dot every I, cross every T. She may have some scar tissue and adhesions."

"That was my first instinct, too, especially given the clean blood work."

"Well it could be anything. You know how stomach pain can radiate and really screw up the diagnostic process."

"Sure. Thanks." Stacy began to stand from the chair, then sat back down with an audible exhale.

"Something else?" Gen looked expectantly at

Stacy. The easy question about her patient surely was not the reason Stacy had sought her out.

Stacy's eyes squinted slightly as her mouth quirked up on the left side. "Man, what am I going to do when you are no longer here to bitch with me about the men in the department? To cry in our beer together?"

Gen stood up and pulled Stacy into a light hug. She rested her hip on the edge of her desk. "I don't know what I would have done without you these ten years. Especially when Jack Morris wanted to fire me when he found out that I was seeing Rachel." Gen quirked her lips and Stacy shook her head. "Boy, you gave him hell about his homophobia," Gen said.

"We kicked some ass didn't we, Dr. Lambert?"

"Who's going to help me put on my ass-kicking boots in Colorado?"

"You know, there's this little thing called the smart phone, with chatting and messaging, and all these twenty-first-century marvels," Stacy said.

"Smart aleck." Gen grinned. "But Dan won't appreciate my texts at two a.m. when I'm bitching about losing funding. Or better yet, when we're being sued by the cowboy puffing away at his cigarettes who thinks we missed his lung cancer because we didn't report the tainted water he's *sure* caused it." Gen let out a small groan. "I remember what Jack kept saying about being department chair—having to run interference all hours of the day. I'm going to be medical director of two rural clinics. I am pretty excited, but also kind of trembling in my heels. You've got to promise to be there for me for a few months, kid."

"Don't worry, Dan and I'll have your back. You can text, any time of day or night, he'll understand.

He's not the most sensitive of husbands, but he has his good points. And you know he loves you. Sometimes I see him smirk when you parry with the big guns at the faculty meetings. He celebrated when you and Rachel got together. You were grinning like a Cheshire cat that first year of your residency."

"Yeah, Rachel…she took me on a long and painful ride," Gen sighed, wincing. "To this day, I can barely look another pathologist in the eye without wanting to deck them."

"I know. We held on every step of the way, and you made it to the other side."

"Live and learn, huh, my dear?"

Stacy looked at Gen with tenderness. "Maybe there's a white knight in Colorado waiting for you. Or, you know what I mean, the female equivalent of white knight." She laughed. "Someone who loves you as Gen, not Dr. Lambert. Who takes you as you are, not as eye candy or trophy. You're so good looking. Look at that fresh face, that voluptuous set of curves that can't be hidden by a white coat. And those legs. My short self is so jealous of you sometimes." Stacy chuckled, then quirked her head to the side and became silent. "But, seriously, our friendship won't suffer just because of a couple of flat midwestern states between us. We have too much history."

"Reminiscing just the other day, I remembered good old Dr. Stanley. That time we campaigned to hand out free condoms in the waiting room on the women's clinic days?" Gen bent slightly with laughter.

"My God, he nearly had a stroke. Or when you took me with you to that gay bar in Cincinnati—"

"We ran into those two medical students. What were their names?"

"Sheena?"

"Dina...Dina and Jessie. Those innocent kids from eastern Kentucky. Out on their first date or something. They turned fifteen shades of red."

Tears coursed down Stacy's face as she continued to laugh. "And, of course, they thought we were a couple. I still laugh about us egging them on by dirty dancing!"

"Hey, can I get in on the fun with my two favorite ladies?" Dan rounded the corner and took in the women doubled over with laughter in Gen's office.

"Hi, honey."

"Come on in."

"What's got you two in stitches?"

"Nothing, really. I think we're trying not to get too maudlin about Gen's move next week."

Dan stepped closer and pulled both women into his long arms.

"You're the only guy I know who does such warm group hugs," Gen gently said.

"Now, now, no waterworks." Dan wiped Gen's tears. "When are we leaving for the party?" he asked Stacy.

"Oh, God. What time is it? We've been shooting the bull and I totally lost track of the time. We need to get the kids from their after-school program, get them home, and feed them, then get to Thoroughbred Tavern by six thirty." Dan and Stacy both gave Gen a quick hug and hurried down the hall, Stacy calling, "See you in a couple of hours, Gen."

Gen finished some last-minute paperwork in her office. This was her final day at UK and her office stood ready for the movers on Monday. She would miss Stacy and Dan, the camaraderie, certainly. But she longed for more control over her clinical work. She craved the challenge that total supervisory responsibility over residents in a rural setting would bring. Here at Kentucky she answered to all the old white men in power at the university. In Colorado, she would run the show. It would be lonely at the beginning, as all geographic moves were, but worth it professionally.

And what about Ms. Delaney, who had occupied her mind since that interview? In their meeting, they had clicked. She felt it. The rancher was quite handsome, intelligent, and experienced at rural health care issues, all features that attracted Gen. But there was something more. Was it an underlying conceit in her manner? A flirtatiousness just below the surface that Ms. Delaney kept under control because she was in a professional situation? Gen had had her fill of games over the years, not only with the male docs surrounding her, but with Rachel. Since the divorce, even though she had dated a few women, she had been squeamish about getting involved in an exclusive relationship. She knew she didn't have the energy or wish to parlay with a game player. Just as well, because she had too much work to do once she landed in Babcock County, Colorado, to worry about getting involved with anyone, least of all a flirtatious rancher, even if she looked as good as Mary Ann Delaney did.

Gen packed her briefcase, lifted a box of personal items she'd kept in her office, shut off the lights, then closed the door, on her way to the good-bye party.

# Chapter Four

"Hey, Connie." Yancy's voice was morning-raspy.

When Yancy hit the bottom of the open stairway, her friend and housekeeper glanced up from preparing strawberry pies. "You're up. Ready for some 'cakes and eggs?"

"God, no. Just some coffee. Quick."

Pausing from measuring flour, Connie peered at her and said, "You're losing weight again."

Yancy grunted. Connie sometimes was like a second mother. Not in a good, caring way, but an in-your-face, bossy way. Yancy's mother, Nina, was a Denver socialite—no ranch wife, never had been. Connie had been hired by Nina fifteen years ago to keep the house running when Yancy first started to manage the ranch. But Connie also kept communication lines open between Nina and Yancy, sometimes running interference between them, or reporting information she thought Nina should know.

Yancy clasped her fingers around the handle of the coffee cup Connie handed her, grabbed the straw Stetson she wore on hot days, then banged out the door.

"Thanks for the coffee. Yes, I will be back around twelve thirty, and no, I don't want anything hot, just a salad or sandwich," she yelled to Connie as she strode in her determined way to the corral.

Yancy stepped into the dark, cool stable, inhaling her favorite mixed aroma of horse sweat, manure, hay, and musty air. "Morning," she called to Victor. He was his usual, steady, quiet self, decked out in old jeans and a checkered shirt, his lined brown face exuding calmness. "How're we doing for today's lessons?"

"Pretty well. Marsha and Virgie arrived at seven to get the horses into stalls for the girls, who are supposed to get here"—he glanced down at his wristwatch—"in about forty-five minutes."

"I'm going to finish the north part of the fence this morning while it's still cool," she called back to Victor. She continued down the main aisle of the horse barn right as Virgie led a horse from the corral toward its stall.

"Morning, Yancy," she said brightly. "Blaze and Honey look to be in good form this morning. It's getting hot again today, so they probably won't give us much trouble."

Yancy's eyes scanned Virgie's bright green shirt that outlined her generous chest, and got stuck imagining those breasts in her mouth. Absently, she replied, "Good, good."

"Eyes up here, sport," Virgie said in a chastising tone, pointing to her face. She glanced down the barn aisle, got closer to Yancy, and said in a low tone, "Listen. I know you have your conquests, but you're barking up the wrong tree with me. I told you a month ago when you hired me for the summer lessons that I'm not interested. I am happily married. I told Bobby about your come-ons, and let me tell you, he said if you pulled anything he would personally come out and kick your butt."

Yancy put her hand up in a surrender gesture.

"Whoa. Who said anything? I was only looking. I can't help it if you are one helluva good-looking woman." Yancy smirked. "But, baby, you are so easy on the eyes."

"It won't take much for me to take my boobs and teach at another ranch. Remember that the next time your eyes wander where they aren't supposed to go."

Yancy watched as Virgie led the horse into the stall and slammed the door shut, spooking the horse a little. Then, still frowning, she slid past Yancy on the way to the corral without a backward glance. Yancy smiled to herself. She shrugged, wondering what it would take to get through her armor. She continued down the aisle, saying hello to Marsha Stansberry, the other riding teacher Yancy had hired the last two summers. Marsha nodded to Yancy.

After Marsha passed, Yancy turned around to look at her best feature—her ass—as it swayed with her walk down the barn aisle. But Marsha was not Yancy's type. Too schoolteacher. Too straight in all the wrong ways. Not flirty, all business, and a little on the mousy side. Also married to a dull accountant with three dull children. Normally, she was up to that level of challenge for its own sake, but since she didn't find Marsha attractive overall, the teacher was far too valuable an asset to risk losing over a potential roll in the hay.

Yancy exhaled. She checked on Marquette in the north corral. At the wooden-slat fence, she clicked her tongue and Marquette trotted over. "Hey, boy. How you doing? Want to go for a ride?" Marquette nuzzled Yancy for any treats she might be hiding while Yancy stroked his neck and muzzle. Treating him like the friend he was to her, she murmured to him about how she loved him and his companionship. Marquette snorted and whinnied in reply. She climbed over the fence slats, haltered him, and led him through the gate to the barn. While picking up the grooming kit, she spoke softly to him again, telling him what a good horse he was. Yancy brushed him with a stiff curry comb, followed by a softer brush, until his coat shone. Looking grim and avoiding Yancy's glance, Virgie led another horse through the aisle to a stall. Yancy decided to give it a rest, and paid no attention to her. After Yancy finished tacking up Marquette, she led him out of the barn to the ranch road. Stopping at the beginning of the dirt path, she tightened the girth again, gave him a solid pat on the neck, then mounted him swiftly while he stood stock-still for her.

"Okay, boy, let's go see some ranch and fix some fence." She and Marquette loped easily along the ranch road, kicking up dust as they entered one of the north pastures of the Triple D, where she hoped to spy some of the new calves in the herd. Another day of hot, dry, ranch work. This was Yancy's stock-in-trade, a way to keep her grounded, absent a personal life. Her workaday world cast her into a self-imposed exile, but she didn't know how else to cope. Loss was not easy for anyone, but her heart felt especially trod upon. She needed to protect her heart, because she knew she didn't have it in her to lose again.

𑁋𑁋𑁋𑁋𑁋

A few days later, Yancy prepared for the first board meeting with Gen at the helm as new medical director. When Yancy entered the conference room, she noted all the staff, including Administrator Jim

McDonald, Business Manager Gerry Bailey, Nursing and Allied Health Professions Director Helen Delong, and others, along with Gen, ringing the perimeter of the room around the large walnut table. She deliberately caught Gen's eye, and nodded and flashed her dimples at the pretty physician.

Yancy took her seat at the head of the long table and confidently initiated the flow of information and discussion. As board chair, Yancy's skills lay in summarizing the issues that came up on the agenda and moving the meeting forward. But today, as the discussions wore on, she became increasingly fidgety. Muscles twitched under her shoulders. Her hands fiddled with her pen, signaling her impatience with the prolonged argument about the financial report, between the banker Mike Scott and James Edwards, a Denver financial analyst and Marlene's husband.

Finally, Yancy brought the detailed dispute on equipment depreciation methods to a halt. "Let's continue to consider these reimbursement issues. Jim and Gerry, for the next meeting, would you have someone prepare a short summary for us on the pros and cons of different methods of medical equipment depreciation?" After receiving a nod from Jim, who typed on his laptop, she looked directly at Gen. "Next on the agenda, we have our first report from the new medical director, Dr. Lambert. First, I want to personally welcome you, Doctor. We all are thrilled to have you finally here at Valley View. I will say more about the barbecue for you under new business. What do you have to report for us?" Calming, Yancy quit fidgeting and directed all her attention to Dr. Lambert.

Gen stood at a small lectern, thanked Yancy, returned her own remarks about being happy to work at Valley View, and began her report. "I've scheduled initial meetings with the Family Medicine Department at the university medical school. I will be following up with the director of the residency program, who's very supportive of working with Valley View and its two clinics. We already have a good working relationship from our work together on the accreditation board for family medicine departments. We are both keen to start the program as soon as we can get the accreditation paperwork completed."

Board members listened raptly as she detailed a preceptorship for second- and third-year residents at both clinics. She outlined the kinds of medical experiences they would participate in. Finally, she discussed the costs and benefits to Valley View for hosting medical residents. The board made noises of approval. Yancy noted that Gen had successfully met the first hurdle of her work at Valley View.

Gen went on to announce the new Saturday walk-in clinic, which the board had tried to get instituted for some time with the last medical director. He had repeatedly delayed the clinic, assuring them that no staff would be willing to work on Saturdays. Gen reported that she gave staff compensatory time off and other incentives for Saturday work. The first clinic was scheduled this week. Again, the board members smiled and congratulated Gen on her swift work in improving services.

When the other business had concluded, Yancy announced, "I am sure y'all have your invitations to the Triple D for the party to welcome Dr. Lambert. Of course, I hope your spouses will accompany you. Jim and I consulted the list of our best donors and have invited them. We are being catered by Del's Barbecue.

They will also run an open bar, which is being donated by the Triple D, so we'll have a good welcome for Dr. Lambert." She smiled politely and tipped her head in Gen's direction.

"Yes, I want to take the opportunity to thank the board for this party. I can't say how hospitable you all are being." Gen's smile lit up the whole room. The board members, especially the men among them, along with Yancy, of course, grinned in appreciation of their new medical director.

After the business of the board meeting had wrapped up, Yancy met Gen at the door, her hands in her pockets, her demeanor all business. "How are things personally for you, Doctor? Are you settling in all right?"

Gen gazed at Yancy. "Thanks, I have a rental property in town, the old Butterfield place. Maybe you know it?"

Yancy nodded.

"I like it quite well. The movers arrived with my stuff, and I'm mostly unpacked, but still doing my best to get totally settled in. Of course, the kitchen was ready first." Gen laughed lightly.

"Of course." Yancy smiled.

Gen paused for a minute. "I'm a fairly accomplished cook. Would you like to come for dinner sometime next week?"

Yancy raised her eyebrows. "Is there something about the clinics you need to discuss?" Her heart rate increased with the idea of spending time with Gen.

"No, nothing. I would simply like to try out my new kitchen. With you not being the cooking type, I thought…I hope it's not out of line, but I'd like to get to know the area. Who better to ask than you?"

Yancy perked up considerably with this news. "Let me know the day and time."

"Since I'm working Saturday, my day off next week is Wednesday. Let's say seven?"

"See you then." Yancy's dimples deepened with her smile, as she watched Gen turn and leave the conference room.

≈≈≈≈≈

After the board meeting, Gen got groceries and tiredly arrived at her new home in the early evening. Cooking helped her decompress from the day. Tonight, she made a new recipe her mom had sent for beef tips in mushrooms, scallions, and red wine. It was a simple recipe, and she reduced the liquid at the same time the rice finished cooking. It smelled marvelous. Her mom always sent the best food ideas. She filled her plate and took it to the small kitchen table, poured a Bordeaux to accompany it, and sat savoring the quiet of her house and the aromas coming off the beef. As she had learned so long ago, she tipped the wineglass to complete the "five S" steps: see, swirl, sniff, sip, savor, noting the tannins and tastes of blackberry, currant, and something else. The wine's complexity pleased her. The ritual took her away from the clinical, the scientific, and back to her own humanity. Her way of unwinding.

Her report for the first board meeting gave her a sense of accomplishment. Although many pieces still needed to be put together before the first resident arrived around the first of the year, her many days of hard toil had reaped fruit, and the board's response to her hard work gave her a thrill. She had chosen this job well, it was all she had hoped so far, and going as planned. She raised the wineglass in a self-salute and sipped gratefully.

Now, what about Yancy Delaney? Gen shook her head. In the gossip hotbed characteristic of medical facilities, she had heard a few stories about one-night stands and an affair with a married woman—the party refused to divulge a name. What possessed her to offer Yancy an invitation to dinner without any forethought whatsoever? Had she lost her mind? Had Yancy's mere presence bewitched her? Gen sighed deeply, relishing the wine, enjoying the beef and its rich sauce. Well, it was done now, nothing she could do. She certainly couldn't take back the invitation. And, who knew? Maybe Yancy and she would have a mature discussion, free from playing games. It depended on which Yancy showed up, didn't it? The buttoned-up board chair, or the philandering rancher.

# Chapter Five

After spending early Saturday mornings in her ranch office, usually paying bills and ordering supplies, Yancy liked to ride awhile. Riding allowed her to keep on top of the ranch, its livestock, fences, water, and pastures. Especially during the pressures of this unusually dry, early summer heat, which promised to worsen as June wore into July, riding also helped Yancy to decompress. That and sex, she acknowledged to herself, helped her relax.

The Saturday after the board meeting, Marquette cantered along the south pasture rimming the small river that ran through the ranch. White-hot June sunlight washed out the already gray look of the pasture. Yancy took in the smells of the plains grasses. A Western Meadowlark sang. She heard the "Bob White" call of a quail. Watching a few clouds scud along in the blazing sky, Yancy felt her shoulders relax a little. While riding always seemed to give her energy, today she couldn't quite shake the feeling of lethargy that overtook her. Maybe it was the temperature rising precipitously in late morning, combined with the lack of sleep yet again last night.

Maybe the latest encounter with Marlene had taken more of a toll than she realized, or even the fight with Cheyenne earlier in the spring. She couldn't help that she was constitutionally incapable of long-term attachments. She'd had one, which was enough.

As comfortable as Trisha's sweet tenderness had felt, Yancy vowed never to give in again. Damn these women and their predatory ways, always assuming possession of her, enticing, yet fearlessly conquering. Yancy should put a stop to it, but she wasn't sure how.

Yancy brooded over her loneliness. The farther she rode, the more lost she became in the pain, trying to put it out of her mind, but failing miserably.

She remembered her brother Ryan, her sidekick, and their lazy summer days together as teens, riding companionably through the plains. At the local rodeo, she cheered him in calf roping, and in return, he cheered her in barrel racing. She missed the easy way they had together. When he confided in her that he wanted to be a physician, she was surprised, but she later understood his interest and encouraged it. On the day she came out to him, he squeezed her in a bear hug and said, "I knew it." He was fighting leukemia even then, in his late teens, and didn't make it to his twenty-second birthday. Yancy's eyes welled up recalling the day of his funeral: his college buddies, Chip and Jaime, who served as sad pall-bearers; her whole family inconsolable at their loss.

A mere four years after Ryan's death, her father died of a sudden heart attack, right as she was ready to assist him as ranch manager at age twenty-eight. He had always been her hero, the kind of rancher she always wanted to be. As a girl, she followed him around, mimicking his stride. Many times, she watched how he, quietly and with tender care, worked with the horses and cattle. Neither of her brothers were interested in the hard ranch work. Phil, more like their mother, read books, and had played tennis and soccer in school. After college, he had chosen financial work and moved to Denver. Ryan, the caretaker, always interested in helping hurt things, often fed the orphan calves or took care of sick foals. But Yancy hung on her dad's every word, clung to him in the corral like a shadow, wanting to be with him in the barn or in the pastures, learning how to run the ranch.

Then, Trisha died five years ago. She had come into Yancy's heart without her realizing it. Yancy first ran up to Denver to see her every few weekends. These visits grew to nearly every weekend, either at the ranch or in Denver. They had been a serious couple for only a short year, when what would be Trisha's last months were spent at the ranch. Yancy watched her closely, helped the nurse with her care, and surprised herself by how attentive and caring she could be. Trisha died of an aggressive form of breast cancer seven years after her dad. Since then, Yancy felt like her heart had been frozen, paralyzed, with no life or heat. Her personal life became only quick trips to Denver for sexual release, to break the constant work both at the ranch and on the health center's board.

She ruminated on loss. Contemplation seemed to be her new normal these days, while she had lost the easy, positive way of her former life. Even though she loved her work, she no longer held deep passion for the ranch and the clinic. Yancy wallowed in self-pity, the dark thoughts swimming through her brain.

Caught in the undertow of her stewing and ruminating, Yancy loped along, only barely aware of her surroundings. She took no note of the scorching sun causing sweat to course in rivulets down her neck and back. She paid little attention to the heat of the day or to the twelve hundred pounds of horseflesh moving under her. The only feeling was a heart thudding with dull sadness.

Marquette's hammering hooves stamped a steady rhythm for her mind's dark wanderings. The terrain passed by: treeless pasture, hill, small gully. Then, on uneven ground, he suddenly stumbled in a hole.

The jolt awakened Yancy from her brooding. But, because her brain was preoccupied, she failed to react quickly enough to prepare before she felt herself tossed out of the saddle and catapulted over the horse's head to the ground. She struck the hard, dry dirt with a sickening thump, accompanied by a snapping sound. The forward momentum flung her some ten feet in front of Marquette, into brambles. She blinked, confused for several breaths. After a minute of total nothingness, agonizing pain encompassed her.

Marquette stopped and stood, like the well-trained horse he was. She raised her head, then succumbed to the ground in anguish. Yancy groaned, then muttered, "Damn it." As she lay in the dirt, she mentally checked what had happened to her body. The pain in her shoulder radiated into her chest, down her left arm. Her wrist felt wrong, too. Nausea washed over her, so she took some deep breaths to get it under control. She sat up slowly to gauge the damage as the sun beat down relentlessly.

After what seemed like hours, but was only a couple of minutes in the brambles and heat, she rose to her feet, holding her shoulder with her right hand, which seemed to quell the pain a little. Her hat lay on the ground where the violence of the fall had thrown it. With her right hand, she leaned over to pick it up, immediately fighting dizziness. Gingerly, she grabbed Marquette's reins under her right elbow, rested her forehead on his neck, and breathed deeply to assess and soothe the excruciating discomfort. She lifted herself into the saddle slowly, and, even in her carefulness, jostled her arm, causing her to wince and swear when spikes of sharp pain pierced her. After she settled carefully onto Marquette's back, she reined him to a slow walk, with as little movement of her upper body as possible, down the way she had ridden, wanting to cry out with each jolt of the horse's hooves hitting the solid ground.

❧❧❧❧

Connie was beginning lunch preparations for Yancy and Victor when she saw Yancy on Marquette, riding at an uncharacteristic, dawdling pace into the backyard from the ranch road. Something was not right. Then Victor ran out from the barn to take Marquette's reins. Holding her left arm close to her body, Yancy weakly slid off Marquette to the ground. She was grimacing, her eyes closed. Connie hurried out the screen door, hearing Yancy's curses the closer she got.

Connie shuffled into the yard as fast as she could, and knelt in front of Yancy. "What happened?"

Yancy slurred an incoherent curse while Connie pried away her hand from her shoulder to see to the damage.

"Is Marquette all right?" Yancy whispered.

Victor ran his hands over the fetlock and pastern of Marquette's leg that Yancy pointed to. "No problems as far as I can see. Leg looks and feels sound." He glanced at Connie, then turned to lead Marquette into the barn, calling over his shoulder, "I'll just get him cooled down and back into the corral."

Virgie and Marsha had emerged from the barn in all the commotion. Connie waved them off and they returned to their barn cleaning. Connie looked at Yancy with concern. "We need to get you to the hospital. Your wrist is all bruised. I think your shoulder might be dislocated."

Yancy weakly answered, "I'm fine. It's a sprain. Not going all that distance to the hospital." Yancy may have been hurt, but Connie could see she was still determined.

Connie sighed and closed her eyes briefly, thinking this was the worst-case scenario: Yancy in pain, in denial, and in control. She screwed up her face. "Well, then, we're going to the clinic. You said that the new doctor started opening the clinic on Saturdays. Here's the deal—you can get yourself into the truck, or I can have Victor carry you." Connie put a grim, unwavering look on her face. "You choose."

Yancy looked into Connie's eyes. She raised herself up, swatting away Connie's extended hand, and walked hunched over, her face contorted in pain. "Damn," Connie heard Yancy whisper. Connie walked nearby and steadied Yancy while she shuffled to Victor's truck parked in the side driveway. Given Yancy's paleness, Connie hoped she didn't pass out, and she was amazed that she didn't put up more of a fuss. It must hurt like the very devil, she thought. No other thing could subdue Yancy. Of course, when you have passed forty, your body doesn't bounce back like it once did.

This accident reminded her of Yancy's broken ankle the last time she barrel raced, right before Trisha was diagnosed. Trisha had taken over in no uncertain terms, getting Yancy to the university medical center in Denver in short order. Yancy had required surgery to repair her ankle and was a bear to live with until she could muster walking around. Connie thought at the time that Trisha had been a saint to endure Yancy's childish whining. Yancy's immature reactions to being sick were widely acknowledged by her mother Nina. Connie herself had tried to be gracious whenever she nursed a grumpy Yancy through the years. But Yancy had responded well to Trisha's care. She had been much less sullen with Trisha, who seemed able to calm the beast in Yancy. But Connie now saw the same immature, cantankerous Yancy before her. Yancy had changed again, and not in a good way, since Trisha's death.

"I'm going to open the door for you and buckle you in," Connie announced firmly when they reached the Ford.

Yancy sighed heavily. When she was bundled into the front passenger seat, Victor slid into the driver's seat and Connie took up a seat in the extended cab.

ॐॐॐॐ

"We've got Yancy Delaney out here, Doc." Gen barely heard the receptionist's voice through the intercom at the nurse's station. "She was out riding and had a bad fall."

"Give me five minutes, Betty. I'm finishing up with Justin Carlton's poison ivy, then Mrs. Schwartz's prescription. Sheila will be out to get her," Gen returned into the intercom. She looked at her nurse and asked, "Why is Betty talking so low?"

Sheila grinned and said, "Oh, Dr. Lambert, you'll soon see."

Gen shrugged and continued with her two patients. After sending Justin out with some topical cortisone, she finished with Mrs. Schwartz's refill. Then she heard a woman's loud, "That hurts. Damn it, don't touch me." Gen poked her head out into the hall. A chunky, light-coffee skinned woman in her fifties or early sixties guided Yancy Delaney by the elbow. In a quick assessment of her, Gen noted the paleness of Yancy's dusky complexion, her dark brown hair in a messy ponytail. Her clothes were covered in dust, her jeans were torn, and her shirt was ripped on the left side, which Yancy cradled to her stomach. Gen grimaced when she heard another round of cursing as Sheila showed Yancy and her helper into Room 3.

Gen reentered Room 2 to finish with her patient. "That refill should hold you for six months, Mrs. Schwartz. We'll see you then for more blood tests." She patted her on the shoulder.

"Thanks, Dr. Lambert. It sure was nice to meet you. It's great to have a doctor with a bedside manner around here."

Gen smiled as Mrs. Schwartz left the room. She spent some moments typing into the medical record on her tablet and took a deep breath before striding into Room 3.

"Good morning, I'm Dr. Gen Lambert." She shut the door behind her. The woman rose, smiled, and shook her hand.

"I'm Consuela Martínez, Dr. Lambert. You know my boss, Yancy."

"I do." Gen paused. Yancy remained still with her eyes squeezed shut. When nothing was forthcoming, Gen said, "Let's see what we have. I hear there was a riding mishap."

At that, Yancy opened her eyes and glanced up at Gen's face. Her pale scowl turned into a slight smile as she perused Gen's body. "Well, howdy there," she said quietly. "I should have had an accident sooner. The clinic has certainly been beautified by your presence, Doc."

"Glad you waited, then, Ms. Delaney," Gen stuttered, not sure quite what kind of reply Ms. Delaney's flirtatiousness required. She decided she needed to gain control of the exam, so she removed Yancy's hand off her hurt shoulder in order to survey the damage. "We'll need to get this shirt off. You can put on this gown, and I'll be right back."

"Don't you want to take the shirt off, Dr. Lambert?" Even in Yancy's noticeable pain, she shot Gen that ogling expression again.

Gen backed out of the room, not wanting to grace the comment with a reply. This was not the Yancy who had appeared so professional in the interview, or a few days ago at the board meeting. Gen didn't like this lascivious Yancy.

When she returned to the exam room, Yancy rocked back and forth, her lips in a tight line. Gen got her to lie back on the exam table and probed the shoulder carefully, gauging the pain level by the contortion of Yancy's face. Gen palpated her left wrist lightly.

"Holy mother of God!" Yancy spit out in a low voice.

"Don't curse the Virgin," Connie chastised from the corner of the room, looking on with tension in her face.

"Ms. Delaney, I'm going to X-ray both your wrist and your shoulder. Your shoulder is not dislocated, but probably is separated. You've sustained some torn ligaments. That will resolve itself by keeping your shoulder joint rigid with a sling, but I want to check that neither the clavicle nor anything else in your shoulder fractured in the accident. When you fell, it looks like you landed on your hand. The impact put stress on both your ulna and on your shoulder ligaments. The wrist break is pretty common with this kind of fall. After we confirm what's going on, and assuming no other fractures, I'll send you to Bernie to cast your wrist. Do you have any questions?"

Yancy looked as if she was only partly able to take in what was going on. During the exam, Gen noted the other signs of shock in the continued paling of her complexion and in her clammy skin. Yancy moaned as Gen grabbed a small pillow and gently propped her legs above her heart. "I'm going to give you something for the pain, then let's get you in a wheelchair and into X-ray. Sheila, will you do the honors?"

≈≈≈≈≈

Two hours later, Connie wheeled Yancy out of the clinic. Her left arm rested in a sling, while a blue cast covered her arm below the elbow all the way to part of her palm, but left her fingers free. Her eyes were glazed over and her head bobbed woozily. Connie held a white paper bag with two medications, a schedule for administering each of them, and printed instructions for caring for the wrist and shoulder.

Gen looked at Sheila after they left, realizing it was nearing time to close the clinic. "That wasn't so bad, now was it?"

"Sure, Doc, whatever you say." Sheila giggled a

little. "How do you like our own Donna Juana? She actually was pretty subdued after the pain meds kicked in, but look out when Mary Anne Delaney comes in for her checkup in two weeks."

Gen frowned at Sheila's assessment.

That evening, relaxing with her feet propped up, Gen wondered about the two Mary Ann Delaneys—the professional one who captured her attention and her mind, and the womanizing one who showed up today, whom Gen most feared. It conjured up her memories of pushing, tugging, and pulling Rachel into her own emotional life, so they could have a relationship of integrity. *So much work, so little return,* Gen thought as she sighed and took a deep drink of her white wine.

# Chapter Six

"Knock, knock!" Roxie yelled into the ranch house great room as she opened the unlocked front door without knocking, per usual. "Yoo hoo. Hey, dorkhead, you up here?" She crept up the stairs to Yancy's room, suddenly feeling stupid for yelling, in case the patient was sleeping. As she got to the top landing, she heard retching, and she stepped up her pace to get into the bathroom in the master bedroom that Yancy used. "Oh, honey." She knelt beside Yancy, who was bent over the toilet. Roxie moved Yancy's hair away from her face, and went to the sink to wet a washcloth to clean her up. "God, you look like shit-on-a-biscuit."

Yancy squinted her eyes at Roxie. "Thanks a lot. On the other hand, I think I look about how I feel," she said with a low snarl.

Roxie scanned her friend, seeing the results of vomiting across the sleep shirt Yancy wore. Her dark brown hair lay matted around her forehead. Yancy's glassy eyes stared sullenly back at her. "Baby cakes, I'll bet you've had more pain meds than you could handle. How much have you taken since you got home yesterday?"

Yancy slowly shook her head.

Gently taking Yancy's good arm, Roxie asked, "Think you're ready to get back to bed?"

Yancy moaned.

"When did you eat?"

"I dunno," Yancy slurred. "I think I ate some lunch on Friday. Nothing yesterday. Don't give me those 'mother eyes' of yours. I was out of it after I got home yesterday afternoon." Yancy drew her hand over her forehead. "Christ, I'm going to hurl again." She turned from Roxie back to the toilet and continued to lose the meager contents of her stomach. "I'm so dizzy. Every time I move my head, I get nauseous all over again."

"When did this start?" Roxie asked tenderly.

"Not sure. Before Connie and Victor left for mass, I think, while they were still down in the kitchen."

Roxie stroked her back. "Come on, get all that nasty medicine out of your system." She waited until Yancy apparently had ended this bout of vomiting, then said, "Stay right here, let me see what's going on." While Yancy clumsily collapsed on the tile floor with her back against the wall, Roxie found Yancy's bedside table and picked up the bottle of narcotics, counted the number still left, and knew that Connie had been giving her the maximum dose of two pills every four hours. They were supposed to be taken only as needed for pain up to the full dose, not the full dose as a matter of course. "Shit," she mumbled under her breath. Next to the pill bottle and water glass was a tray of food, including some juice, cold toast, and soggy cereal, all untouched.

She reentered the bathroom. Yancy still sat propped against the tile wall, her eyes closed. "Come on, let's get you back to the bed."

Yancy muttered as Roxie helped her to stand, "I feel like that time we tried LSD. Everything is kind of floating, my head feels like it's barely tethered to my neck."

With Roxie's arm around her waist, they reached the bed. Yancy pointed out the vomit sprayed across the pillow and top sheet. "I can't go back there."

"Um, okay, right...let's see. How about the guest room?"

Yancy nodded wearily, leaning on Roxie's smaller frame. They reeled together down two doors in the hallway, to a lilac-blue room with a flowered bedspread on a canopy bed. An oak dresser and an overstuffed chair, covered in the same material as the flounced bedspread, completed the ensemble. "This room makes me want to puke some more. Look at all that frill. Mom and her decorator," Yancy said in disgust.

"Okay, baby cakes. You'll only be in here until we can get your sheets changed." Roxie fussed while she got Yancy situated under a light cover. As soon as Yancy's head hit the pillow, she closed her eyes and was asleep. Roxie shook her head at her friend's state, the blue tinge under her eyes, the pain etched across her lips.

The front door opened downstairs and keys clanked onto the foyer table. There were multiple voices, one male and two female. Wondering who was with Connie, Roxie made her way down the open staircase into the great room.

Victor greeted her with a small wave and sat on the couch with the *Sunday Denver Post*.

"Roxie, hi. Thanks for coming by while we were out." Connie hugged Roxie, then pulled her to meet an attractive woman with curly, light auburn hair, smiling widely. "This is Dr. Lambert. Doctor, this is Yancy's childhood friend, Dr. Roxanne Campbell. She's the town head-shrink person."

Roxie extended her hand to the pretty doctor, noting a warm smile and bright green eyes. *Something about her eyes...Is my gaydar on alert?* "Actually, I'm a clinical psychologist, not a psychiatrist. It's great to meet you, Dr. Lambert. Everyone calls me Roxie, by the way."

Gen took her hand, continuing to smile while taking in Roxie.

Roxie said, "I sent you an email welcoming you. I would really like to have coffee sometime to go over mental health protocols for the clinics."

"Yes. Great to put a face to the name. First, please call me Gen. And yes, I got that email. As soon as I get settled in a bit more, I certainly want to get together. Rural mental health is an interest of mine, and I hope—"

*Crash.* A weak, "Son of a bitch" came from upstairs.

"Oops, better check on the patient." Connie launched her short frame up the steps. "Doesn't sound good."

"And that, Doctor, is our friend Yancy. Might be a good idea for you to take those oxycodone." In a near whisper, she added, "I think Connie overdid it on the dosage. Yancy's been vomiting all morning. It's a miracle there's anything left in her system, because she hasn't eaten since Friday."

Gen's eyebrows rose slightly. "Let me do a quick check," she announced and walked up the steps. Roxie followed. Gen asked over her shoulder that someone get her medical kit from the back seat of her car. Victor, who had been reading his newspaper away from all the commotion, bounded out the door, and in no time came trotting back in and up the steps.

"Good morning, Ms. Delaney."

Yancy looked up in surprise. "The beautiful doctor, making house calls. You couldn't keep away after you checked me out yesterday, huh?" The words sounded like Yancy's standard come-on, but the delivery was a little garbled.

Roxie saw that Yancy had tried to get out of bed, but had knocked over a lamp in her careening lurch.

"Let's get you to sit down," Gen said, taking her right arm while Roxie stood on the left side to protect the injuries, and together they helped her to the bedside chair. "I'm going to do a quick exam. Blood pressure, heart rate."

Victor laid the medical kit on the bed and excused himself, making his way back downstairs to safety, while Connie and Roxie stood off to the side of the chair. Yancy watched the doctor in a semi-drunken haze, with her head canted onto the back of the chair. Roxie guessed that she probably wanted to taunt the doctor, but couldn't muster the words.

"Having any pain this morning, with either of your injuries?" Gen asked in a professionally aloof tone as she attached the automatic blood pressure cuff. She swiped a temporal scanning thermometer across Yancy's forehead.

Connie offered, "She was not able to sleep much last night. I stayed here at the house, down on the couch, but kept coming up when I heard her moaning. I would give her two of those pills every four hours."

"Mm-hmm." Gen kept a detached, professional visage while she finished her exam by softly pinching the skin on Yancy's arm. "I am going to take her off those pain medications, first, and prescribe something a little less harsh. She's dehydrated from the vomiting. Is there someone who can be here with her, help push liquids and maybe get some food into her?" Gen looked up, then took her phone out of her purse. "I'll phone the pharmacy."

"I'll stay the rest of today, Doct—er...Gen."

"No, no, Roxie. I can stay," Connie said.

"Not going to happen, Connie. Sunday's your day off." Turning to Gen, Roxie said, "I'll call my wife, Kate. She and her brothers run the ranch just down the road. It's her turn to check on livestock later today. She can bring what we were going to grill out from our house in town. Yancy usually comes to town every Sunday and joins us. Instead, we'll have supper here."

"Good, but I think our patient is going to be having crackers for a few more hours. She'll stay nauseous until tonight probably. Clear liquids as she can tolerate them." Gen looked around the bedroom at Connie and Roxie. "Any questions? I probably should get going."

Yancy, through half-lidded eyes, glanced up at the three women surrounding her chair and slurred, "Geez, if I'd known I had attracted all this pulchritude, I'd have dressed for the occasion."

Roxie shook her head. "Hey, dorkhead, keep it together. I don't think your puking is attracting any pulchritude this morning."

Gen put a hand over her grinning mouth.

Connie stepped toward Gen and extended her hand. "I'm so glad you came by. I'm sorry. I had invited you from church to have coffee with us and Yancy, but I didn't think you'd have to make a house call."

"No problem. I'm glad I could help with our colorful patient. I trust that things will calm down tonight. Bye, everyone."

"Thanks. Good-bye," Roxie said as she and Connie got Yancy back into the canopy bed.

Victor called out as he went out the door with Gen, "See you in the truck, honey."

"Yeah. Be there in a minute." Connie stood over the bed where Yancy had again fallen into a drugged stupor of fitful sleep. "I'll have Victor run to the drug store and get that new prescription."

"No, he doesn't have to do that. When I talk to Kate, I'll have her pick it up on her way over. You guys get home and relax."

Connie sighed. "Never a dull moment with my Mary Anne, huh?"

Roxie chuckled. "It's been that way since I knew her in junior high. If it was like this at age thirteen, I don't think anything's going to change now."

# *Chapter Seven*

Two weeks later, Yancy travelled systematically around the ranch yard, checking on the caterer, the band, and the bar, and asked Victor to direct guests who had begun to arrive where to park their cars. She glanced around at the tables decked out with red-checkered tablecloths, the smell of barbecue redolent in the air. With all the preparations in place, she walked in the back door of the ranch house.

"Hello, my darling girl." Nina breezed into the great room, threw her purse onto the table, and stepped forward to wrap her arms around Yancy. She was impeccably dressed in a crisp, summer-weight pantsuit in contrasting shades of red, her favorite color now that she had begun to wear her hair a natural gray. It was short, but styled with flair to look as if she had just combed it casually.

"Hey, Mom."

"You're looking better than the last time I saw you, all sleepy, your eyes squinting with pain." Nina looked intently at Yancy's face while holding her at arms' length.

"Yeah. Hardly a twinge now, though I still don't want to move too quickly. This damn shoulder."

"But one thing, darling."

*Here it comes.* She lowered her eyes from her mother's face and sighed.

"I thought you said you were going to eat better.

I love a svelte woman just as much as the next person. But darling, you're skin and bones. You know, Connie's job is to keep things in tip-top shape, and you, my sweet girl, aren't in good shape."

"Aw, Mom. Come on. I'm an adult. I'm busy. I don't have time to eat the mounds of food that Connie prepares."

"Look at me. I'm still active, I'm busy, but you wouldn't be able to count my ribs. I always think some flesh on an older woman is to be expected. Attractive, even."

"Geez, Mom, I'm not that old." In fact, her mom played tennis and golf, and swam in the winter. She was in fantastic shape, trim and firm, even though she would be sixty-nine on her next birthday.

"Well, I've spoken recently to our new doctor... what's her name, Genevieve? I've told her to make sure you get all your annual exams this year. Daddy would have expected you to be in robust health to tackle the responsibility of the ranch, you know."

"Yeah, sure, whatever."

"You sound like a sullen teenager." Nina shook her head.

"Why do you think I sound like one, Mom? You treat me like I've just learned to do bookkeeping, not like I'm a professional business manager."

"I'm not talking about your intellectual abilities, I'm talking about how you take care of yourself, your body and soul." Nina stroked Yancy's hair gently, looking with loving eyes at her only daughter.

"Hey, I'm no longer in Sunday school classes."

"Well, now you know what I expect. Let's change the subject. How did the new doctor strike you? Did you like her? Is she good?" Nina asked.

A smirk crossed Yancy's face. "Oh, her?" She feigned disinterest, looking out the window at the crowd beginning to form around the outdoor bar. "By what we saw at the first board meeting, she's going to be a great medical director. As far as her skills, I didn't pay much attention, was kind of out of it at the clinic when she got me fixed up. I have to go for my checkup this week."

"I liked her when I talked with her on the phone the other day. I'm looking forward to meeting her and working with her on board development. You're the president now, but I still want to keep my hand in to make sure there are good folks coming up the ranks on the board."

"Sounds good, Mom. I'll do whatever you want."

"Let's go greet our guests, shall we? Phil is parking the car and we'll meet him outside."

&#x273F;&#x273F;&#x273F;&#x273F;

Later in the afternoon, James and Marlene Edwards approached Yancy, each holding a drink.

"How y'all doing? This is a very fine party, Yancy." James raised his bourbon on the rocks in her direction. Marlene gave her an appraising look and a small smirk.

Yancy inwardly groaned when she saw Marlene's face. *Please, not her today.* "Thanks. Glad you and the other board members could come to welcome Dr. Lambert."

"She's gorgeous," Marlene noted, her eyes glancing at Yancy over the glass of white wine she sipped.

"She's a real catch. Did some amazing work

there in the Kentucky mountains." Yancy refused to be baited by Marlene's jealousy.

"Yeah, we did well snapping her up," James put in, oblivious to the looks crossing from Marlene to Yancy.

Marlene sidled up to Yancy. "I wanted to go over some things about my last lesson." She put her hand possessively on Yancy's arm.

"What?" Yancy tried to step back from Marlene's hand. She squinted.

Marlene led her away from the bulk of the group surrounding the buffet table and bar. "Are we getting together as usual this Tuesday?" Marlene's sultry voice bit into Yancy's libido like a snake and woke it up.

Yancy sighed. Despite how Marlene turned her on, she had to do this. "Marlene...I...I don't think we should see each other anymore."

"You don't mean that, babe," Marlene said sweetly. She drilled her hazel eyes into Yancy.

Yancy's head swam as the heat of Marlene's body mingled with her perfume. She gasped slightly for air. "I do mean it," she managed to mumble. "You're a married woman, dammit."

Marlene puffed out, then narrowed her eyes. "Don't tell me Yancy Delaney cares about the marital status of anyone she fucks. You are so full of shit."

"There you are." Gen appeared from behind Marlene, looking at Yancy, and glanced at Marlene. "I'm sorry, I don't mean to interrupt."

Yancy met Gen's eyes with gratitude. "Dr. Lambert. Have you met Marlene Edwards? James's wife?"

Marlene turned to meet Gen's eyes with a glinting appraisal. "Hello, Doctor." She turned and eyed Yancy with her wolfish grin, and winked. "See you Tuesday for our regular lesson." Her hand ran seductively down Yancy's shirt placket. Marlene twisted away from Gen, gave her a haughty look, and passed by.

Yancy met Gen's face with chagrined embarrassment. Gen cocked one eyebrow in a question.

"Um…sorry for Marlene's rudeness. Did you have something you wanted with me?"

"I just hadn't had time to touch base with you. Everyone, er, almost everyone"—she looked in the direction Marlene had just walked—"has been very welcoming. It's been fun to get to meet donors and all the families of the staff. It will make my job easier when it comes to scheduling, to know what family life looks like for each of them." She gave Yancy a sincere look of gratitude. "I also wanted to say that you're a good board president. I like the way you conduct business while keeping the patients' welfare at the forefront."

Yancy smiled. "Thanks, Doc. I enjoy my work on the board." She was enthralled by Gen's gaze upon her.

"Yes, I can see it means a lot to you." Gen smiled back.

"I need to see some other donors. I'll see you later this week for my follow-up appointment." Yancy stood rooted to the spot. She then woke herself up from her dreamlike state staring at Gen, and stepped away, nearly tripping on her boot.

⁂

After four hours of schmoozing with donors, board members, clinic staff, and county health officials, Yancy was ready to stop. She never drank at these events because she was constantly aware of her responsibility to be on her good game. Clinic supporters and board members always asked her opinion on any number of health policy issues affecting Valley View, but they especially focused on the ongoing fear that they could lose federal funding. Lately, they concentrated on the effects of federal health policy changes on uninsured patients. It was work, not play, these Valley View social events. Exhausting. And, today, to top it all, Marlene goaded her about the new medical director.

Yancy drew a deep breath. Relieved to catch Roxie's eye across the dwindling crowd, she beckoned her over subtly with her eyes. She blew out her cheeks and turned to Roxie.

Roxie looked summer-comfortable in a billowy, turquoise cotton dress that complemented her fair complexion and blue eyes. Yancy loved the way her blond, braided hair draped down her shoulder. Roxie brushed her hand across the back of her wife, Kate, who walked beside her. Kate, taller and bulkier than Roxie, had spiky brown hair, and wore her ubiquitous jeans and crisp Western shirt. They couldn't look more different, Yancy thought, the rancher and the hippie.

Kate sidled up, looking equally as bored as Yancy. At least Kate was holding a cold beer in her hands, Yancy noted ruefully. "Can we vamoose from this rodeo yet?" Yancy said.

Roxie, holding onto Kate's waist, said, "This is nice, Yancy. It's a beautifully sunny summer's day, not horridly hot like it's been. The barbecue's fantastic. Bobby Bernard's band is very popular. Why don't you like these things? You used to love them when Trisha came with you."

"Well, yeah, a good-looking woman makes it tolerable. I like my board work, but, standing around without Trisha to make jokes with and keep me pumped, social events are torture. I hate schmoozing."

"Don't talk about Trisha that way. We both know you cared for her." Roxie took a deep breath before continuing. "Baby cakes, you don't seem to be moving on very well. I know for a fact you wouldn't have crashed on Marquette the other day if you'd had your head screwed on right." Roxie's soft eyes looked compassionately at Yancy. She took a moment before continuing. "I think you are clinically depressed."

"You're kidding." Yancy shot her a look of disdain. "Depression is for people like my mom's Junior League friends who have nothing to do all day but spend their husbands' money."

Roxie leaned in. "Okay, fine. I get it. Yancy Delaney can't be bothered to consider that she may have some emotional issues to deal with. She hides behind a tough butch façade, casually screwing strangers. She overworks on the ranch, over-functions with the clinic board. Much more important than weighing her behaviors, or God forbid, doing something about them." She took a deep breath, scrunched her brows together. "You know, I have been your friend for a hell of a lot of years, dorkhead. But this is the lowest I've ever seen you go. Your appetite is for shit. Your sleep is for shit. And you, my friend, are for shit." Roxie punctuated her last statement by poking Yancy in the chest.

"Wow, Rox, why don't you tell me how you *really* feel?" Yancy laughed. She leaned toward Roxie, feeling her temper rise, and whispered, "You know your problem is that you take care of everybody but yourself. You stick your little shrink-a-fied nose into other people's business and tell them what's wrong with them, but you don't look at the glass house you're living in."

With a reddening face, Roxie answered, "I get that I'm not perfect. Just ask Kate here. And you know what? I've been taking anti-depressants for about a year now, because I had some stuff I needed to handle that was kicking my butt. I'm not too proud to take care of some issues." She poked Yancy in the chest again. "Deal with it, Delaney!"

Kate, having quietly witnessed all the bantering between them, chimed in. "You're toast, buddy. This woman is like a bucking bronco. She won't give up till you're whipped into shape. Look what happened to me." Kate smiled at Roxie and threw her arm around her shoulders.

Yancy held her hands up in surrender. "Geez, give it a rest. I don't need to fight with y'all, too. My mom is already on my case." She brushed an imaginary piece of dirt from the front of her shirt, then looked up into the distance and closed her eyes for a moment, blowing out a huge breath.

Roxie spoke up again, "Will you think about getting some help? I can't stand to watch you wasting away any longer."

"Don't I have a life?"

"No, I don't think you do. Working long hours into the night every day, then fucking some chick in Denver every Friday is not a life, dorkhead." Roxie leaned in again, and said in an undertone, "And messing around with James Edwards's wife is the last straw."

Yancy opened her mouth to reply. Instead she stuffed her right hand in her pocket and frowned at Roxie. She huffed in and out for some time in the silence between them, and gave her a withering look. Finally relenting, after mulling over Roxie's diatribe, she said in a soft voice, "I have to see the doc on Tuesday, so tell me what I've got to do, dammit."

"All I'm asking is that you take the depression screening questionnaire. The clinic has it online. I helped them get registered with the website recently." Roxie was still standing close to Yancy, and she put her hand over her shoulder. "I love you, but your stubbornness can really bug the hell out of me sometimes." She pointed with her head to the doctor talking a few feet away with a board member. "Gen and I met last week about mental health screenings, especially for depression. She's totally with me about the need for primary care docs at the clinic to have more mental health resources. All the medical staff are on board."

"Hell, Rox, if I do that screen at the clinic, it will be all over the county by the end of my appointment. I won't have any privacy." Yancy roughly shoved Roxie's hands off her arm, and took a few paces in the yard. "Shit, here she comes now."

"I'm about to head home, but I wanted to thank you for this wonderful party. How nice of the board to set this up." Gen held out her hand to Yancy, a sincere smile playing on her lips.

Yancy cased her from head to toe while taking her hand and holding it a little too long. *Wow, great legs in that little dress that brings out the red highlights in her hair. Nice legs, nice breasts, nice everything. A smile that goes on forever, and those piercing eyes.*

Gen bent in to speak in Yancy's ear. They were still holding hands, and Yancy thought for a minute she was coming in for a kiss. Her heart beat like a drum. *What the hell?*

Gen said quietly into her ear, "I noticed, Ms. Delaney, you are not wearing your sling. It's best if you keep it on to help the healing in your shoulder, you know." She drew back and smiled a little less sincerely. More professional tone, Yancy noted.

"Sure, Doc, but it's been so damn—I mean it's been pretty hot to be wearing that thing."

Then Gen surprised her by winking. "It's your healing, Ms. Delaney." She turned to Kate and Roxie. "Good to talk to you again, Roxie. Great to meet you, Kate. Hope to see more of you both. Bye."

Yancy watched Gen walk to her car, mesmerized by her grace. Suddenly, Yancy trotted toward Gen's car. "Wait a minute, I forgot to ask you something, Doc."

"Oh?" Gen turned to meet Yancy's eyes.

"I, um…" Yancy shocked herself by standing in front of the doctor about to ask her for a date. *Damn, get it together, Delaney.* "Somebody told me that you ride. When I met you at the interview, I mentioned you could ride here on our trails. I wanted to ask you to come ride with me on one of your next days off. Actually, y'all can come anytime. I've got several good trail horses. I'd show you some of the better trails." Yancy felt herself rambling, so stopped and held her breath.

"I've mostly done English riding and dressage, but I'm fine with Western too. I'd love to ride sometime. I'll have Betty give you a call with my schedule, okay?" Gen's smile was back to the wide genuine one that showed the crinkle of her eyes.

"And, I'd…just another…Actually it's none of my business. I, uh, kind of thought you batted for my team, so to speak." Yancy broke off her glance. She couldn't believe this had spurted out of her mouth. She waved off the question. "No. Never mind, you don't have to answer that. I'm…God, I can't believe I asked that! You must think I'm a total jackass. I'm sorry."

Gen paused briefly and looked up, as in thought. "So, you want the scoop. I'm sure the scuttlebutt has been flying." Gen drilled her eyes into Yancy's.

"No, no. Dr. Campbell, I mean Roxie, heard from one of the lab techs…oh hell, I'm sorry." Yancy put a hand out in dismissal, then turned to walk away.

Gen lightly took her arm, drew close to Yancy's ear, and said, "Yes, I bat for your team. Not only that, I'm first string." She winked, walked to her red Camry hybrid, and drove off down the lane, leaving Yancy standing with a small smile. *I like her.*

❧❧❧❧

"What the hell?" Roxie came to stand at Yancy's side. "Did she kiss you? My God, Yancy Delaney is blushing!"

"Shut up, dorkhead."

Roxie hugged Yancy.

"Get off me, you crazy shrink!"

"Now that's the old Yancy I know and love."

Nina sauntered up and put her hands on both women's shoulders. "Well, girls, I'd say the day went well." In the background, the band packed up and the caterers broke down tables and bagged trash. "All but one board member made it, most of the clinic staff came." Then she whispered, "And I think we'll be able to milk another twenty grand from Mike Scott. All in a good day's work, eh?" She looked directly at Yancy.

"Hello, darling, are you there?"

"Uh, sure, Mom. Yeah. A good party."

Yancy's brother approached them wearing his casual uniform of Polo shirt and khaki Dockers. "How did we do on the ask?" Phil inquired of Yancy and his mother.

"Geez, bro, this wasn't a fundraiser, it was a welcome party."

"But I saw you and Mom talking with Mike, so I assumed. We're always trying to get Mr. Skinflint to pony up, and since he'd had a couple of bourbons, I thought y'all were doing what you do."

"While we didn't bother him today, he did mention to me that he planned to write a check before the end of the month. He seemed enamored of Dr. Lambert." Nina turned her face back to Yancy and peered at her, slightly grinning. "I saw you talking with the new doctor. She's very attractive, isn't she?"

"Better go write the checks for the caterers and band." Yancy avoided Nina's glance to flee to the house.

After Yancy left, Roxie caught Nina's sly look. "Not sure what's going on, but I would say that woman has had her feet taken out from under her."

Nina turned to Roxie and said, "If Yancy could find what she had with Trisha...Connie and I worry ourselves sick."

"I know, so do Kate and I. Five years is a long time to grieve without moving on."

"What do you think? You know about these things. Does she need some medication or therapy? All our losses have been difficult for the whole family. But Yancy, since she was a child, always hid her emotions, even when she took things harder than any of us."

Phil snorted. "That'll be the day, when she does something healthy."

Roxie said, "I'm trying to get her to take the first step and admit she has depression, so that things can get rolling. You, of all people, know she's not the easiest person to convince."

Nina sighed. "If I can help in any way, please call on me. You know only too well that I'm the last person she'll listen to. She acquiesces to my wishes when we're together, but then does whatever she wants when I return to Denver."

Running his hands through his hair, Phil nodded.

Roxie did a double take.

Nina smiled smugly at Roxie and winked. "Oh, I've got my daughter's number. I thought Connie would be a good influence, and God knows she tries. I've always been happy that you've been her friend," she said, patting Roxie's arm. Nina sighed. "It's about time for us to go. See you in September, dear?"

"Yes, I'll be here for the fundraiser. Maybe by then the ball will be rolling on Operation Yancy, huh?" All three grinned ruefully. "We can only hope."

"C'mon, Phil." Nina took Phil's arm.

# Chapter Eight

"Sheila, is this the only record we have for Ms. Delaney?"

"Yancy?" Sheila peeked over Gen's shoulder at the medical record on her tablet. "I guess so, Dr. Lambert. What are you looking for?"

"Results from her last annual physical. Nina mentioned something about her not having regular physicals, but I thought it was just the overanxious mother talking."

"Gee." Sheila screwed her mouth. "Now that I think of it, I can't remember Mary Anne Delaney ever coming here for an annual."

"Oh. Where does she go? It's not odd that a board member might want to have a physician somewhere else."

"Nowhere I know of. We've never sent any test results to any other primary care, as far as I know. At least not the ten years I've worked here. She's never come here for anything but a few cuts and sprains."

"Okay, then, never mind." Gen knocked and entered the exam room.

"Ms. Delaney, good to see you." Gen continued to scan the vital signs that Sheila had recorded minutes before. "Blood pressure looks good, everything normal. I would like to see your shoulder."

"Hi to you, too, Doc." Yancy took off the sling, unbuttoned her shirt, and lowered the sleeve off her left arm. She smirked.

Gen tried not to notice the ribs she could see, the muscular shoulder, or defined abs. She gently prodded the injury site and checked range of motion in the joint. Yancy grimaced. "Feel that?"

"I'm fine."

"Mm-hmm. How're you sleeping? How's the pain level?"

"Fine."

Gen squinted her eyes. "Ms. Delaney—"

"Can we get to first names? Yancy?"

"Okay, Yancy." Gen knew a side-step when she saw it. "So?"

"Fine and fine."

*Oh boy, one-word answers.* "Your shoulder is healing nicely. You don't have to wear the sling any longer." Yancy smirked again. "Although I imagine that won't change what you've already been doing," Gen added.

Gen typed some notes into the tablet and made a show of scrolling up and down. "Since this is your first non-urgent visit with me, I was trying to find some baseline vitals on you, and test results, like chest X-ray, PAP, mammogram, routine blood work. Where do you receive those services?" Gen drilled her best "clinically removed" look into Yancy.

"Don't have any." Yancy made a show of reading a poster about asthma on the wall, then pointed to it. "This is good info."

Perusing Yancy's medical record on her tablet, Gen decided to lay it on thick. "Let me see if I understand you correctly. You have never had a routine physical as an adult? You are...forty-one? Right?" Gen waited a beat and realized Yancy was not going to respond, because she continued to peer intently at the asthma poster. Gen crossed her arms to gird herself. "I would expect this in someone with no insurance, or perhaps no car to get to appointments. But what I don't understand is why someone in your situation would forgo basic health services. Not only that, you and your family have built the best rural health clinics in the state. You are high-risk for both cancer and heart disease, given your brother and father's histories." Gen stopped and took a breath. "If I understand your board work correctly, one of your jobs is the health of this community. What kind of example are you setting?"

Yancy continued to look busy reading the asthma poster. She shrugged.

"Where is your sense of self-worth?" Gen waited a moment, then added, "Do you have a death wish?"

Yancy's head jerked up. She looked at Gen and quickly looked away.

With a gentle look of compassion Gen said, "What are you afraid of, Yancy?"

Yancy slid off the exam table, not glancing at Gen, and buttoned her shirt quickly. So softly Gen wasn't sure she had said anything at first, she spoke. "I guess my shoulder's doing well. I'll see Bernie in two weeks to get the cast off. Let me know when you want to go riding." She shut the exam door quietly behind her.

The closed door with the damn asthma poster mocked Gen. *What a person of extremes. One minute she's all seduction, the next she's a petulant child, then a professional board member. She's smart. Her clinic work shows her conscience and compassion. But what a button I pushed when I brought up illness and loss. And what about a death wish? She masks her fear with anger, macho sexuality, bravado. I wish I could have hugged her to me and taken away all that hurt right now. Beautiful chocolate eyes, graceful movements in those damn Levi's and boots. Even disheveled in bed she looked great. Oh God!*

Gen closed her eyes a moment, puffed out, and called to her nurse. "Sheila? Who's up next?" Gen poked her head out into the hallway.

❧❧❧❧

Yancy answered her phone the next afternoon when Roxie's name popped up.

"Where you been?"

"Went for a ride. Then Victor and I worked in the barn. One of the horses kicked the shit out of a stall. Got little kids arriving all afternoon for lessons. I'm working on the books right now and ordering some more hay, because of the damn dry weather."

"You sound tired. What's going on?"

"Have a pounding headache, too." Yancy blew out a gust of air and rubbed her head. "Not sleeping."

"Are you still there?"

Yancy weighed her next sentence. "Have you kept up with all your woman exams?"

Roxie laughed. "Woman exams? What are you, thirteen? You mean PAP test, mammogram, that kind of stuff? Sure. Once a year, I go and spread 'em for some dork in a white coat to feel me up. Then my breasts get smashed in a machine and I'm good for another year or two. Piece of cake. At least we'll have a woman doctor doing these icky exams now. And she seems to be a good listener. I like her."

"Yeah, whatever."

"You can't fool me. I know you like her, too." Roxie laughed.

"Don't be so sure. She can be an asshole."

"I don't believe it."

"Take my word for it. She's a bitch sometimes."

"You're full of shit, Delaney."

"She went on for about ten minutes about my lack of annual exam records yesterday. It's not her business if I don't think I need that stuff. I'm not screwing some dude, so I don't need exams to get the pill and I'm not old enough to—"

"Wait, wait...did I hear you correctly? Are you crazy? You've never had preventive care?" Roxie's voice raised considerably.

"Why would I get a test to find cancer? Who wants to find it? Don't call me crazy."

"Don't take it out on me. I'm your friend. I can't believe I didn't know that you didn't get exams. I would have kicked your ass. And not only that, don't you head up the health care for this county? Aren't you always trying to get Mike Scott to loosen his tight grip on his millions so uninsured ranch hands can have a regular doctor?" Roxie huffed, then finished. "What the hell's the matter with you?"

"Now you sound like Gen. Why can't people mind their own business?"

"For your information, this is what friends do. They help take care of each other and point out their faults when they are being total dorkheads. Jesus, what about relationships don't you understand?"

Yancy paused. "Is there a reason you called me?"

"What? Wait...We're not done with this conversation. And yes, I called to see if you wanted to come over for supper, because you won't eat unless someone puts it in your mouth. You're driving poor Connie and your mother, not to mention me, to an early grave. Also, while we're on the subject of the clinic, I assume what you are griping about is that you saw Dr. Gen and she rained on your stoic parade. Did you do that depression screening you promised to do?"

"Why don't you go screw yourself? And, what time do you want me for supper?"

"See you at seven, dorkhead. Bye!"

☙ ☙ ☙ ☙

Because she had waited to shower until the lessons had finished and the seven kids, Marsha, and Virgie had left, Yancy ran late. For a relaxed night with Roxie and Kate, she put on her worn, most comfortable, clean Levi's, her broken-in boots, and an old, faded shirt. But as she pulled up to their house in town, a red Camry hybrid was parked in front. *Damn. At least I'm good at improvising.*

"The cavalry has arrived. Beer for you, my dear." She handed the six-pack to Kate. "And wine for you." She handed the wine bottle to Roxie, bowing slightly. She flourished a bouquet of flowers from Connie's prized flower bed, bowed deeply from the waist to Gen, and in her best French accent, intoned, "*Et pour vous, ma chère, beauté pour la belle*, beauty for the beautiful. Or something like that."

"Boy, you must be feeling better," Roxie said, laughing.

Yancy gave her the evil eye while pointing to her old, worn clothes, then said in an undertone, "If I'd known she would be here, I would have dressed better."

"Sorry," Roxie mouthed back.

"Gen, long time no see."

Gen smiled and nodded to Yancy.

"What's up, Kate? Didn't get to talk to you much at the barbecue for our heartthrob of a doctor." Yancy glanced at Gen to see if she reacted. Gen continued to smile, and shook her head a bit.

Roxie kissed Yancy on the cheek and patted Kate's shoulder as she walked by her chair. At the door to the kitchen, she slid her arm through Gen's and announced that they were going to finish a couple of things for supper. Yancy appreciated Gen's hips' sway in khaki chinos, and the lovely auburn highlights in her upswept hairdo.

"Don't like this dry spell we're having. How're your pastures holding up?" Kate was all matter-of-fact, down to earth. She propped her shined boots on the ottoman.

Yancy sat across from Kate in another club chair, then inclined toward her to whisper conspiratorially. "What's up with the ambush? I didn't know she was going to be here."

Kate shrugged. "You know me, I'm not the matchmaker in the family." She chuckled.

Yancy said, "Damn." Kate was always clueless when it came to gossip.

"What? Everybody can see how you look at her. Don't be too grateful."

"Sarcasm. That's a new one for you, buddy." Yancy punched her lightly on the shoulder. "I enjoy a nice body and a smart mind like anyone else."

"Whatever you say, stud. But I think you have something for her. Better watch out, she's not one of your gals from Spanky's."

"Sure. Hell, don't you think I know that? Time

for a beer." Yancy took in Kate's comment. Maybe Gen wasn't a Spanky's type, but she was still a woman, wasn't she?

At supper, Yancy fidgeted with her food, taking small bites here and there. "Delicious, Roxie." Gen looked at Roxie, then, pointedly, at Yancy. "Wouldn't you say?"

"Yeah, yeah. Roxie's a great cook." Yancy did not take the provocation to react to Gen's not-so-veiled hint about her lack of eating, and changed the subject. "So, Gen, when're we going riding? I get my cast off soon, but I've been out a couple of times already. Rode this afternoon for an hour. It's going to be sunny this weekend, if you are off and want to come out."

"Sure. I'm off Saturday." Gen ate. She looked up and smiled.

"Good." Yancy felt her heart do a little dance. "You said you did dressage as a teen. Where did you learn?"

"Dad was an army doctor. When I was in high school, he worked at Bethesda, so I took lessons in Virginia." She put her finger on her chin, pausing. "His last posting before retiring was at Ft. Campbell, Kentucky, and I did a few dressage competitions while I was at UK. I stayed for med school, and the rural medicine track in my residency. I practiced there about eight years total." She looked at each of them. "Kentucky's the only place I've ever lived that looked like its postcards." She laughed softly, and Kate and Roxie nodded their agreement.

"I've been to the Keeneland thoroughbred sales a couple of times, but that's my only time there," Yancy said. "That was something else, all the Arab horse farm owners, Queen Elizabeth's horse people. It was way too rich for me. I was looking only for quarter horses at a local farm. Did you own a horse there?"

"I really wanted to, but no. I didn't have time to ride in med school and I didn't want to just board a horse and leave it. My friend Dan Philpott's family ran a horse farm, which is how I met him in college, taking lessons. He, his wife Stacy, and I all went into rural medicine together. Stacy is slated to be the next director of the UK program."

"Sounds like good people," Kate announced. She mopped up the remaining morsels on her plate with a piece of bread.

"Time for dessert, ladies," Roxie said a few minutes later, beginning to gather plates from the table.

Yancy caught her hand. "No way. Gen and I will clean up and bring the dessert, right?" She winked and Gen nodded.

As Yancy brought in another stack from the table, Gen loaded up the dishwasher. The sight of Gen bent over, those chinos hugging the round butt, made Yancy's core melt, and something clicked inside her, compelling her to move closer. She sidled up behind Gen, cupped her rear, and pressed her crotch into her backside. "Nice ass, Doctor."

Gen shot straight up, turned around with blazing eyes, pulled back, and soundly slapped Yancy across the face. "Don't you ever touch me again without my permission!" she said in a low, fierce voice.

Yancy put her hand to her cheek, squinting her eyes. *Oops, a tactical error. Kate just told me this woman wasn't like Spanky's Friday night girls.* Yancy slowly grinned. "So…" She cleared her throat and looked Gen in the eye for a full minute.

Gen returned her look with a challenging,

unblinking glare, breathing rapidly, her face flushed. After a while, her breathing slowed.

"Okay, Doctor," Yancy said finally. She turned to go back into the dining room. *So much for trying to seduce the doctor. That way.*

Roxie, with a look of distress on her face, had leapt up from her chair. Kate looked puzzled. Controlling her emotions into a neutral face, Yancy motioned Roxie back down. "No problem."

"What the hell, Yancy?" she whispered.

Yancy shrugged. She stacked the remaining dishes and carried them into the kitchen. A few minutes later, both she and Gen returned carrying dishes of cookies-and-cream ice cream, neither betraying that anything had happened. Yancy got busy spooning ice cream into her mouth.

It was Gen who broke the tense silence. "Kate, how long have you been doing ranch work?"

Kate's shoulders visibly relaxed a little. She warmed to her tale of her two brothers and one cousin, all of whom she worked with, to maintain the ranch that had come into the extended family back in the late 1890s. Kate, never one to talk at great length, surprised Yancy by spreading out the conversation over the next fifteen minutes, until all traces of the women's uneasiness were forgotten, and jokes about calving season and her brothers' horse training mishaps warmed the icy air.

They left the table to drink coffee in the living room. Roxie and Kate sat together on the love seat, leaving Gen and Yancy on opposite ends of the couch. For the rest of the evening, they all talked together easily. Gen shared stories of some of her eastern Kentucky patients. Yancy recognized local Babcock county "types" in medical lore. Patients were the same all over.

After another hour, Yancy yawned and stretched, and made going-home talk, followed by Gen's thanks to the hostesses.

Yancy asked Gen gently, "Can I walk you to your car?"

Gen, not replying, picked up her shoulder bag and gave Kate and Roxie each a light hug, saying good night. Yancy waved to them, quirked her mouth in a rueful grin, and escorted Gen out the door.

"Look, I'm sorry." Yancy stood awkwardly next to Gen's car door.

Gen eyed Yancy for a moment, her arms across her chest, as she leaned against her sedan. Sighing, she said, "I don't get you. You seem to be a perfectly fine person that I would like to get to know better, but you seem hell-bent on shooting yourself in the foot. Right now, I'm not sure I want to see you again."

Yancy's heart fell, but she immediately wiped off any traces of feeling from her face. She cleared her throat. "I went for a ride this afternoon to my favorite thinking place…Don't look at me that way. Yes, I really do some wool-gathering occasionally. I came to the conclusion that you might be right."

"About which of the catalog of things I said to you at the clinic?"

Yancy chuckled. "Can't remember them all. I guess the part about being scared." Yancy ran her fingers through her hair, looking up at the sky. "Will you take a walk with me? It's a beautiful night, the moon is nearly full. I promise not to make any moves."

"Why should I?"

"Hell, I don't know. I heard you say you would

like to get to know me better. Oh, forget it." Yancy threw her arms up and slapped her hands against her thighs, then made to turn and leave.

Gen grabbed her arm. "I may be nuts to do this, but let's walk. I do have to leave soon. Working tomorrow."

Yancy led her down the sidewalk. "I like you, Dr. Lambert. You don't take my bullshit."

They shuffled down the sidewalk of Roxie and Kate's street.

Yancy's heart gave little skips, and her breath came rapidly. She couldn't get the silly grin off her face. "Tell me, when did you know you wanted to be a physician? And were you out before you went to medical school?"

"Boy, you don't beat around the bush, do you?" Gen's eyebrows shot up and she snickered. "Yes, I was out in college, after about three semesters of dating men. Then I met a woman who was an art major. We were opposites. Where I was the studious pre-med student, she was carefree and laid back. Even so, we clicked. We had a relationship until we graduated and went our separate ways. We're still friends." Gen looked at Yancy, who focused on listening. "I really didn't date much until my residency, when I met my partner, Rachel. She was a pathology resident. I don't know if you know anything about pathologists, but the main reason they like their patients to be dead is so they don't need to have much bedside manner." Gen shook her head slightly. "Not the best girlfriend material, I later found out. We divorced two years ago."

"What are you, in your thirties?"

"Thirty-eight. Why?"

"Let's see, you were together, what…a good ten

or twelve years? You're not a quick study, Doc."

"You said it. She was truly an interesting person. I kept thinking things would get better between us. I guess I hoped I could bring her out of herself, or something. I learned never to try to fix someone I was married to, but not until I caught her in bed with one of the med center administrators."

"Ouch."

"How about you? What's your history?"

"Trisha is the only long-term thing I've had. I dated some at U. Denver and saw a couple people at Wharton."

"You have an MBA from Penn?"

"Uh, yeah…"

"I have to say, you take me by surprise."

"Is that a good thing?"

"As long as the surprises are not like the one I had in the kitchen." Gen stopped walking, turned to Yancy, and gazed into her eyes. "Go on, about Trisha."

Yancy looked away from Gen's gaze, studying the pavement, stuffing her uninjured hand into her jeans pocket. It surprised Yancy to have someone pay attention to her. It felt good. "We met at Wharton my last semester. She was a year behind me, but five years older. After she graduated, Trisha had to return home to Albuquerque, to meet the obligations to the company that supported her MBA studies. But when she completed her contract, she came to Colorado to work in marketing for the women's health system in the metro area. She did some riding lessons for me on the weekends. We were together on and off. Finally, we became serious. A few months later she was diagnosed with Stage Four breast cancer." Yancy inhaled audibly. "The treatment didn't do anything. She was gone in another six months, only forty-one years old."

Gen was quiet for some moments, then gently said, "Hard stuff." She placed her hand on Yancy's arm.

Yancy choked, fighting the welling tears. She wiped her right hand down her face, then shoved it back into her pocket. "Have you been dating lately? Is there someone back in the Bluegrass State?"

"No. No one." Gen paused. She placed her hand on Yancy's forearm. "Yancy, I'm not a psychiatrist. I don't want to butt into your life, but in my opinion, you seem to be suffering from what is called complicated grief."

Yancy's lips froze into a hard line on her face. She took a step back from Gen.

"Please, know I'm only saying this because I feel we are making a connection." Gen removed her hand from Yancy's arm. She turned and continued to stroll down the sidewalk.

Yancy contemplated whether she should follow her. Did Gen really want to know her better? No one but Trisha ever wanted that. Right then Yancy's phone chimed, signaling a text message. She read it and quirked a small smile. "Roxie and Kate think we've been eaten by wolves. Both our cars are still in their driveway."

"I've got to go." Gen looked at Yancy with those piercing eyes.

Yancy stared back into that perfectly wonderful face.

"This has been nice." Gen smiled. "You're right, I wouldn't have wanted to miss such a pleasant moon."

Neither of them moved. Yancy licked her lips, eying Gen's mouth. "Have I made up for, you know, the kitchen?"

"You don't get off that easy. Also, that was just one of your little forays into sexual harassment. You've just begun to redeem yourself." Gen gave Yancy a steely look.

Yancy thought she might as well plow forward. "You're still coming Saturday? We have a date with some horses. We don't want to disappoint them. It will give me another chance to…get to know you. Let you see I'm not a total jackass."

Yancy saw the hesitation in Gen's eyes before she spoke. "I hope you take to heart what I said about grief. And, um…sure. See you Saturday."

Yancy nodded, numbly watching her get into her car. Then, realizing her car was blocking Gen's, she did a quick jog to her Rover and got in.

ℵℵℵℵ

"What a piece of work," Gen said into her phone, her legs on the couch. "Does Jack still think it's the nineties? I can't believe he wants to appoint only men to the task force on women's health, which was our idea in the first place!"

"I'm really missing you, my dear. There are only two women in the department now. How can I make a stand for us, get Jack to back down, without you here? I need your keen wit and pithy comments." Stacy's voice sounded sad.

"I could use you out here, too. I've got a board member who's been somewhat of a pill. Even moving toward sexual harassment."

"Holy crap. Can you get the guy off the board?"

"No, no. It's not like that. She's the board president, the daughter of the founder of the Valley

View Medical Center, and really knows her stuff about rural medicine. I don't want to get rid of her, I just want her to get some help."

"What kind of help?"

"Kind of a complex situation. She had to go through the deaths of both her dad and brother when she was only in her twenties. Then her partner died five years ago. She's still wallowing around in heavy grief. She acts out all over the place, womanizing, everything a sexual innuendo."

"Man, I'd slap her face."

Gen snickered. "I did, a few nights ago."

Stacy gasped. "No way! It's like…you know. That older doc in Pineville. The guy who pinched you when you got caught alone together in the elevator?"

"Oh, my God, yes. I had forgotten all about him. Then there was the surgery resident, Kevin, who thought he was such a stud muffin. He kept asking me out and wouldn't take no for an answer. What a jerk." Gen blew out a huff.

"Well, you finally told him to bug off, that you were gay. I was in shock when he tried to convince you that you only needed a real man. I saw you slap him after he grabbed you. He turned fifteen shades of pink."

"Thank God he never spoke to me again."

They both giggled for a minute. When Gen's laughter died down, she said, "But seriously, this woman is really smart and has a heart for health care. She runs a ranch all on her own. And did I tell you she looks like Angie Harmon? She's not hard to look at!"

"Whoa. The actress? The one you watch on *Law and Order* reruns? And that cop and doc show?"

"After Rachel, I could never again watch that cop and doctor thing. Remember? The doctor was a pathologist. Ugh!"

"Right. So, what's happening with Angie Harmon the rancher? You've got to work with her on the board. That's got to suck."

"That's the kicker, Stace. She's great in professional situations. She gets the issues we're balancing, between making the clinic financially viable and keeping services low cost. Recruiting docs to the boonies. The whole thing. She's pretty cute when she's telling the banker that we need his millions. She can be a real charmer."

"But she's got this asshole thing going on?"

"You know, there are deep waters there. I can sense it. She shows little glimpses of total vulnerability, but quickly hides behind the sexual stuff. I've heard she's had only one-night stands since her partner died five years ago. She uses her cockiness as a shield, which is too bad." Gen took a deep breath. "God, I sound like I have a thing for her."

"Ooh, boy."

"I'm afraid. I'm terrified that she's another makeover project, like Rachel. And you know how well that worked. She didn't have much self-awareness to work with, and by the time I figured that out, I had invested all my emotional capital, while she was sleeping with the director of marketing."

"Oh, come on. You're older and wiser now. I hear a difference in your voice when you talk about your rancher. You haven't even told me her name."

"Yancy. Actually, Mary Anne Delaney."

"Delaney from Colorado? You know, that name sounds familiar." The phone was silent for a few moments. "I know. She was on the Rural Health Association's development committee, when I worked with our Kentucky chapter. She was great. You're right, she's really smart. I liked her a lot when I worked with her. But she didn't attend the social mixers, so I didn't get to know her very well. Geez, she's a mover and shaker at RHA. You have a lot in common. I hope you can make a go of this relationship."

"There is no relationship. She's barely an acquaintance, because I only met her two months ago, and most of that time has been between my interview and actually starting the job. We've worked together so little, she is still an enigma." Gen was exasperated.

"Yeah, but once you have slapped someone and continue to talk to them, maybe you've made an impression...Ha! More than the impression of your hand on their cheek, I mean. Maybe there's hope. Sounds like she has Princess Charming possibilities."

# Chapter Nine

On Tuesday, Marlene arrived at her usual time, right as Yancy tied her horse to crossties in the barn for her to groom and tack up. Walking up the aisle of the barn, Marlene edged up to Yancy. "Hi, good looking," she said, pressing along Yancy's legs and wrapping her hands around her waist.

"Your horse is ready," Yancy mumbled, disengaging from Marlene's grip.

"Well, I can certainly see that." Marlene sighed. "What's with the cold shoulder?"

"Nothing, I just have things to do today, so let's get started with your lesson." Yancy did not look at her.

Marlene huffed. "Okay." She grabbed the grooming brush from her roughly. "I can see where this is going. Or should I say, where it's not going." Yancy looked up to Marlene's fierce stare. "Someone else in the bed these days?"

Yancy jerked her head to glower coldly at Marlene. "Not your business, is it?"

Marlene grunted and turned to her horse.

❧❧❧❧

Saturday morning dawned beautifully bright, with a warm breeze over the plain when Yancy woke earlier than normal, feeling excited. She bounded down the stairs in scuffed riding boots and old jeans, and streaked through the back door, yelling behind her, "Coffee and lots of it. Maybe some toast. Back in a few after getting the horses in the stable."

In ten minutes, she sped back into the kitchen. The coffee was bolted down, two bites of toast barely chewed. "Dr. Lambert will be here around eight thirty. Please tell her to come to the stable. Thanks, Connie." And she banged out the back door again.

Marquette and his dam, Golden Girl, were both in the barn. Victor brushed the mare with a curry comb. "I'll get started on Marquette," Yancy told him, and she ducked underneath the cross-tie to get to her horse.

"Both of them seem pretty good today. Going to be another hot one," Victor said, keeping to his task. "Later this morning, Chuck, Alan, and I'll drive the herd into the north pasture, because the cattle have taken care of all the grass to be had south toward the bluff."

"Mm-hmm." Yancy hummed distractedly, getting the clumps of dirt from Marquette's coat. When she finished with brushing, she picked up his back-left hoof and carefully picked out the dirt and debris around the soft frog. When she had finished, she leaned into the horse's body and hefted the back-right hoof to repeat the procedure.

"Morning, ma'am," Victor said, doffing his hat slightly. Yancy glanced up from her job bent over Marquette's hoof.

Gen walked farther into the barn aisle. "Looks like a beautiful day for a ride, Victor. How're you?" Gen had a large smile.

Gen looked luscious in her riding outfit. Yancy's

heart did a little happy dance. "Morning." Yancy stood and beamed at Gen. Motioning to the mare, she said, "If you want to take over Golden Girl's grooming from Victor, I'll be a few more minutes with my horse." Reluctant to break the connection, Yancy slowly bent back to her work on Marquette.

Golden Girl whinnied softly at Gen. She laughed, and spoke softly to her, smoothing her hands across her withers and back. "You mind? I brought a carrot."

"No problem, but don't make a habit of it. It encourages them to bite."

When the carrot was put under her muzzle, Golden Girl immediately bit into it and crunched loudly. "You're a beauty? How old are you? About six or seven?"

"She's eight. Marquette is her son."

"They are both wonderful. I like Palominos." Gen took the soft grooming brush from Victor, who then left the barn for the truck. Yancy heard Chuck and Alan's Jeep drive onto the ranch road, to join Victor in the cattle herding.

Gen continued. "Palominos remind me of Roy Rogers's horse, Trigger. Boy, that was a while ago. Watching those really old reruns. Did you ever want to be a cowgirl like Dale Evans?"

"Are you kidding?" Yancy laughed quietly, looking up from the hoof in her hand. "I wanted to be Roy Rogers. No sissy girl for me. He always got to shoot guns and ride fast to get the bad guys. All Dale did was sing songs after it was over." Yancy finished Marquette's last hoof. "I thought I was going to grow up to be Roy Rogers, in fact. It wasn't until I started filling out that I realized I was really a girl after all."

"Wow, that *is* a tomboy! Me, I had visions

of being a medieval lady riding with my knight in procession. Later, I caught on that my fantasy knight was a lady dressed in armor. But it took me awhile. I don't imagine you ever played with Barbies?"

"Ha!" Yancy guffawed. She saw the small smile that lit Gen's face and smirked back. "You about ready? I'll run in and see what kind of picnic Connie put together, then we can get on the trail." Yancy smiled all the way to the house. She loved their playful banter.

༄ཉ྄ཉ྄ཉ྄

They rode in silence, taking in the early morning breeze. As the sun rose higher, the heat shimmered. Yancy pulled Marquette back and rode beside Gen.

"How many acres here?" Gen's arms swept across the landscape in front of them.

"About two thousand, give or take. The river meanders to displace the geography every few wet years. Not exactly like a Kentucky horse farm, is it?"

Gen nodded. "But this has a whole other kind of beauty. The long views. The distant snow-covered peaks give me chills. And the air here has a distinct quality. Not as humid, and a different smell of sage or something. It's unmistakable."

"Glad you like your new home." Yancy glanced over at Gen, watching her small grin as she took in the vistas of the ranch. Yancy felt her insides doing flips, her eyes unable to leave the vision that was Gen.

To get herself out of the trance, she suddenly yelled, "Wanna race?" Marquette was spurred into a gallop nearly before Yancy finished her challenge. "Go to that big tree."

"Hey, cheater!" Gen called out, and followed her at a good clip.

They raced flat out, Golden Girl coming up fast. They both reached the tree at about the same moment. Yancy had lost her hat, and Gen's previously carefully clipped hair strung along her reddened cheek. They both laughed and caught their breath, reining the horses to a halt.

"You're a good rider," Yancy said, as she took in the heightened glow on Gen's face.

"Thanks. It's so beautiful."

"Yes, it is." Yancy stared at Gen and licked her dry lips.

Gen caught Yancy looking directly into her eyes. She shook her head slightly. "You and your Princess Charming thing."

"What if I told you it wasn't a thing, but the truth. That I find you very attractive in every way."

Gen scrutinized Yancy's eyes, a small scowl wrinkled her eyebrow. "I never know when you're going to be good Yancy or bad Yancy. I've seen you be so ornery, and I don't like being caught in the crossfire of your sexual taunting."

Yancy reined Marquette closer to Golden Girl. She peeled off the leather riding glove from her good hand, and it trembled as she stroked Gen's cheek. Even with a dry mouth, she managed to say, "Oh, darlin'. I'm having a hard time, too. I'm scared because my heart has taken about all the beating it can handle." She lowered her hand. "Don't you get it? Don't you see me stumbling around you and getting all tied up?"

Gen's eyes squinted. Yancy felt Gen's challenge. "What makes me different than all the others? How can I be sure this isn't a bait and switch, that you won't drop me like yesterday's news when a hot cowgirl walks into your path?"

Yancy held Gen's steely gaze, and whispered, "I
don't…" She leaned over her saddle and kissed Gen
lingeringly. She continued the kiss until Gen pulled
back and gasped, staring at her, eyes wide, clutching
her throat.

"Is that my answer," Gen whispered, taking
shallow breaths.

Yancy stroked Gen's cheek again with a feather
touch. The spell was broken when Yancy inhaled and
said, "Whew." It's probably time for lunch."

After a quick picnic of sandwiches and apples,
they trotted and cantered back to the corral. Yancy
occasionally looked at Gen, and occasionally caught
Gen looking at her. She found it hard to speak, so she
broached mundane topics for a few moments, and then
lapsed into silence again.

Finally, trotting into the ranch yard, they led the
horses for a rubdown before they released them into
their corrals. Still in the barn, Gen turned to Yancy with
sparkling eyes. "It was a lovely day. I enjoyed seeing the
ranch. And I enjoyed our ride, and especially getting
to know you better." She bent to brush dust from her
riding breeches, and when she rose up, she locked eyes
with Yancy. "I was wondering, the last time I invited
you for dinner, you broke your wrist. Would you like
to try for dinner again?"

Yancy ran her hand through her hair, unleashing
her ponytail. She rubbed her hand along her pants, and
shoved her hand into the jeans pocket. "Sure. What
day?"

"I'll text you after I look at my schedule for the
next couple of weeks." Gen leaned in and gave Yancy a
quick kiss on the cheek, and left.

Yancy dreamily grinned, watching Gen walk

down the aisle and out into the ranch yard to her car. She knew Gen was trouble. Something real was happening to her heart and it scared her to death. On her way to the house, she alternated between grinning stupidly and looking up to the sky, as if expecting an answer to fall on her.

❧❧❧❧

Later that week, Yancy typed away in the ranch office, surfing the web. Connie startled her. "When do you want lunch?"

Yancy quickly shut the laptop lid. "Oh, whenever, I'm just looking up some…stuff."

"You look kind of guilty. Porn?" Connie laughed.

"No, it's not porn." Yancy stood and met Connie in the doorway. "I'm going to Denver tomorrow to have lunch with Mom, so I'll be gone all day. Wanted you to know."

"Good for you to get away. Midsummer can be kind of slow. Families going on vacation, then getting kids ready for school. Why don't you go somewhere fun? You haven't been on vacation for a while."

Yancy ran her hand through her long hair, tendrils spilling out from the ponytail. "I'll think about it. I am going to the Rural Health Association conference in October. It's close, in Phoenix this year… Don't scowl at me. I know it's business, but I always enjoy those things. They're good networking for the clinic. I meet interesting people. Gen, I mean, Dr. Lambert is also representing the clinics." Yancy felt her face redden.

Connie raised an eyebrow. "I see. You'll not be alone, then. Good, good." She turned to go back to the kitchen. "Lunch will be ready in five minutes."

# *Chapter Ten*

Yancy got on the road to Denver early. She was dressed in her "meeting with Mom" clothes: a more upscale, ecru, linen pants outfit. Nina had high standards for dress and comportment, which Yancy had bucked as a teenager. But the older she got, the more she had given up and played by her mom's rules, dressed up, and acted polite, but it rankled her a little that her mom still had this control over her. At least she drew the line at wearing dresses.

The heat had abated a bit, for which she was grateful. In her back seat were clothes for later at Spanky's; it wasn't a trip into the city without stopping to see who was at the Country Friday Night. She hoped to hell it wasn't going to be Cheyenne.

"Hello, darling, you look very nice today." Nina brushed her red lips over Yancy's cheek. She pulled back to appraise her daughter. "You seem less pale, too. I'm so glad."

Yancy smiled. Always aware of her mom's scrutiny, she'd taken no risks today with her appearance. Nina had on her more casual pants and top, both high-quality raw silk, Yancy noted.

Nina continued the top-to-bottom scan. "I'd still like to see you put on some weight. Those slacks seem to be hanging off you. How are you doing?"

"Great, Mom." Yancy squirmed in Nina's arms like a three-year-old, getting free and taking her seat at one end of the huge table in Nina's formal dining room. It was set for a light lunch, but with the usual china and crystal.

"Phil couldn't come today. He says there is too much happening with the markets. Iced tea?"

"Well, the futures market is all over the place this summer because of the heat and dry spell. I can imagine he's working his ass...butt off."

They ate their Cobb salads, making small talk. Yancy fidgeted in her chair. They talked about the barbecue and the clinic, and about the hard, dry summer at the ranch.

When they finished, Yancy put her napkin next to her plate, cleared her throat, and began. "I have a question."

Nina raised her eyebrows, but said nothing.

"I, uh...geez, I can't believe I am going to ask this." She looked down at her plate. She took a deep breath, knowing how much may be riding on her getting herself in hand. "Do you know of any good shrinks?"

Nina's eyes grew wide for only a second, her face became neutral then. "Yes, a few here in the metro area." Nina placed her napkin next to her plate. "I know them primarily from my work on the hospital volunteer board over the years. Why do you ask?"

"I can't see anyone back home. I need some privacy, and well..." Yancy looked up from the table. Her heart pounded. She wiped her hand on her pants.

Nina reached across to stroke her hand. "Oh, darling, I know this is hard." Nina gave a gentle and caring look at her daughter. "Let me get you the names of two or three good psychiatrists. I'll be right back."

While Nina went to her office, Yancy fiddled with her spoon. She stood and paced to the window and back to the table, sitting when Nina came gracefully into the dining room with a folded piece of linen paper.

Yancy took the paper and said thanks in a small voice, then looked around, feeling lost. Suddenly, she rose from the table, looked at Nina's raised eyebrows, kissed her mother on the cheek, and quietly let herself out.

When Yancy reached her Rover, she looked over the list. There were two female names and one male name. "No sense dragging my feet." She blew out under her breath. With slightly shaky hands, she typed the first number into her phone.

An hour later, she found herself headed to a street near the medical center complex to have an intake exam with a Dr. Jillian Foster's office. It was enough to make Yancy's head spin. She hadn't given herself time to think twice about what she was doing, to stew about it, to back out, or to call herself on how incredible this all was. Or to talk herself into being the stoic person she had become since life started running all over her heart.

As she located the street number for Dr. Foster's office building, she wiped perspiration from her upper lip. Her stomach fluttered. Her breathing was a little ragged. She steeled herself and stepped onto the pavement, walked intently across the parking lot and through the glass doors into the mauve and beige reception area of a multiple-practitioner, mental health practice.

A pleasant, middle-aged receptionist took her name. Yancy handed over her insurance card, and received a clipboard with a form attached. Yancy sat in a comfortable chair, looked over the form, then, taking the pen that had been given to her, filled in the blanks about her address, contact numbers, and health issues. She came to the question, "What brings you into Dr. Foster's office today?" After taking a minute, she quickly wrote, "depression, grief." After Yancy handed in the completed form, she was asked to enter a small room down a short corridor.

"This is the depression screening checklist that Dr. Foster asks you fill out before you see her. It's private and confidential, only you and her will be able to see the results. You start here at this website, and just follow the prompts." With a mouse, the receptionist pointed to an icon on a laptop. "When you finish, open the door, but stay in this room and someone will come for you shortly."

Yancy nodded and mumbled thanks as the receptionist closed the door. For a few minutes, she sat at the small table in front of the laptop, taking big, fill-out-your-chest breaths. Finally, she thought, *What the hell, let's just get this over with.* She clicked the icon. The program came up, all bright colors and easy-to-read fonts. She read the prompts and began. In a about half an hour she had answered all types of questions, from eating habits to sexual habits. She sat back from the table and inhaled deeply. Her eyes were a little blurry from the screen time, causing her to blink. She opened the door, and waited until a petite woman with salt-and-pepper hair knocked lightly on the doorframe.

"Mary Anne?"

"Yes," Yancy answered and stood up. The woman beckoned her to follow down the same corridor. The room was well decorated, with an oriental rug, a large beige leather couch and two matching armchairs, a couple of end tables with lamps, a small coffee table, and a wooden credenza-type, horizontal filing cabinet. One wall held floor-to-ceiling bookshelves crowded with books. On the other walls hung abstract prints and oils in bright reds, blues, and golds. The overall feeling was warm and inviting, yet professional. Yancy's shoulders relaxed a bit.

The woman closed the door, turned to Yancy, offered her hand, and said, "Ms. Delaney, I'm Jill Foster. Before we begin, I understand the time slot opened rather suddenly when one of my clients cancelled this afternoon. I hope you are free for the entire fifty minutes?"

Yancy took her hand, which was neither too firm nor too soft, but didn't return the small woman's smile. She stuttered, "Sure, no problem. I…" The doctor took one of the armchairs and motioned for her to find a seat. Yancy swallowed hard and wondered what the hell she was doing in this office. "The time works for me. It's…it's my first time to do something like this. I'm not even sure why I'm here." She stared at the art on the wall behind the doctor's head, and gave a small laugh. God, she felt pathetic. She fiddled with the buttons on her shirt. Her stomach did somersaults.

"Let's start with just a few questions about you, and then we can discuss why you came in today." The doctor quirked her head to the side. Her smile was compassionate and kind, Yancy thought. A few deep breaths loosened her tight shoulders some more.

For the next forty minutes, Yancy gave the basic information about herself, her family, and her work. Then, she launched into the details of the deaths of her brother, her father, and Trisha. As she was relating the litany of loss, she found herself getting closer and closer to the huge cauldron of emotions bubbling deep within her. Finally, she burst into sobs and cried uncontrollably. The doctor waited quietly, saying nothing.

After a couple of minutes, which seemed like hours, her sobs relented. She grabbed some tissues from a box conveniently sitting on the coffee table. With a few small, last sniffles, Yancy tore a tissue in her hand. She made eye contact with Dr. Foster and spoke softly. "God, I'm so embarrassed. I never cry."

"Mm-hmm." Doctor Foster nodded. "Mary Anne, do you think that may be a problem?"

"Everybody calls me Yancy," she stated. Dr. Foster only nodded assent but didn't reply. "What is a problem, you mean me crying in front of you? I'm so sorry, Doctor."

Jill Foster scrunched her eyebrows. "That's not what I meant at all. I was more concerned that you never cry, not that you cried right now. Seems you needed to let out some emotion. Is that normally hard for you to do, be in touch with your emotions?"

Yancy stared at her for a second, then chuckled. "Well, I do pissed-off pretty well."

Jill smiled kindly. "Let's look at the results of your depression screening survey before our time is up." She picked up her tablet from the side table, found Yancy's results, then moved to sit next to Yancy on the couch.

For the last minutes of the session, Yancy was led through the results that signified her symptoms of chronic depression. She was fascinated by the way the doctor matter-of-factly detailed the items Yancy had answered, without judgment. Yancy's breathing slowed, the tightness around her mouth eased, but she pursed her lips and squinted in thought.

"I thought people who were depressed lay in bed crying all day."

"That's a common misperception. The truth is that depression can manifest in any of a number of symptoms. You listed quite a few that figure into a diagnosis." Jill Foster met her eyes with gentle observation. "Given this information, how would you like to proceed? I can give you my opinion, but it's more important to find out what you think may work for you."

Yancy asked several questions about the options. They considered several types of medications, talk therapy, a regimen of other kinds of therapies, and combinations. Dr. Foster felt Yancy's symptoms severe enough to begin treatment as soon as possible. Yancy left the office with a prescription for an anti-depressant, and an appointment for the next Friday.

After she got into her Rover, she immediately phoned her mother with the outcome of the day's appointment. Both she and Nina were a little astounded that Yancy had followed through.

"I am so proud of you," Nina gushed.

"Mom, you're not crying, for fu—Pete's sake!"

"Oh, let me care a little about my only daughter. I love you, darling. If this new path helps your happiness…You've been suffering for too long, and all of us who love you have suffered with you, I can tell you."

"Oh," Yancy replied sheepishly. "I'm sorry I've caused people any trouble, Mom."

"Well, you have a good weekend. Let's talk next week. You could have lunch with me again next Friday," Nina added brightly.

"I'll think about it. Bye."

༄ ༄ ༄ ༄

Yancy could hear the twang of guitars and pumping of the bass nearly a block away from Spanky's. Her eyes adjusted to the dark as she entered, and she finally spotted a seat at the bar. "Hey, Carla. The usual." Carla slipped a sweating bottle of High Country Pale Ale in front of her. Yancy scanned the crowd while sipping the cold beer, her back to the bar, her elbows resting on it. She was relieved that Cheyenne didn't seem to be there. She saw a group of women a little younger than her at a round table. The bleached blonde with spiked hair was sizing her up, so, after some time pondering her but not wasting any time, she grabbed her beer and ambled up to their table, and asked her to dance. The blonde smiled, and took her hand. Yancy placed her beer on her table and led them to the dance floor.

"I'm Morgan. Did anyone ever tell you that you kind of look like that actress, Angie? Angie Harmon? What's your name, tall, dark, and handsome?" Morgan gave a small giggle.

"Yancy."

"Nancy?"

"No, like Nancy but with a Y. Yancy."

"Interesting name. You from here?"

"No. I live on a ranch south of here. What about you? You live in Denver? What do you do?"

"Yeah, I live not far from here in an apartment building. I work at a tech store, selling electronic stuff. You know, computers, tablets. How did you hurt your arm?" Morgan looked down at the blue cast on Yancy's left arm.

"Just a riding thing. I wasn't paying attention." Yancy maneuvered a leg between Morgan's and ground against her, groaning a little. Morgan gave it back, grinding her hips. She was about three inches shorter, her breasts rubbing below Yancy's. After the first song, Morgan began to nestle against Yancy's neck.

Yancy's hand came up her back and caressed the sides of her breasts. Morgan murmured, "You want to go back to my place?"

Yancy nodded. They left the dance floor walking hand in hand, and Morgan told the group at the table she was leaving. Yancy shuffled her feet. The throb in her pants had begun, but she felt a little bored by the whole scene tonight.

They arrived at Morgan's in two cars—Yancy had learned her lesson with Cheyenne. As they entered the apartment, Yancy took her hand, leading her to the couch in a small living area. They plopped down together. Yancy immediately reached under her flowing blouse and stroked her skin, found her bra clasp, and undid it. She kneaded the medium-sized breasts until the nipples stood at attention.

"You're beautiful," Yancy murmured into Morgan's neck, pulling the loose blouse up over her head. She quickly unbuttoned Morgan's capris, and pulled them over her hips, along with her bikinis. Still dressed, Yancy moved over top of Morgan. She caressed her shoulders. She nuzzled her neck. Morgan responded like all the others, with moans and thrusts of her hips. Yancy kissed progressively down her torso, not slow at all, until she came to her hot wetness. Her tongue plunged into the wet folds and she stroked, sucked, and licked slowly, then in a lust-filled fast clip, making Morgan buck. In a few minutes, Morgan was yelling, "My God, oh my God," and shaking with orgasm.

Yancy rolled off of Morgan, feeling oddly

disoriented. She lay down on her side next to her, until Morgan's breathing returned to normal. Finally, Morgan looked at her. "Come here, sexy. It's your turn."

Yancy felt she was not present in the same room, not sitting on a couch with a hot young thing. Her mind drew a blank; she was thinking in slow motion, nearly paralyzed. Knowing she didn't want or need anything else this night, Yancy leaned over to kiss Morgan softly. "Sorry, I've got to go." She came up from the couch, tucking in her shirt where Morgan had pulled it out of her jeans. She pocketed her keys and phone.

"You're not serious, are you?" Morgan sat up on the couch. She grabbed at Yancy's arm. Yancy jerked it back, closed the last button on her shirt, and turning to Morgan, blew a kiss and left. Yancy stumbled to her car. Before getting in, she stared into the dark night without seeing. Shaking her head to clear her vision, she got in and started her Rover.

෴෴෴෴

As she pulled onto the main highway, Yancy felt like Roxie's proverbial shit-on-a-biscuit. The tears began about fifteen minutes out of Denver and didn't stop until she parked in the garage. Her shoulders ached from tiredness and tension. The day had been long. The visit to the psychiatrist plagued her with so many questions: Why was she cloaked with stifling darkness? Where was her heart, her mind, her soul?

She sat in the Rover for a while, a few minutes, maybe longer—it was hard to tell how long—until she felt she was under more control from the crying jag. When she entered the kitchen from the garage, the house was totally dark. With dragging feet, she tromped slowly upstairs.

## Chapter Eleven

The next Wednesday morning, after taking care of the horses, Yancy caught up on a huge pile of July paperwork, until she was cross-eyed from staring at the laptop screen. When she finally finished around four thirty, she stretched her arms above her head. After she changed into dusty work clothes, she walked to the barn where Marquette greeted her with a whinny. Her heart sang with his unconditional love. Together they went for their usual canter around the pastures.

Gen was constantly on her mind: their ride and the easy conversation they had had. After the last time at Spanky's, she increasingly appreciated Gen's warmth. Gen listened. She gave her opinion freely, but not with a heavy hand. She knew Yancy's problems, but gave her the benefit of the doubt. They had talked together like they had known each other for longer than a few weeks, yet times of silence also seemed natural. Yancy had never known this kind of attention. Gen cared about her. This gave Yancy a twinge of anxiety, yet her heart fluttered whenever she thought of that kiss.

What the hell was happening? She'd lost her edge with Gen, like with no other woman since Trisha. Gen was so enticing. She was onto Yancy's usual bullshit, and was no one-night stand, for sure. Yancy needed to work with her on the board, but if she screwed this up, they would be staring awkwardly at each other across that board table for a long time. She could quit the board. Her mom would really hit the ceiling. Phil would kill her. And damn it, she didn't want to leave the board. It kept her sane, gave her something fun and interesting to do, challenged her intellectually, and she loved the policy work.

Beads of sweat formed on Yancy's forehead. Yancy thought there was something there between Gen and her. It felt a little like it did with Trisha, but so much more...Yancy couldn't decide what. The French would say that Gen had that *Je ne sais quoi*. She remained thoroughly turned on by her: her eyes, her tinkling laugh, her quick wit, and her smarts. All of Gen made her heart feel again. There's so much they shared—not only the riding, but the clinic, RHA, and friendship with Roxie and Kate.

After paddling in stale backwaters these last few years, Yancy felt like she had been thrust into roiling rapids. She struggled with the different feelings swirling around her. Gen, all her friends, her mom and Phil, and now this new psychiatrist...it was a lot to take in, all of them asking to be let in, to know the real Yancy Delaney. Did Yancy even know herself? Not since Trisha left her all alone had she felt like the old happy Yancy. Life had become rote work and Spanky's. Yancy was ready for something more solid; she felt spent with the craziness eddying around her.

Totally lost in her introspection of the dilemma of her life, especially where a certain lovely doctor fit into everything, Yancy rode for longer than the hour. When she realized how long she'd been riding, she put Marquette into a gallop to the stable, and dashed into the house to get into the shower and dress for dinner at Gen's.

She was so late, she didn't have time to do much with her hair. But luckily, she had picked out what she was wearing already, so she only had to throw on her nice jeans, a new chambray shirt, and polished boots. She bounded down the stairs two at a time, stopped in the kitchen to get a bottle of wine, and rushed out the door, where she quickly clipped some of the zinnias from Connie's front flower garden. She exceeded the speed limit all the way into town and finally slowed in the twenty-five-mph zone of the treelined street of mid-century ranch houses where Gen lived. She didn't have time to check herself in the rearview mirror, so she did a slapdash run of her hand through her still damp hair.

Gen opened her door, smiled brightly, and motioned her to come in. Yancy offered the bottle of French Rosé and flourished the home-grown bouquet, leaving Gen with a quirky grin. "Did you know that I love flowers? Come on in. I'll just get something to put these in. Thank you." She lightly kissed Yancy's cheek.

Yancy smiled back and murmured, "You're welcome. These zinnias are Connie's pride."

"Well, then, thank Connie for me. Would you like to see my place, then maybe we can have a drink?"

Gen led her on a tour of the house she was renting, a traditional siding-and-brick ranch style. Kentucky landscape photographs, two of horses, hung on the living room wall. A framed picture of a good-looking older couple stood on the mantelpiece of the stone fireplace.

The dining area held a table to seat eight. In the kitchen, Yancy noted updated and modern appliances, and several fancy pieces of culinary equipment dotting the counter. Yancy pointed to them. "Do you use all that?"

"I certainly do. My mom taught me all I know, in her good French fashion, so I love to cook and bake. I'm the regular Keebler elf at Christmas. I love hosting dinner parties, so get ready to receive some invitations in a few months. I plan to entertain the clinic medical staff later this fall." Gen grinned mischievously. "I still am wrapping my mind around the fact that you don't cook."

"Impressive," Yancy noted. "No, no cooking for me. Connie is my salvation. I hate housework, cooking most of all. I'm good at making coffee because I live on it, but after that, I could subsist on a diet of cold cereal, ice cream, and bananas."

Gen looked at her with soft eyes. "Would you like to learn to cook? I could teach you."

"Please, let's not give Kate and Roxie more ammunition against me. They already think my domestic skills are pretty pathetic, I don't want to screw up even more. They'd never let me live it down." They both laughed lightly.

"They are good friends, aren't they? How long have you known them?" Gen asked, then turned to busy herself making a salad at the counter.

Taking a stool at the small island, Yancy watched Gen at the countertop. With quick and efficient movements, she chopped vegetables. Her hands were slim, her backside moving with the chopping. Watching her mesmerized Yancy. Finally, she answered, "Roxie and I went to school together, after her dad was transferred here in the sixth grade, from some eastern state, New York, maybe Pennsylvania, forget which one. Kate was a couple years ahead of us, but they really didn't get together until we were all at

U. Denver. They started dating our sophomore year, and have been together ever since. I'm always blown away by how people can be together for twenty years."

"How so?"

"I don't know. I mean, don't people get bored? Drive each other nuts? I can't imagine someone wanting to hang with me and my quirks that long." Yancy played with the salt and pepper shakers on the island.

"I've never had as long a relationship as that, but I have always imagined that couples have to exert themselves to keep things fresh, keep the feelings real. Communication is important. It's hard work and doesn't happen on its own. I don't know it for myself, but it seems self-evident."

"Your parents been together a long time?"

"Let's continue our conversation somewhere more relaxed, why don't we. Patio or living room? Beer, wine, iced tea?" Gen placed the salad in the fridge and kept the door open, waiting for Yancy's answer.

"How about on the patio with iced tea?" Yancy snorted. "Sounds like the murder mystery board game."

Gen shook her head, grinning at Yancy. "Go on out. I'll bring the drinks. Dinner should be done in about twenty minutes."

Yancy found a comfortable chaise lounge in the shade of the canopy on the patio, put her feet up, and breathed in the summer smells of cut grass and neighborhood grills. The July sun wouldn't set for some minutes. The breeze wafted around the patio, creating a restful, moderate temperature. When Gen brought two iced teas out, Yancy took the opportunity to take a look at the white jeans hugging her ass and a blue UK College of Medicine T-shirt outlining those enticing breasts.

Yancy took a sip of her iced tea, lowering her eyes to attempt to keep herself from staring. Gen had spotted her eyes roving over her chest. "Sorry," Yancy muttered.

Gen's index finger flitted to her lips briefly, and she seemed about to say something.

Yancy, taking advantage of the lull in the conversation, picked up the topic from the kitchen, asking Gen again about her parents. They had been together since they met when her dad was stationed at the Army hospital in Germany. Her mother was born in France to American parents. "That's where your exotic first name, Genevieve, comes from?"

"Something like that. Both Mom and Dad liked the name. How about the nickname Yancy?"

"My older brother Phil was three when I was born and couldn't say Mary Anne, so Yancy stuck."

"It seems to fit you." Gen had an amused smile. "I noticed you have a good relationship with your family."

Yancy blew out a long breath, and raised her eyebrows. "My mom and me...big subject. Growing up, it took a while for her to come to grips with the fact that her only daughter was more boy than Phil. Phil was the studious one, good grades, tennis star. Ryan was the class clown, the baby. I was the rowdy one." Yancy lifted one side of her lips. "I know, I know, hard to believe."

Gen laughed gently.

"Then when I came out my first year of college, Mom didn't seem surprised. Both Mom and Dad sat me down. I will never forget that day. They had asked me to the great room after a Sunday lunch. I was scared shitless. But when I walked in trembling in my boots, Dad hugged me really tightly, and Mom began stroking my hair and calling me darling, like she does. They told me they had known for a while that I was gay, just hoped I would be happy, and if that meant I would have to leave the dinky town we were in, they would understand."

"Why didn't you leave? I would imagine it was hard to live openly here."

"I did go to Denver for school, where Kate and Roxie and I became the three stooges. We were a great support team for each other after graduation. I couldn't have gotten through Ryan's death without them." Yancy took an audible breath. "I kept looking for Miss Right. They just looked at each other and it was over for them. When I graduated, I decided I needed some time away from the Triple D and Babcock County, so I took a couple of years traveling with a group that did agricultural tours around the country, and some abroad. It was a great learning experience. After that, I knew I wanted to get my MBA to put together with my farm management degree so I could come back to the ranch with Dad." Yancy's fingers rubbed the condensation from her frosty glass. She looked out at Gen's backyard, sighed, then continued. "Dad had his heart attack some months after I started at the ranch. He planned to gradually let go of day-to-day operations and fully retire when he was sixty-five, except, well, he was fifty-seven when he…" Yancy's eyes welled. She took a deep, shuddering breath.

A soft hand wrapped itself around Yancy's hand, stopping it on the glass. "You still feel his loss. Is it still this hard to talk about Trisha, too?"

Yancy wiped her eyes and shook her head. "I

can't seem to get on with life. As I said before, we met at Wharton. About a year after I left, she got a nonprofit job in Denver. I would drive up to see her some weekends, then more over time. It led to us announcing ourselves as a couple. Right after that, she was diagnosed with cancer. When she couldn't work any longer, I brought her down here with a nursing service. Finally, hospice came in. I had to watch..." Yancy choked.

Not looking at Gen, Yancy sipped more of her tea. They sat in silence for several minutes and watched the early evening sky. A colored pattern of passionate reds and oranges belied the heaviness in the air around them.

A ding could be heard from the kitchen.

"That's dinner," Gen said quietly, and she got up from her lounge chair.

"Can I help?" Yancy spoke through a froggy throat.

"Sure, come set the table, get the salad, while I take care of the chicken."

Yancy stepped into the kitchen and took the plates to the dining table, laid them out, and finished with the cutlery and glasses, right as Gen came in with chicken cordon bleu. "Salad's on the counter." She went back and picked up a bowl of rice.

"Wow. You didn't have to go all out. And it's beautiful, too." Yancy noted all the food and bit the inside of her lip. She hoped this wasn't a test of how much she could eat.

They sat. Yancy poured the wine for them both. "Cheers." They clinked their glasses. Yancy didn't feel particularly cheerful. They passed food to each other.

"How's your appetite these days?" Gen asked.

Yancy had taken a little of everything on the

table, but not much filled her plate. Looking down at her hands, Yancy took a big breath, then glanced up. "I want to…"

"Yes?" Gen looked at her with tenderness.

"I wanted you to know…geez." Yancy threw her napkin on the table. "Oh hell. I'll just say it. I've started treatment for depression. I thought you should know." Yancy's eyes focused on the napkin.

Gen stopped the forkful of food halfway to her mouth and laid her fork on the plate. "That's a big move for you. Do you want to talk about it?"

Something in the air suddenly shifted. Yancy's tone became biting. "Listen, I'm not your reclamation project. You shouldn't worry that you need to overhaul me. Everyone seems to want to suffocate me, to 'fix' me. Why not you, too?" Yancy abruptly pushed her chair back and stood up. She paced to the dining room window and back.

Gen stood up and caught her arm, her voice quavering. "You can listen to me now. I am not your mother. I am not even your lover. I am a physician who saw you medically and noted some things that your mother and friends have been harping on. Don't you dare start treatment for them, for me, for anybody else. If you can't do something for yourself, there is nothing magical going to happen that will fill your life with whatever you're looking for. I know there seems to be something here." Gen pointed to each of them. "But, you have to love yourself before anyone else can, you big dope." Gen puffed out and dropped Yancy's arm, then moved to the living room to flounce down on the couch. "Why am I even doing this?" she said into the air.

Yancy crammed her right hand into her pocket,

shuffled into the room, and sat gingerly at the edge of the couch. They looked at each other with imploring eyes. "I'm sorry...Damn. I'm apologizing for every fucking thing I say and do around you. Damn it."

Gen gazed gently at Yancy and took her face in her hands. Leaning closer, she whispered, "So can we acknowledge that we both want to have some kind of way forward? God help me, I don't know why, but I can't get you out of my mind."

"I think of you all the time, too." Yancy looked at Gen intently. "But you implied the other day that there was nothing between us unless I got my shit together."

"Is that why you're in treatment?"

"Hell, I don't know." Yancy paused to look around the room. Gen's hands dropped from her face. "No, it's not. I want to be happy again. I want to feel something." Her fist pounded her chest above her heart. "At least feel what it felt like when Trisha and I had our good times. When Dad and I loved riding the ranch. When Ryan and I were playing horseshoes and drinking beer." She stood and paced to the same window, her back to Gen, her uninjured hand again pushed deep into her jeans pocket. "I have felt so few feelings for so long. You have opened up a spigot that I can't seem to close. These damn feelings are pouring out all over me." Yancy turned and met Gen's gentle gaze, shaking her head sadly. "I feel overwhelmed. I am so damned confused," she said with glassy-eyed sadness.

Gen rose from the couch and gathered Yancy into a tight hug.

Yancy stiffened in her arms. She relaxed her shoulders, leaned into Gen, and let the tears fall down her cheek. Gen continued to hold her tightly, rubbing her hands along Yancy's back. The emotion overwhelmed the air in the room. Yancy felt she was drowning. She took deep breaths and backed away. Her hands rubbed over her face and she sniffled.

"You okay?"

"I can't believe I did that." Yancy said dully, staring at the floor. "I never cry, and I've cried more this past week than I ever have." She looked at Gen briefly, her heart aching with sorrow. "I have to leave."

Gen brushed a hand over Yancy's cheek and bit her lip. "You're safe here," she said softly.

Yancy met her eyes again, turned from her, and paced toward the dining room and back. Abruptly, she gathered her keys and phone from the foyer table, looked at Gen, and mumbled quietly, "I'm sorry. I... uh, thanks for dinner." She leaned in to kiss Gen on the cheek. Quietly she opened the door, left, and clicked it shut.

❦❦❦❦

The silence of Yancy's leaving, and the vacuum made by the absence of her body, sucked the air out of the room. Gen flopped back onto the couch, unable to move, trying to get control of her breathing. She laid her head back, shaking it. Her eyes were scrunched closed. Yancy had opened something deep within her, a connection so charged, she felt the loss of her in the room like the loss of oxygen. A piece of herself had left through the door with Yancy. But it was craziness to be falling in love with a woman who so pulled at her, brought her to the brink of wanting to kiss her senseless, or to shake her to bring them both to their senses.

She wasn't ready for this. Was she? It seemed so fast—she hardly knew the woman—but every time she was in her presence, all the signs were there that she was falling for Yancy. Her clinical skills could not miss the change in vital signs, but she also felt the non-clinical symptoms: her heart lurching, her stomach fluttering, constantly thinking about Yancy. On the other hand, her rational self still posted a warning. Yancy was dangerous. She could turn into a playgirl in a heartbeat. This may all be an act to get her into bed, to seduce Gen with her vulnerability. Yancy poked at Gen's weak spot—her need to help an emotionally stopped-up woman, assist her in adult conversation, and the sharing of feelings. Was Gen trapped into another role as caregiver? As champion of expressiveness and integrity?

Several minutes later, Gen's phone dinged with a message. *"Sorry about dinner. It looked very wonderful. Would u go to dinner w me Sat nite? Partly to make up for 2nite. I would like to see if I can get my act 2gether w u."* The text ended with an emoticon of two women holding hands.

Gen groaned. "God help me." She rose from the couch, looked into the dining room at the remnants of the dinner she had prepared that were congealing into a cold mess on the table. Her eyes overflowed with tears, and she grabbed a tissue from a box in the kitchen. *Oh God, what is this, what's going on? Why can't I be on my own? Why did Yancy have to show up in my life, with her Angie Harmon brown eyes, and those dimples that appear when she is being a total flirt? Why does her little-girl vulnerability bring me to tears?*

In a slow walk around the room, Gen peered at her phone, smoothing the screen with her fingers for some minutes. Her loud sighs echoed in the living room. How much should she get into with her? Where will it end? If Gen said "yes" now, could she say "no" later? She felt so confused. She may very well be impeding Yancy's healing from her losses. But damn, she was so attracted to her! Ugh.

Finally, she texted back, *"CU Sat."*

# Chapter Twelve

"Hi, Dad!"

"It's so good to hear your voice, Gennie. Email's okay, but it doesn't compare to a phone call. How's Colorado treating you?"

"I'm doing really well. I love the clinics. The people are friendly here, different than Kentuckians, but just as open and welcoming. I have settled into the house. A nice older ranch style with a fantastic kitchen."

"That's important. Can't wait to taste your banana crepes again. And I'm glad the work's going well. How is the medicine?"

"It's good, too. We have a solid staff of nurses, nurse practitioners, and physician assistants, and even a lab and X-ray so that folks don't have to travel fifty miles to the nearest ER. I've started a Saturday clinic for walk-ins. The patient flow works. I like the patients I've seen so far. It's your usual mix of Medicare patients with chronic problems and younger patients with regular checkups and school exams. It's all good."

"I'm happy to hear it. I was afraid you wouldn't be as well-staffed and equipped as the clinics in Kentucky."

"We've got a really knowledgeable board, which helps. The board president is the daughter of the founder. She's got an MBA from Wharton, serves on the RHA development committee."

"Impressive. I'm thinking you're pleasantly surprised." The pitch of her dad's voice rose like it did when he found something of interest.

"The work with the academic guys is also moving forward. We plan to have our first preceptorship starting in January. Locals have talked with the clinic about starting a riding therapy program. A friend who's a psychologist is outlining a proposal to present to the board. I'm pretty pumped about being their medical backup. We need the board approval in a few days. Tonight, I'm having dinner with the board president, who I really like working with."

"Hmm," Paul said. "Is there something you're not telling Mom and me about the president? You talk about her in every email, now dinner."

Gen paused. "Second dinner. She was at my house Wednesday night. It got cut short. Anyway, we're making it up tonight. Maybe it is only one dinner after all." She gave out a small, high-pitched laugh.

"Well, kiddo, sounds like things are doing well in Colorado. I look forward to meeting this interesting board president. Maybe at Christmas, huh? I'll email our travel plans sometime later, probably in October. Don't want to wait too long to book something during the holidays. I miss you and love you. Here's Mom."

❧❧❧❧

"How you doing with the wrist?" Roxie pointed to Yancy's arm, now free of the cast.

"Stiff, but okay."

They were sitting at a table for two in town at Mosley's Diner, having lunch. The waitress had just left their orders of chef salads and iced teas.

"Okay, what's up? We never have lunch. You're not the lunching type, and I can tell something's on your mind. Spill it." Roxie searched Yancy's face.

Yancy glanced over the glass of iced tea she was sipping. "I…uh." She cleared her throat.

"C'mon, Studly DoRight. It's me."

"I took your advice."

"Okay. What advice? I need a little more to go on."

"Depression."

Roxie didn't like it when friends came to her for mental health advice. But Yancy's friendship went deeper than that. Yes, she brought her professional expertise with her into her two closest relationships, it couldn't be helped. But she never overtly analyzed Yancy. Psychology could ruin a good companionship. Nevertheless, her training kicked in, and, as Roxie waited quietly for Yancy, her motto was "don't scare the wildlife."

Yancy moved her knife and fork around the tabletop. Finally, she took a cleansing breath. "I've had two sessions with a psychiatrist in Denver, and I started medication, too." Yancy still hadn't met Roxie's eyes.

Roxie felt a huge weight she hadn't known had been there leave her shoulders, but she retained her professional remoteness, nodding her head and drawing out the word, "Okay." She slid her hand over to Yancy's to still her, stroked her knuckles lightly, then quickly removed it.

"I'm a fucking waterworks. I was at Gen's for dinner Wednesday. I was doing pretty well until I… wasn't. I ended up in her arms crying like a baby. I was so embarrassed, I left. She is a gourmet cook, made this amazing dinner, and I didn't even stay to eat it." Yancy looked up at Roxie, who kept her eyes from widening at this news.

Roxie looked gently at the misery on Yancy's face, and said softly, "Well, baby cakes, nothing is set in stone. Nothing is irreversible." They both laughed lightly.

"Thanks for the reminder. We are having a makeup dinner tonight. I'm taking her to the new place in Aurora, Roberto's."

"You know I love you. I know it took a huge amount of courage for you to open up to Gen. That's pretty damned amazing for you. I'm so proud of you." Roxie took the chance to grab Yancy's hand.

Yancy's face turned pink. "Well, I have a lot of redeeming to do. The shrink and I have talked about that. How much of a jackass I've been, and this is just my latest need to apologize."

Roxie moved back into friend-face, raising her eyebrows. "I have to say, when I heard that slap in the kitchen at our house, I was astounded that she spoke to you at all the rest of the night. Let alone riding with you, then asking you for dinner. You didn't pull another stunt, did you?"

Yancy shook her head rapidly. "Nothing like that. I knew when I grabbed her ass in your kitchen and got that slap, that Gen wasn't going to put up with any bullshit. I realized she was a person who cared about herself, respected herself, and that if I wanted to get any closer, I had to do that, too. I have to say, though, it's damn hard not to stare at those tits…uh, breasts, and curvy hips. Her hair has this sheen of red highlights. Man, I just drool every time I'm around her. I'm a mess." Her eyes glanced up at Roxie.

Roxie smiled crookedly.

Yancy continued, "I figured I had to get my act together. But it's not just with her. It's everyone, really. Mom, you, and Kate. I'm really tired of being unhappy with my life. The shrink and I have figured out that I've had a big grudge against the world. Not just since Trisha, or Dad. It's come on since I lost Ryan, I think. Anyway, hell, I don't know…"

"Baby cakes, I am so happy you've done this. We've all been stewing over you and there wasn't a damn thing any of us could do. But, the most important thing is that I see some of the old Yancy. The one who found herself, and went for the things she wanted."

"Thanks, dorkhead. I love you, too."

Roxie swatted Yancy's arm, and they ate their salads. They both had silly grins on their faces.

# Chapter Thirteen

Saturday night continued the rainless, dry, hot spell that had reappeared after the barbecue. Yancy drove up to Gen's house at seven, having spent more time than usual on her appearance, especially getting her straight locks to fall to shoulder level, out of the ubiquitous ponytail. She had on a pair of her "meeting Mom" linen pants and a nice tank-type shell, feeling a little naked without her boots because she was wearing black flats. Her hands were slightly clammy. She inhaled deeply and rang Gen's doorbell.

"Wow...I mean, hi. You look, uh, beautiful." Yancy's eyes felt like they were bugging out of her head as they were treated to Gen in a navy, halter sundress whose neckline plunged several inches, revealing luscious mounds of flesh. It draped to her knees, showing taut calves. Petite feet rested in little navy sandals. Some kind of fresh perfume wafted up to make Yancy feel a little lightheaded. Gen's light auburn hair was in a French braid. Finding her voice, Yancy finally said, "Some more flowers from Connie's garden," and handed Gen a bouquet of black-eyed Susans and purple cone flowers.

"Lovely," Gen said, looking Yancy up and down, cradling the proffered flowers. Gen smiled and stood aside for Yancy to enter the living room. "Be right back," she said as she raised the flowers in a salute.

Yancy's hands went to her pockets, and, finding

none in the slacks, she grasped them together in front of her, twisting them around.

On the drive to Roberto's, Yancy and Gen first made small talk about the ranch and the clinic. The upcoming market of the Triple D cattle was keeping Yancy busy at home. Gen continued her work on planning for the rural residency.

Yancy licked her lips, glanced at Gen, cleared her voice, and said quietly, "I want to apologize for losing it at your house on Wednesday night."

"Losing what?" Gen looked at her blankly, her eyebrows raised.

"You know, blabbering about my problems, bawling like a baby with you. I'm...embarrassed."

Yancy melted when Gen grasped her hand and stroked her fingers. With an affectionate look, Gen said, "You are so adorable, you big doofus. I loved that you shared with me." Gen's look then changed from tender to fierce. "And don't you ever apologize for having feelings. I know what you're thinking."

"You do?"

"You think that being strong means being in charge of yourself. But, you've got it all wrong, rancher. It's when you let yourself be a little open with someone that a relationship has a chance. When you're real."

"Real. You're saying I wasn't being real when I grabbed your ass at Kate and Roxie's?"

"No, you weren't. You were being some macho version of yourself. Let me tell you, it turned me completely off."

Yancy snickered while stroking her own cheek. "Oh, Doc, I know you were turned off." She quickly looked at Gen, then gave her attention back to driving. "Are you saying that I'm more real when I'm blubbering on your shoulder?"

"When you were 'blubbering,' as you call it, I felt emotions I could relate to. I could feel your grief and your confusion. Something real to me, yes. When you have come on to me with your smooth lines, it puts a barrier between us. It feels like a role you're playing. Is it to keep people at a distance?"

Yancy raked a hand over her face and sighed deeply. "Geez. You can cut right to the core of me. I never met anyone like you. You see through me, and you scare the shit right out of me."

Gen looked at Yancy with a soft gaze. "I'm not trying to scare you. I just want to know you better. You intrigue me, too. I've seen so many facets of you. You're both the horsewoman and the board president. I see you bantering and laughing with your friends. I see your commitments and integrity. But don't like the rumors about the rogue who takes women hostage for sexual pleasure, then discards them."

"That's a little harsh. It's not like they're coerced." Yancy frowned.

Gen laughed ruefully. "No, I imagine they follow you into the bedroom very willingly. They may even be doing the seducing. But how does it feel when you leave?"

Yancy sighed as the restaurant came into view. "Saved by Roberto." She blew out a huge breath and pulled under the restaurant's canopy entrance. "I hope you like Italian food. I know you like French food."

"I love Italian food. I especially love ordering things I normally wouldn't cook myself."

"What wouldn't you cook?"

"Veal, for instance. I don't like how calves are raised so inhumanely, so I don't eat veal often."

After Yancy tossed her keys to the valet, she met Gen on the passenger side and put out her arm to escort her. They entered the restaurant, where a darkened atmosphere met them and violin music wafted around them. The maître d' escorted them to a small table in its own corner away from other diners.

"This reminds me of eating once in Florence. Another summer night."

"Were you alone?" Yancy furrowed her brow.

Gen laughed softly. "No. I was with my dad and mom."

"Oh." Yancy smiled as she relaxed with this information. "Will you tell me more about Rachel?"

Gen's eyebrows lifted in surprise.

"Oh, hell, I'm sorry—"

"No, don't be sorry for stating what you're thinking about. That was one of Rachel and my problems. Her ideas about relationships were very cut and dried, all about tallying who did what and when. All about keeping score. You know, who carried out the garbage last, whose turn it was to cook. Who initiated sex."

"Didn't talk too much?"

"Well, not about us, no. When I tried to bring her out of herself, to even talk about her work, it was torture for both of us."

"Was she a reclamation project?" Yancy smirked.

"God, I hate that phrase." Gen scowled. "Yes, I tried to make her into someone I wanted her to be. Does that satisfy you?"

"Why would that satisfy me? Maybe I'm on your list for renovation. That scares the hell out of me."

Gen sighed. "I am trying my best to stay out of your own reclamation. I have feelings for you."

"You do?"

"Yes!" Gen cried. "What about this electricity between us are you missing?"

"Doc, I'm not missing any electricity. But electricity can sometimes just mean that a lot of current is running through the lines. It doesn't necessarily mean that there's a real connection." Yancy gazed into Gen's eyes and held them for some time. She hesitated, then said in a low voice, "But, I feel a real connection with you."

Gen was quiet. "I can't seem to help myself around you. I have great admiration for you as a person, your hard work, your passion for the clinic. But I see the undercurrents of your past, and God help me, I can't do anything about what you have suffered."

The violin music came closer, a man in a tux playing "Memories" softly.

"It wasn't all suffering." Yancy looked down at her hands fidgeting in her lap. "I loved my brother and my dad. And I think I loved Trisha, too. I must have, because it hurt so much when she died." Yancy looked up at Gen and smiled briefly. "They tell me love is a good thing, Doc. Wouldn't you prescribe it?"

Gen turned a light pink. The waitstaff's approach interrupted her answer, and they ordered dinner and a bottle of wine. This suspended the solemn tenor of the conversation for the rest of the night, and they continued to learn more about each other. They laughed often, sharing their likes and dislikes, their childhoods, and their dreams. Yancy realized she had not felt this lighthearted for some time. By the time the check arrived, she was surprised that they had spent two and a half hours talking.

On the drive back, Gen caressed Yancy's hand gently. They listened to the quiet strains of guitar and sax on the satellite radio's jazz station. The silence was comforting, although a slight tinge of anxiety began to creep up on Gen the closer they came to town. Yancy parked in front of Gen's house.

Gen hesitated, then said with a smile, "Would you like to come in?"

Yancy swallowed hard. "I, uh. I'm having a hard time."

"What?" Gen asked softly.

Yancy looked down at their clasped hands. "I'm not sure what to do. Oh, hell." She put her head back on the headrest and looked out her window.

"Tell me." Was Yancy just as nervous as Gen was?

"You're the first person I have felt anything with since Trisha. I don't know how to be. You're not the fuck of the week." Yancy beat her hands once on the steering wheel. "Damn! I'm so sorry. That was crass. I didn't mean it like that." Yancy's eyes implored Gen. Gen weighed Yancy's statement while confused feelings of fear and regret wrestled with attraction, sexual excitement, and fascination. She looked into Yancy's eyes, drew Yancy's face to her, gently stroked her jaw, then kissed her lips softly. Yancy responded, deepening it. They kissed for what seemed like several minutes.

Gen contemplated how to proceed. She broke the kiss and said breathlessly, "You mean something to me, too, Yancy. But I need to take things slow. Can we do that?"

Yancy blew out a breath, kissed Gen harder,

grasped the back of her head and stroked the nape, and nuzzled her neck. "Oh, God. I want to go slow, but I also can hardly stand what's building up inside me. I feel like a horse that's trying to take the lead away from the rider, who keeps reining me in. Damned if the rider isn't me, too."

Gen felt relieved in a way, knowing Yancy felt as confused just as she did. She looked on her with compassion and understanding as she leaned her forehead on Yancy's, her hands stroking Yancy's arms. "Nothing need happen. I am not going anywhere."

"I want so much to happen. I want to be near you, I want my hands all over you. But I can't yet. I'm still caught up with whatever craziness has me. I swear, Gen, I am trying to get past it. I hope I can be the person you need me to be."

"Oh, rancher." Gen sighed into Yancy's neck. "You're going through a lot of inner searching right now. I don't feel you and I together need to wade into the waters you have just begun to dip into."

"Yeah." Yancy let out a small moan. "I should let things go at a slow trot until I get the lay of the land. But damn, part of me wants to gallop into the night with you." She kissed her deeply, then pulled back. They locked eyes. Yancy took a shuddering breath. "If we were to date, what would that look like?"

Gen's heart took flight with happiness. She searched Yancy's eyes. "Well, like this. Dinner. Maybe a ride on the ranch with a picnic. A movie? Hearing live music? What we have already done? You know I love to cook, even if you aren't into eating so much. Just promise me one thing?"

Yancy raised her eyebrows.

"If you come for dinner, please don't leave again

before you've eaten it?"

Yancy laughed lightly and kissed Gen. "I promise." She looked deeply into Gen's eyes. "So how about you come for a picnic ride on your next day off?"

They kissed again lightly. Gen caressed the front of Yancy's linen top. "Good night. I had a very nice evening. I'll see you for a ride next Sunday." Gen nearly skipped into the house. Yancy seemed so heartfelt in their conversation and she had shared her feelings, thank God. Gen prayed that something real had taken off between them.

❧❧❧❧

"What are the tears about?" Dr. Foster sat in the usual armchair while Yancy sat across from her, her eyes gritty, her hands wiping up and down her jeans.

"I don't know. I…Hell, Doc." Yancy threw her hands in the air and slapped them down on her thighs. "How do I know what I'm feeling? I guess I never paid much attention. I just thought of doing something and did it. I met Trisha, we had sex. It didn't occur to me that I might feel something more for her until we got together. Suddenly, she was dying."

"Um-hmm," Jill Foster responded quietly.

"I didn't really treat her with respect until those last months. Then, I did everything I could for her. She came to stay at the ranch, hospice came to take care of her." Yancy choked and lost her composure for some minutes, unable to speak. Dr. Foster sat watching her, compassion in her eyes.

As she regained her voice, Yancy said, "How do you know when it's okay to love? Is it ever safe?" She clenched her fists and lightly pounded the arms of the chair. "I hate the feeling of being out of control, of not knowing if something will last, whether I'm going to lose someone else, like I lost all the others." She gazed directly at Jill Foster and whispered, "I can't take another loss."

"What do you think will happen? What's the worst that might happen should you lose someone else?"

Yancy studied the pictures on the wall, the carpet. She met Dr. Foster's eyes. "I don't know," she murmured. "It feels like something in me would die, too. That I would just dry up and blow away with the wind across the pasture."

"That you would cease to be?"

"Part of me, yeah."

"What about the other part of you? The strong, rancher part?"

"Oh." Yancy laughed. "That part? That part would saddle up and ride the ranch, go to town every Friday at Spanky's and—"

"Run?"

Yancy fiercely looked up at Jill Foster. "I don't run."

"What does all the Friday night activity mean to you?" Dr. Foster asked neutrally.

"It's entertainment. It's getting away from all the crap." Yancy pulled herself up straighter on the couch. "It's keeping myself under control."

"Why do you need control? What does control give you?"

Yancy looked at Jill Foster, the streaks of gray in her hair, her light aqua skirt suit, and her brown, unwavering eyes. "Control keeps me...it makes it... I need it, Doc. I need it so I can live. So I don't lose myself."

"Do you equate loving someone with losing yourself, losing who you essentially are?"

Looking down at her hands in her lap, considering, Yancy spoke quietly. "My mom loves me so much. And I love her. But she constantly harped on me when I was a kid to be more ladylike, to wear dresses and makeup. To take an interest in how I looked, you know, for boys. When I came out to her and Dad when I was back from college that first summer, I figured she would blow a gasket. But neither of them did. They both hugged me and said they wanted me to be happy. When she met Trisha, she liked her." Yancy looked up from her lap and smiled. "Mom really likes Gen, the woman I was telling you about. I try to believe Mom loves me, but sometimes, I feel I have to be that put-together, ladylike person she always wants me to be. You know, to fit in with her social set in Denver, be the woman she can show off to her friends."

"You want to please her?"

"Yeah, something like that. I never feel I'm quite enough, you know? Not the daughter she really wants."

"And Gen, the woman you had dinner with, the same thing?"

"Yeah, a little," Yancy said in a small voice. "I...I want to be what she needs me to be, I think."

"And how does your concept of love link back to the losses you have had, Yancy? Do you think that if you please people, they won't abandon you?"

Yancy chuckled. "Well, that's pretty dumb. How can I keep people from dying?"

Dr. Foster closed her notepad quietly. "Our time is up for today. I'll see you next week," she said, smiling and rising from her armchair.

# *Chapter Fourteen*

"All in favor of adjournment, say aye." Yancy wrapped up the monthly board meeting.

As the mental health consultant for the riding therapy program, Roxie had presented her plan to the Valley View board. "What did you think of my proposal?" Roxie edged up to Yancy as she was collecting her papers into the meeting folder.

"Good. You all did a great job putting everything together." Yancy smiled genuinely at her friend. "I can't wait for us to begin the program. Virgie and Marsha are on board to help out with the kids. I may want to get another lesson horse, don't know yet, but let's see how many kids we have signed up by the time the program starts."

Roxie nudged Yancy. "And it doesn't do any harm that Gen's the volunteer medical liaison either, huh?"

"Ah, cut it out."

Roxie peered at Yancy closely. "Okay, I get it. We've got something happening, don't we Studly DoRight?" She slung an arm across Yancy's shoulders.

Yancy grabbed Roxie's arm. She hustled her out of the conference room, down the hall, out through the clinic's back door, and into the parking lot. "Damn it, Rox. Broadcast it to the whole board, why don't you!"

"What the hell's wrong?" Roxie's eyes went wide.

"It's personal."

"Since when has any of your conquests been a secret?"

"For Chrissake, it's not like that. This means something. She is not just a passing thing."

"Holy shit, Yance." Roxie grabbed Yancy by both shoulders and faced her squarely. "Do you mean you're really serious? You, the heartbreaker?" She grinned wickedly. "Are those meds kicking in?"

"Lay off, damn it." Yancy shrugged Roxie's arms from her shoulders and strode to her car, Roxie following closely.

"Wait a damn minute, you can't just spill something like that without more information. Give it up, baby cakes."

At the car, Yancy's eyes scanned the parking lot, and she turned to Roxie and stated matter-of-factly, "We're dating."

"Dating? Like bed-and-breakfast dating? Or dinner-and-a-movie, kiss-at-the-door dating?"

"Kiss at the door." Yancy looked down at her boots.

"Holy shit!" Roxie held her hand over Yancy's forehead. "Are you all right? Have aliens taken over Yancy Delaney?" She giggled.

Yancy swatted her hand away. "Jackass."

Roxie eyed Yancy with mischief. "That's wonderful. I mean, who would have thought you, the stud of the Triple D, would be kiss-at-the-door dating? I think it's so cute."

"Damn it, it is not cute. I'm seriously in trouble. I can't sleep at night for thinking about Gen. Every time I see her, my throat goes dry. I feel like the first time in college. I'm a mess. There is nothing remotely cute going on."

"You are in trouble. I love it." Roxie grinned widely and grasped Yancy around the neck for a tight hug.

"Get off me before I get violent."

"Tell me more. I want the scoop about the dates."

Yancy dug her boots into the gravel of the parking lot. "Get in," she said as she unlocked her Rover and Roxie slid into the passenger seat.

"Geez, you're being really cloak-and-dagger." Giggling like a teenager, Roxie turned in the seat to look directly at Yancy. "Are you trying to maintain your stud creds?"

Yancy yanked her hand through her hair, redoing her ponytail. "Shut up, will you? This has me tied up in knots. I feel like I've been corralled or something. And the hell of it is, it feels good."

Roxie continued to look intently at her friend as Yancy fidgeted with the keys in her hand. "Well, that's a good sign. Isn't it?"

"Damned if I know. I am totally out of control with this whole situation."

"Hmm," Roxie murmured. "And that scares you."

"Hell, yes!" She shut her eyes tight and hit her head against the back of the driver's seat.

"Have you heard about just taking things as they come? Going along with what you feel? It's not a new thing, dorkhead."

Yancy jerked her eyes open to glare at Roxie. "Thanks, Roxass. I'm not a child." Her eyes then went to the keys in her lap. "I'm not the best at keeping in touch with feelings."

"Oh, really. Big news flash," Roxie answered. "I remember a similar conversation when Trisha was sick and came to stay at the ranch. There were a lot of feelings swirling around then."

"Don't remind me."

"Those feelings had a lot to do with fear of loss, though, Yance. This is totally different. I can see by the way Gen looks at you that she likes you a lot, and you don't need to save her, or take care of her. This time, you're playing on an even field."

"What do you mean, even field?"

"You don't control her."

"Hell, I'm not even controlling myself."

"Sounds like love, stud. What are you going to do?" Roxie reached over and stroked Yancy's arm gently.

"Damned if I know. She's coming over to ride on Sunday. I guess I'll just—"

"Have a good time? Enjoy yourself?" Roxie held the back of her hand to her forehead. "Heavenly days, what is the world coming to? Mary Ann Delaney having fun."

Yancy knocked Roxie's hands playfully and bit back a smile. "You're really a dork!"

## Chapter Fifteen

Gen went to nine o'clock mass on Sunday morning. It afforded her a time of peace and quiet, even as she knew the priest may not say things she agreed with, and, if he decided to, could exclude her from taking communion because she was gay. None of this mattered to her. Her faith was rooted in a sense that God loved her and had made her exactly the way she was. She couldn't be distracted by the politics of a church that gave little responsibility to women leaders. She had friends in Kentucky, Roman Catholic nuns, who were strong leaders of their communities. Some of her non-religious friends could not understand her need for her Christian faith, but for her, it grounded her, gave a sense of her identity, and a tether to her family. Because of her father's Army career, and the every-three-year moves as a teen especially, keeping her faith meant stability to her: knowing she could enter any church and be comforted and encouraged by the silence, the music, the words of the mass, and Holy Communion.

On her way down the aisle to leave, she nodded across the church to Connie and Victor. She drove home and changed into her riding gear.

She wondered yet again what this attraction to Mary Ann Delaney meant. Yancy was nearly the opposite of Rachel in many ways. Rachel had grown up in Chicago, was sophisticated and urbane. She dressed always in professional attire. Her favorite hobbies were going to the theater in Louisville, the opera in Cincinnati, and concerts in Lexington and all over. Her parents were both physicians, so she had been bred with all the perks of a private education on the north side of Chicago. Coming to Kentucky for her residency had been part of her small rebellion against them, even though her family was connected to a physician in Lexington who owned a modest horse operation. It was he who encouraged her interest in pathology and forensic medicine, and the residency at the university.

But the contrast seemed to die there. Like Yancy, Rachel had trouble with commitment, emotions, and, by extension, relationships. Gen had tried mightily to bring Rachel out of herself, to talk with her openly. While Rachel often engaged people in scintillating discussions about politics, art, or music, she could not seem to function in the realm of emotions. She was much like her father in that regard: a nice enough man, but not genuinely friendly or open on a deeper level. He practiced psychiatry, a field where emotional control in the client's presence was paramount.

Gen liked Yancy very much, but tried to proceed cautiously. Any time she was near her, Gen's heart rate rose rapidly, and she could feel herself flushing from sexual arousal. Yancy seemed to hold sway over her body and her brain both. She ardently wished not to take on the responsibility of bringing Yancy along into a relationship, and thankfully, Yancy's friends and family also were encouraging her to be more self-aware, and to take better care of herself.

Nevertheless, despite her misgivings about Yancy's recent past, Gen felt she was drawing nearer and nearer to her, a magnetic pull that felt both exhilarating and terrifying, given the warning signs of Yancy's reputation as a player.

Gen knew she could not, would not, be involved with anyone who treated her with disrespect. She was not wired that way. Her very being chafed against any treatment that smacked of misogyny or macho swaggering. The moments where Yancy's armor let in the small pinpoint lights of vulnerability gave Gen hope that she could love her. And the more Gen saw of Yancy, the less armor Yancy seemed to be wearing. Gen could only hope that Yancy wanted what she wanted—a chance to see where this relationship might go.

❧❧❧❧

Watching for Gen's red sedan, Yancy drank iced coffee on the front porch, shaded from the eighty-eight-degree sun. Her heart felt like it was beating out of her chest in excitement about their second ride. She took a deep breath as she watched the dust behind Gen's car billowing up the lane.

As soon as Gen stopped the car, Yancy leapt up and went to the driver's door to open it. Gen's smile nearly knocked her off her feet. They both stood next to the car for a minute. Yancy ducked her head and lightly kissed Gen on the lips. "Ready for a good lope?" Yancy pointed to a green cloth grocery bag Gen pulled from the passenger seat. "What's that?"

"My turn to bring the picnic." She grinned.

"I can only imagine your gourmet picnic." Yancy leaned over to see what was in the bag.

"Get out of that." Gen swatted her playfully. "You'll see later. I hope you like white wine."

"I'm more of a beer gal, but if you remember, I enjoyed wine at your house and Roberto's. Let's get the mounts tacked up. I groomed them both before you got here. We want to get going, because it's another scorcher today."

☙☙☙☙☙

They rode into the pasture, along the stream called Cutback River that bounded Triple D ranch.

Yancy stood in her saddle and swept her arm to the west of their position. "We've tried to pasture our herd here this summer, but even the river's dryer than normal for August."

"What's the dry weather doing to your ranch?"

Yancy yanked the straw Stetson from her head and wiped the perspiration from her forehead, then pushed it back on. "Price of hay is off the charts, for one thing, so because some pastures are brown, we have to supplement with hay and it's costing us. Also, as the dry heat browns the green grass, we've got a fire hazard. If it ever decides to storm, a good lightning strike could set off the dry grass and then we'd have to move the herd faster than hell." Yancy glanced at Gen and saw her compassion. "Got me jittery. Losing some sleep."

Gen breathed deeply and nodded. "Who tends the herd?"

"Victor deals with day-to-day stuff with our two ranch hands, Alan and Chuck. I push the paper, and hire and fire, but he's the head wrangler. It's not like when I was a kid, when we'd use horses to move cattle. Nowadays we use our trucks. But we'd all have to pitch in if we needed to move three hundred head of Angus pronto." Yancy smiled ruefully at Gen. "Do you pray?"

Gen smiled back. "As a matter of fact, I do. And I will. I've noted that the prayers at Holy Family, where I've been going, have a lot of petitions about ranch life, for good weather and healthy livestock. I've never lived in such an agricultural area, so I've liked how the church embraces the lives of its ranchers."

"That's cool." Yancy looked intensely at Gen, taking in her lovely hair, scintillating eyes, the graceful curves. Yancy walked Marquette the twenty feet toward Gen, to stand him beside Golden Girl, then she reached over to cradle Gen's face with one hand, and murmured, "*Tu es aussi belle que les paysages du Colorado.*"

Gen flushed a light pink. She covered Yancy's hand with her own, as she shook her head and gave Yancy a look of amazement. "You surprise me every time I'm with you. *Merci.*"

Yancy bent over her saddle and kissed Gen lightly, feeling the soft lips answer her. "*Tu es ma surprise.*"

Gen inhaled sharply, pulled away from the soft kiss, and whispered, "You. How am I supposed to respond to charming words and kisses like that?" She searched Yancy's eyes. "Can I trust you, Mary Ann Delaney?"

Yancy was still inches away from Gen's lips. "God help me, Genevieve Lambert." Yancy moved slightly away. "I seem to have no filter between how I feel about you, and what I say and do around you. Maybe we both should be warned." She backed Marquette away from Golden Girl, but kept her eyes locked on Gen's. She felt her core beginning to melt from the contact with Gen, and while her body reacted just like any Friday night at Spanky's, her heart pounded loudly with something much deeper and more painful. Feeling that she had laid herself open to Gen yet again, her fear rose, and Yancy pressed her knees into Marquette's side as she loped away toward the river.

They rode a few miles more, until just after noon, then stopped by the river under the shade of a cottonwood, which did not provide much relief from the suffocating air shimmering around them. They both dismounted, and, without speaking, Yancy spread a blanket on the ground while Gen untied the picnic bag from Golden Girl, placed it on the blanket, and began to lay out the food she had brought. Yancy grabbed the reins of both horses and tied them to a sturdy, low-hanging branch. She felt a little more in control and sought to lighten the mood.

"Wow, an authentic *pique-nique!*" Yancy eyed a crusty French bread, brie cheese, plastic bags filled with fresh veggies, two apples, a small bag of grapes, and a bottle of Sauvignon Blanc.

"Ms. Delaney, where did you learn such a good French accent?"

"Undergraduate internship at the Agricultural Exchange, you know the agricultural tour company I told you I worked at after my bachelor's. I had some time in France, mostly Normandy, some in Provence. I had taken Spanish in high school, but decided I needed French in college. Internship came open. My dad knew the executive director…" Yancy shrugged and regarded Gen with a slight smile.

They talked about the different towns Yancy had worked in, the dairy farms and apple orchards around Caen and Lisieux, and the vineyards and lavender of Provence. They talked of shared experiences of drinking wine, of meeting the French people, who

Yancy characterized as friendly after a short time of getting acquainted. "I felt they would never accept an outsider, though. The French are very jealous of their culture."

"I know what you mean." Gen laughed. "My mom's parents lived in Europe, working most of their lives with WHO, in either Paris or Geneva. They came back home the last years of their lives, though. They said they never felt they would be received as anything but Americans."

Yancy popped the cork on the wine. Gen held small plastic glasses while she poured.

"*Salud.*" Gen held her glass to Yancy's for a toast, beaming at her. "I hope you like the bread. I made it myself."

"Holy shit."

Gen shook her head at Yancy. Yancy ate a full plate of bread, cheese, and veggies, came back for seconds, and then grabbed several grapes and apple slices. They had nearly finished the bottle of wine.

Yancy pointed to a rise in the landscape up the river. "That's the end of our property, Martin's Bluff. The next ranch over belongs to Kate's family."

Gen followed Yancy's gesture, and Yancy watched her take in the brown grass leading to green trees lining the river, and the rise along one bank. Some Cooper's hawks glided in the distance, making the scene even more peaceful.

Gen yawned discreetly and lay down on the blanket, her eyes hooded drowsily. "Boy, the wine and this heat has kicked my butt."

Yancy leaned over her, stroking Gen's face while propped on one arm. She kissed Gen, lightly swiping her tongue over her lips, which then opened to let in a more probing action. Gen hummed and purred under Yancy's lips, urging her to further explore and to deepen the kisses. Yancy moaned her need, and she caressed Gen's shoulders and sides, then moved under her shirt to cup a bra bursting with supple, silky flesh. Gen wriggled underneath as Yancy's leg came between her legs, pressing the crotch of her riding breeches. Yancy felt her own wetness and Gen's heat come together, and she pressed harder with small thrusts. Both began to breathe and moan more rapidly. Gen's hands caught in Yancy's hair, pulling strands away from her ponytail. She petted along Yancy's back to the belt on her jeans. Her fingers burrowed underneath Yancy's waistband.

Yancy pulled back, panting and sweating. She looked intently at Gen, who continued to explore the plains of her lower back. After Yancy caught her breath, she muttered, "God, Gen." Her hands caressed Gen's stomach and abs, finding sweet softness. "You are so beautiful, you knock me out."

Gen brought one hand to cup Yancy's cheek. She let out a high titter. "Did anyone ever tell you that you look like Angie Harmon?"

Yancy sat up. She began to laugh uncontrollably.

"What? What did I say?" Gen sat up, encircling Yancy's waist with one arm and grinning, but looking at a loss.

"Geez, Gen. You sounded like one of the women at Spanky's."

"What's Spanky's?" Gen's facial expression was so innocent. They both continued to giggle.

"Oh, baby cakes." Yancy snorted, then turned into Gen's arms and kissed her soundly. She looked around at their surroundings. "It's fucking hot out here. We need to get the horses and ourselves back."

They both sighed, rose stiffly from the blanket, packed up, then swung up on their mounts. On the ride back, they loped, but with stops for the horses to rest.

ℳℳℳℳ

"We both need more water." Gen noted her own sweaty face and Yancy's flushed cheeks. "I should have pushed hydration more out there. Are the horses okay?"

"They got watered at the river, but they need to be cooled down. Why don't you get some water for us both from the kitchen?"

Gen came back with a pitcher of water without ice, and poured them each a glass of welcomed relief. "You okay?" Gen asked Yancy, who she noted was sweating profusely, her face flushed. Yancy rubbed her forehead. "Do you have a headache?" Gen asked.

"Fine." Yancy took the glass of water and downed it in one long pull, handing the glass back to Gen. She turned and continued to wipe down Golden Girl.

"You look overheated."

Yancy squinted at Gen, taking off her hat and swiping her forehead with her shirt sleeve. Her face paled. Suddenly she swayed.

Gen grabbed her around the waist. "Let's get you into the house where it's cool."

Yancy put her arms out to push Gen away. "I'm fine," she muttered, then crumpled to the dirt of the barn.

Gen cried out, "Yancy." She rushed to the picnic bag lying in the dust of the barn floor, found a cloth napkin, poured water on it from the pitcher, and knelt next to Yancy to wipe the wet cloth along the back of her neck. She undid the snaps on Yancy's shirt and opened it wide. She noted that Yancy's jeans hung loosely on her, but she unbuckled the belt anyway, then unzipped her jeans.

Yancy was beginning to come around. She tried to sit up.

"Whoa." Gen pressed her hands on her shoulders. "Stay put for a while, okay? You might have sunstroke. We need to get your temperature down, so please rest a minute," Gen said softly, stroking some hair that had fallen over Yancy's forehead. Gen was concerned when she checked the thready carotid pulse. Yancy's pallor and clammy skin worried her. She refilled the glass to have water at the ready.

"I'm okay. Let me up." Yancy again tried to rise, then bit her lip and slowly folded back to the ground.

"Drink some more water." Gen's voice was soft and gentle.

Yancy sipped from the glass. Gen continued to wipe her face, neck, and chest with the cool, wet napkin.

Gen's heart was pounding. She knew she was acting on professional instinct, but she was very alarmed. "Can you stand now? We need to get you into the cool of the house." Gen lifted Yancy's arm to assist her while she raised herself on wobbly legs.

"I'm good, I'm good." Yancy brushed Gen's hand away from the small of her back.

"You are a very obstinate person, Ms. Delaney." Gen grabbed the half-full glass of water and frowned, watching Yancy brush off her hat and put it back on, then step slowly toward the back door of the ranch house, zipping up her jeans as she walked.

"I want you to drink more water and to sit and rest for the rest of the day in the cool of the house," Gen said in her professional tone, but looking with tenderness at her "patient."

Yancy grabbed Gen's hand and turned it to kiss the palm. "I'm sorry, *ma chèrie*."

Gen knit her brow as they walked to the house. "There's nothing to apologize for. If anything, you might want to apologize for not having gotten your annual physical. I imagine there's some medical reason for why you were so affected by the heat today."

When they were safely inside, Yancy squeezed Gen's hand, raised her head to the ceiling as she plopped onto the couch, and huffed in exasperation.

"I know, I know. I'm being a nag just like everyone else in your life." Gen sat down next to her on the leather couch and scrutinized her face. "But I also want you to know you mean something to me. Will you promise to get checked out?"

Yancy nodded. "I can't believe I'm saying this. Yes. Hell, yes! I can't fight all of you." She threw her hands up and slapped them down on the edge of the couch cushion.

Gen leaned in close. Yancy caught her breath. "Is this my reward for being a good patient?" Yancy asked. They kissed, lips brushing lightly, then more insistently. Yancy held the back of Gen's head to pull her in for a closer and deeper kiss, as their tongues played over teeth and lips. Gen's hands circled Yancy's strong back, feeling the muscles tense.

Gen backed away slightly, her head lying on Yancy's shoulder. She murmured in her ear, "You need to rest." She pulled back reluctantly, grabbing the front of Yancy's still-opened, sweat-stained shirt and smelled the rich aroma of her, mixed with the smell of desire in them both. She shrugged out of Yancy's embrace, cupped her face, and kissed her tenderly on the cheek. "I'm going to call Roxie to come over. I'm going home and coming back with supper."

"No, no. You have things to do for work tomorrow, I'm sure. I have some bookwork to catch up on. It's a good way to cool down. I promise not to do any outside chores, as soon as the horses get put away."

Gen covered her mouth. "Oh, my God. I forgot about the horses." She got up to leave.

"Don't. I can do it." Yancy made to stand, but faltered, her eyes closing.

"No way. I'm going to get you some more liquid. You're not going anywhere." Gen went into the kitchen, poured some orange juice from the refrigerator into a fresh glass, refilled Yancy's water, and brought both glasses to Yancy on the couch.

"Geez, you don't have to wait on me."

"Don't be a whiny patient," Gen said, shaking her head as she placed both glasses on the cedar plank that served as the coffee table. "I want both these glasses drunk by the time I've taken care of the Marquette and Golden Girl." She looked intently at the woman on the couch who was wan and pale. "I want to take care of you. Please, let me." Yancy opened her mouth. "And I know what you want to say. It's a strong person who can sometimes let themselves be taken care of a little when it's needed, so don't give me that stoic butch crap."

Yancy gave her a steely look, picked up the juice, and, without taking her eyes from Gen, gulped it down in one go. "How's that, Doctor Bossy Pants?"

Gen laughed. "Keep going. I'll be back soon." She

went out the back, the screen door slapping shut.

Fifteen minutes later, Gen came in from the stable. She washed her hands at the sink and drank more water, then, noting the silence in the house, crept beyond the end of the island that separated the kitchen area from the great room. As she reached the couch, she saw that Yancy breathed rhythmically. Her eyes were closed, her head canted back against the couch. Gen touched her wrist to check her pulse—thankfully normal. She pulled Yancy's boots off, picked up a light throw from near the cold fireplace, and laid it lightly across her.

*Yancy is one stubborn, independent person,* she mused. *What am I getting myself into? At least she seems to be letting me help her. That is something, isn't it? Who am I trying to convince?*

# Chapter Sixteen

Yancy stirred, feeling stiff. Her eyes opened to the great room in waning, early evening sunlight. A wonderful aroma wafted from the kitchen. Water ran upstairs. She remembered falling asleep when Gen went to the barn. Was Gen upstairs? Who had cooked?

She flung the throw off her feet, and, noticing that her shirt was still open, snapped it closed. She gingerly stood in stockinged feet. Feeling more like herself, she padded into the kitchen, finding two pans on the stove. She lifted the lid on boiling pasta. Another pan held clams or mussels in a light sauce. She replaced the lids right as Gen came down the stairs.

"Hey, sleepyhead." Gen toweled her hair. She was dressed in khaki shorts and a kelly green Valley View Medical Center polo that made her eyes pop with color. "I ran home to get clean clothes and came back here to shower. Do you like clam spaghetti?"

Gen's skin glowed peaches-and-cream, and the curves of her legs were set off by the shorts. "You look good enough to eat. I may not need dinner," Yancy quipped with a sly grin.

"Down, tiger. You are still in the doghouse until further notice. Roxie and Kate will be here for dinner in a little bit. You look much better. I hope you're feeling better."

Yancy looked down at her dusty jeans. She

brought her shirt to her nose, smelling dried sweat. "I need a shower, too. I'll be right back." She smiled widely at Gen and pecked her on the cheek as she passed her on the way to the stairs. She leaned in and whispered, "Thanks for taking care of me."

Gen grinned.

When Yancy returned from her shower, she saw Kate in an armchair sucking on a High Country Pale Ale. On TV the Broncos played Chicago in a Sunday night, pre-season exhibition game. Yancy clapped her on the shoulder. "Hey, buddy, who's winning?"

Kate lifted her beer. "I heard you had a good ride today, but the heat kind of got to you. You doing okay?"

"No problem." Yancy waved away the concern on Kate's face.

"Dorkhead!" Roxie called from the kitchen island. "How are you?"

"Geez, Roxass. I'm fine." Yancy gave her an exaggerated frown. "Can I have a beer?"

"Ha, baby cakes. No alcohol for you." She extended each syllable. "Can you spell de-hy-dra-tion? You probably have something else going on, if you ever got any blood work. Until then, you're getting juice and water." Roxie came and sat on the arm of Kate's chair, kissed her neck, and ran her hand along her back. Kate looked up lovingly at Roxie and brought her down for a chaste kiss.

Gen returned from the kitchen with two glasses and handed them both to Yancy with a small bow. "For the jolly rancher." Her mouth quirked into a grin.

Yancy gave her a playful sneer in return. "Thanks, Dr. Mom."

"Don't bite the hand that's about to feed you."

Roxie rose from Kate's chair, grabbing her hand to pull her up. "Come on, supper's on." Roxie grabbed the large platter of pasta from the island and placed it in the middle of the oak table that sat on the west wall of the great room.

☙ ☙ ☙ ☙

Yancy walked into the Ryan Delaney clinic on Thursday afternoon, presented herself to the receptionist, and said quietly, "Appointment with Diane."

She took a seat in the waiting area, her shoulders knotted up, her stomach doing a dance. She played solitaire on her cell phone, then placed it in her pocket and leafed disinterestedly through a ragged *People* magazine.

"Mary Anne?" A coffee-complexioned medical assistant dressed in pink scrubs, her top festooned with cartoon characters and a name tag that read "Valerie," called her back. She first weighed her and asked her height, then escorted her into an exam room, where Valerie took her blood pressure and swiped a dermal thermometer across her forehead. "You're in for an annual checkup, right? I need you to fill out this history form. Make sure you answer all the questions. Also, list all your current medications here. The nurse practitioner will be with you shortly." Valerie smiled politely, then left.

Yancy took the clipboard with a sigh and began to check boxes and fill out lines. She scanned the room, realizing that when she had previously been in the clinic, it was for taking care of a cut or a sprain, an X-ray or two—just a quick in-and-out affair, not this detailed medical stuff. She felt trapped, at the mercy of medical types and their bad news. Ryan. Dad. Trisha. It was almost always bad news. But it wasn't only the prospect of death. That she could take. Before death, she had seen what they did to Ryan and Trisha during treatment. Inhumane. They lost their dignity, their privacy, their control over their lives. Yancy could not abide any of that.

In five minutes, after knocking on the closed exam room door, a medium-height young woman wearing baby-blue scrubs, a short white jacket, and a stethoscope around her neck, entered and brightly introduced herself as Diane Cramer, giving Yancy's hand a firm shake. Yancy took in her tanned face and short blond hair. She noted a wedding ring on her finger.

Diane sat, looking over the computer screen, and scanned Yancy's medical record. Taking the clipboard, she read aloud each medical condition, making sure Yancy had answered them all. She asked her more specific questions about Ryan's cancer and her dad's heart disease, and input the data into the medical record without looking at Yancy. She then turned on her stool to face her squarely.

"We've got work to do today, Ms. Delaney, for your first complete physical exam. You can put on this gown and I'll be right back." She pointed to a blue and white cotton gown folded on the paper-covered exam table. She smiled as she closed the door.

"Damn," Yancy grumbled as she took off her boots, shirt, and jeans, then her socks and underwear, tied the skimpy gown at the back, and tried to gather it around her legs when she sat uncomfortably on the edge of the exam table. The room was cold, and she would be naked in front of medical people who held all the power in this impersonal, sterile space with its shiny instruments and smell of disinfectant. How had Ryan made it through all this medical probing? Had she even paid attention when Trisha had undergone all her tests?

Diane came back in, smiling. "I'm going to start by checking your heart and lungs," she said as she put the stethoscope to her ears and pressed the diaphragm to Yancy's chest, first on the left side then her right side. "Breathe deeply...again," she said as she listened to the sounds around Yancy's back. She next checked ears and throat using a small light. "Say 'aah.'" Her fingers felt the side and front of Yancy's neck. "Looks good, no problems with ears and throat. Now if you'll lie on the table, please."

Yancy laid her head on a small pillow.

Diane pulled a sheet over Yancy. "I'm going to do a breast exam." She explained how she would proceed, then covered Yancy with the sheet on the right side, and pushed the gown aside to expose the left breast. Yancy's face warmed. Diane looked intently at the breast, seemingly inured to a patient's blush, and ran her fingers clockwise. She repeated all the movements on the right breast.

*Holy crap,* Yancy thought. *Why don't I just run around naked in here? As if this gown and sheet cover anything.*

"Okay." Diane smiled warmly again. "We'll do a Pap smear now. Have you had any menstrual problems?" Yancy felt mortified, being probed and poked, and now the most intimate of exams was about to begin. Diane explained what would happen while she pulled up a rolling stool, grabbed a crook-neck light from the side of the room, and positioned it to shine between Yancy's legs at the end of the exam table. She pulled stirrups out from under the exam table and asked Yancy to put her feet into them.

Yancy's eyes grew wide as she did as she was asked. "No, no problems." Her feet felt like ice, and she wished she'd kept her socks on. Her hands clenched into balls. She tried to think of good thoughts, like riding Marquette. Like kissing Gen. *No, don't think about that!*

As Diane covered her legs with the sheet, Diane asked about any issues with other gynecological problems. "Scoot down farther on the table, please. Did we review how many sex partners you've had over the last five years?" Diane shoved the sheet back above Yancy's mons.

Yancy's heart pounded, her stomach heaved.

From her perch on the stool, Diane peeked over the draped sheet into Yancy's eyes. "Yes?"

Yancy stammered out, "I've had quite a few partners, I guess."

Diane retained a neutral look on her face. "Do you have an estimate? Are we talking three, thirteen, thirty?"

Yancy felt her face heat as she licked dry lips. Her mouth felt like cotton. "More like thirty." *Damn it to hell.*

"Okay," Diane responded. "We'll also do some blood work to check your sexually transmitted disease status. Were these sexual encounters safe? Did you use dental dams? Other protection?"

"No. None of them." Yancy felt exposed to the world. She blinked her eyes rapidly. *How the hell could she have forgotten such a simple thing as safe sex?*

Diane then focused the light between Yancy's legs, going about the business at hand with no indication that Yancy had just revealed her most intimate secrets and was now spread bare for everyone to see.

Yancy took a deep breath and focused on what Diane was doing between her legs. "Geez, I feel like I'm under a Gro-Light," Yancy muttered.

Diane peeked over the sheet drape again and quirked her mouth in an apology. "Sorry, it's not the most comfortable exam, is it? I'm going to use the speculum to open your vaginal area now so we can get a good look at your cervix and vaginal vault. First, I will touch you, then you'll feel the speculum." Yancy felt fingers on her folds and her vaginal opening being prodded by hard plastic, then opening wide. She was being invaded, impaled, by this instrument. Her heart beat loudly in her ears. God, she couldn't wait until this was over.

"Relax now. Just a quick swab of some cells. You might feel a poke." Diane stood and swiped the swab across a slide on the counter. "I am glad to say that everything looks healthy. I don't see any reason to think you contracted anything." She had Yancy move back while she opened the exam table to support her legs, now out of the stirrups. Yancy thanked God that the pelvic exam was over. Surely there couldn't be much more humiliation left. "Now I'll do an external exam over your lower abdomen and pelvic region to make sure everything's okay. You'll feel some pressure." Diane moved the gown up and the sheet down to expose Yancy's lower stomach, and probed and pushed into Yancy's belly. Yancy tried to unclench the stomach muscles that Diane was prodding. "There we go, not so bad, huh? You can sit up now."

Yancy pushed her gown back down, sliding to dangle her feet off the side of the table, and yanked the sheet across her lap, grateful for whatever little good it did to retain her dignity.

Diane typed data into the electronic medical record, then looked at Yancy. "That should do it for the physical exam. I want to get some routine blood work, as well as check for the STDs. You can get dressed and go down to the lab. I have the order in the computer so they'll know what to do. I should have the results of some of the tests later today and I'll call to let you know. I would advise you to use protection in the future in your sexual encounters."

Yancy nodded numbly. How stupid could she be?

"Also, this is a test for blood in your stool. Please do this at home. The instructions are pretty explicit." Diane handed her a small packet. "Send that into the address on the mailing envelope as soon as you can."

Yancy nodded again, feeling her lack of control was now complete.

"Do you have any questions? Everything looks pretty good. Heart, lungs. Blood pressure a little on the high side, we'll want to keep track of that. Some people have higher numbers when they're in the clinic than at home. We'll find out about any other issues, like cholesterol or blood problems, from the lab tests. We want to monitor you for heart disease, especially more closely as you turn fifty, given your family history. I also have an order for a mammogram. You can schedule that on your own at the hospital, but since you're forty-one, you're past the date when you should have had your first baseline, so don't put that off." Diane glanced at Yancy's electronic chart. "I don't say this very often, but you seem to be a little underweight for your height. Do you have any eating problems?"

"Um, my appetite isn't what it was a few years ago, but I think it's been stress."

"What has been causing the stress? I see you just started medication for depression with a Dr. Foster."

"Yeah, I'm doing psychotherapy with her in Denver." Yancy was puzzled about how her medical record had that information. "But how did you—"

"Whenever you use a benefit on your health insurance, it automatically populates into one electronic record. It's important that I know this information about your medications. You signed a release of information for your primary care provider at Dr. Foster's."

"I see," Yancy said. "But I don't want my information spread all over the county."

Diane smiled sympathetically. "I understand. This is all confidential. No one can access your record except the medical staff. We all need IDs to access the system, and now that I will be your primary caregiver, I'll be the main keeper of your record. Other clinicians will need my permission to see anything. You'll have to give written permission for outside providers to have access."

Yancy nodded, relaxing a little. She liked Diane. She was kind, but not infantilizing, like some medical types. "I have you as my primary care now? That's good. How often do I need to get these exams?"

"PAP and pelvic every year. But, please call me if you have any problems at all with your cycle, or if you discover any other changes." Diane gave her a meaningful look. "We'll see about the mammogram, since you are not at high risk. The rest will depend on your blood work. If we see any numbers outside the normal range, we'll talk about how to proceed. I want you to be in on all the decisions about your care. I'm here for you, Ms. Delaney." Diane put a hand on Yancy's hand briefly. "Anything else for me today?"

Yancy felt elated she could leave, and she quickly said, "Nothing. No. Thanks, Diane." She rose from the exam table and instantly threw off the gown, even as Diane was closing the door behind her. She felt accosted. She had given over her very self to Diane, who was, admittedly, a fine nurse practitioner, but she'd been treated to every humiliation and couldn't get out of that exam room fast enough. And, now, she was expected to subject herself to this torture every year? Like hell.

&#x0219;&#x0219;&#x0219;&#x0219;&#x0219;

About five o'clock that afternoon, Yancy received a call. The caller ID indicated the clinic.

"Hello," she said uncertainly.

"Hello, is this Ms. Delaney?" It was Diane's voice.

"Yes."

"Hi, this is Diane from the clinic. I have a quick update. I got the results of some of your blood work, which overall were pretty good, good numbers. One thing though, your red blood count is low, which says you are anemic. Have you ever had that before? I want to start you on some medication."

"Not that I know of," Yancy answered quietly, relieved to hear she was clear.

"Also, I want you to monitor your eating. You need to be sure to eat balanced meals, get iron in your diet. I am going to send you some brochures on nutrition."

Yancy closed her eyes and huffed. "You don't need to send anything. I can go to the CDC web site and look over the nutrition guidelines."

The phone was silent for a second. "I didn't know you knew about that. That would be great. After you start taking the medication for the anemia, I want to see you again in six weeks to follow up with more blood work."

"Sure."

"Are you having any stomach problems? Any bowel changes? This medication can be a little constipating."

Yancy and Diane went over her eating habits for a few minutes.

"Looks like you use Dean's Pharmacy, so I'll just send this prescription to them."

"Sure," Yancy answered, blowing out the breath she hadn't realized she had been holding. Okay, it was only one pill, but still. She had never had to take pills before. Well, pain killers occasionally for those cuts and breaks. Damn.

# Chapter Seventeen

On the second Saturday in September the weather continued to be sunny, with temperatures in the mid-nineties, but dark clouds were gathering in the west. The bus from New Hope, the bi-county program for special needs kids, pulled into the driveway of the Triple D Ranch exactly at 10 a.m., discharging ten children between the ages of six and eleven. Some were autistic, some had Down Syndrome, and others a smattering of other neuro-muscular issues. They milled near the barn, excitedly chattering, while three adults from New Hope supervised them.

Virgie and Marsha had recruited five volunteers. Earlier that morning, Kate had pulled up into the drive with a trailer of four horses. Yancy had her six lesson horses. All ten horses were tied by halters to the corral fence, since there were only four cross-ties in the horse barn for grooming. New Hope had acquired riding helmets for all their charges through a donation from the local ranch store, and all the children were wearing shoes with a heel for safe riding, even though they would be led on their mounts by volunteers taking lead reins.

Because Gen attended the riding therapy program as medical backup, she had arrived to see how the program worked and what kind of on-call situation she would be taking for the five Saturdays of the program this fall. As Gen walked from her car, Yancy met her.

"Hey," Yancy said quietly, pecking Gen on the cheek.

"Hey back," Gen said, smiling at Yancy. She scanned the yard of children and the row of horses ready for grooming and tacking. "Looks like they're ready to get going."

"You'll work with me. I have a child with a muscular disorder. The volunteers will get the kids over to the horses. Today we'll spend getting horses and children comfortable together, so they'll ride only a short time."

Gen followed Yancy over to meet Marcus, an eight-year-old child with a buzz cut, who looked anxiously at their approach. They each introduced themselves. Marcus lowered his head and said, "Hi," quietly.

Yancy stooped down to meet him in the eye. "Are you ready to have some fun? I hope you like horses."

Marcus looked at her through his long lashes. "Yes, ma'am."

Yancy took his hand, and they all walked over to Honey. Marcus, after some encouragement from Yancy, stroked the horse's neck. She showed Marcus how to brush her, then handed him the brush. "Here you go. If you are relaxed with Honey, she will be just fine. She likes kids, and I think she likes you, Marcus."

Marcus took the brush and, with halting muscular movement, moved it over the mare's neck and back. He grinned up at Yancy, and she cheered him on with a smile.

As he groomed Honey, Yancy gently and patiently worked with the boy. She made many positive remarks about his progress and joked with him easily, and his tight face began to relax into a smile.

When the children had finished the grooming, volunteers helped them get acquainted with the horses by leading them around the barnyard. Yancy taught them how to behave around horses, warning them not to walk behind their horse, or to make loud, sudden noises. She showed them the different names of horse's anatomy. The children walked their horses in a line for several loops around the perimeter of the corral, until Yancy felt they all were comfortable. Next, each volunteer helped their child to saddle and bridle their horse, and led them to the mounting block to boost the child up and settled into the saddle.

When it was Marcus's turn, Yancy watched him make his ungainly way onto the mounting block, while his eyes got wide. He looked to Yancy, who gave him a thumbs-up. "You'll do great. Honey rides like a dream and she won't do anything bad. She's very gentle." Yancy steadied Honey, and helped Marcus to move his small legs onto her back.

"Now sit up very straight, and let me get these stirrups fitted just for you," she said as she placed his feet into the stirrups and shortened the leather strap into the buckles. "You look just like a cowboy."

Marcus grinned back at her.

The mounting of ten children onto horses took some minutes. As soon as each child was situated atop a horse, volunteers led the horses around the edges of the corral in single file. They spoke gentle words of encouragement to the small riders.

Marcus began to giggle after the first circuit around the corral. Yancy looked up and smiled. They all rode at a tranquil walk for about ten minutes, with most of the children smiling, and some even giggling, the longer they rode.

As the time ended, the horses were led back to the mounting blocks and the children were helped to dismount. Many of the children were talking eagerly, some merely grinning widely. They all took off saddles and bridles, haltered their horses to tie them to the corral fence, and began to groom them.

When Marcus had finished with Honey, he turned with a big grin, and told Yancy shyly, "Thank you, Ms. Yancy. That was fun!"

"You are so welcome. I hope to see you next week, Marcus. You make a very good rider."

Marcus beamed and made a small shaky wave as he was helped back into the New Hope bus.

Yancy made a few comments to Nicole, the New Hope staffer leading the group, until all the children were aboard, then she waved the bus off.

She turned around to the intense gaze of Gen. Yancy wondered how long she had been Gen's subject. She felt herself blush.

As the roar of the bus subsided and other cars were leaving, Gen walked to Yancy with a smile. She stroked Yancy's arm and gazed at her with tenderness. "You were very good with that boy."

Yancy resettled her hat, looking down at her boots. "Thanks. It comes easy to me, being with new riders."

Gen shook her head. She leaned in to kiss her lightly.

Yancy heard a throat clear nearby. Kate walked up to them. "That went well, don't you think?"

"Sure. Yeah." Yancy was distracted by Gen's closeness.

"Better get these horses loaded up then." Kate laughed.

"Sure. Yeah." Yancy finally turned to Kate. "Oh, I'll help." She jogged to get Kate's horses into the trailer.

The sky had darkened over the morning. Now, blue-black clouds roiled over the valley. Lightning flashes had been seen for some minutes in the distance, but were closing in. Thunder rolled, then clapped loudly, startling everyone. Both Kate and Yancy looked up and scowled as lightning lit up the swiftly growing gloom. As another very loud thunder clap resounded, the horse Kate was leading balked at getting into the trailer.

"C'mon, now, Monty." Kate gentled her horse. The horse backed away, his hoofs dancing with fearful energy. Kate patted his mane, keeping the lead short, giving her horse time to calm before trying to lead him into the trailer again.

Just then, Connie came running into the yard, yelling, "Kate, Kate!"

All eyes turned to Connie, who looked like the devil was chasing her.

"I just got a call from your ranch, they couldn't reach you on your cell."

"Darn. I turned it off while we were with the kids." She took the phone out of her pocket and looked at the screen. "I've got two messages from Nathan."

"There's been a lightning strike at your ranch. The horse barn is on fire!"

Yancy glanced at Kate and yelled, "Let's go in my truck. We can finish loading your horses later."

Kate quickly led Monty into a stall in the barn. She and Yancy both sprinted for Yancy's green truck and sped off toward Martin Ranch in a dust cloud.

☙☙☙☙

Gen was left startled by the fast-moving events, standing with Connie in the yard, right as rain began to patter around them.

"I'll get my medical kit and get out to the ranch. I imagine they've already called 911 for fire and medical emergency." Gen ran to her Camry and opened the trunk to check her medical kit. "Connie, please call Jim McDonald and see if he can get some of the clinic staff out to the Martins'. And please call Roxie."

When Gen was two miles from the Martin Ranch, she saw smoke billowing upward in black plumes. Chaos reigned in the driveway. The county fire truck pumped a stream of water from its reserve tank onto the remaining skeletal roof of the horse barn. Two horses were corralled in a fenced pasture upwind of the fire. Gen scanned the ranch yard searching for either Yancy or Kate, but she glimpsed Roxie on the periphery of her vision, watching the barn intently. Gen ran toward Roxie, who, when she saw her, jogged to meet her.

"They're in there!" Roxie screamed over the cacophony of people's yells and shouts, and the pattering sound of the rain that was now falling at a clip.

"Who?"

"Kate went in to get out more horses. Then Yancy followed her in. The fire chief tried to hold them back but they flew in anyway. Damn it!"

Gen put an arm around Roxie's shoulder. "How long have they been in there?" She backed Roxie away from the fire. Between the spray from the fire hoses and the pelting rain, they both were getting soaked.

"I don't know. It feels like hours, but maybe a

couple minutes is all. I hope this rain helps douse the fire."

Firemen with oxygen tanks entered the barn. More pieces of the roof suddenly fell in from the center of the structure in a huge crash. Sparks flew high into the air. More firemen arrived in another red truck, hastily moving ranch hands and others who were watching back from the conflagration. A white Babcock County ambulance van pulled into the driveway and three medics hopped out.

Roxie yelled to them that Kate and Yancy were in the barn. One fireman looked at her incredulously. "Don't worry, Roxie, we'll get them out." He comforted her with a hand on her shoulder, then turned back to the barn to run with others wielding spouting hoses.

"Kate!" Roxie screamed. Gen gently stroked Roxie's arm.

They finally saw two firemen emerging from the dark smoke, guiding Yancy, who held the reins of an Appaloosa whose eyes were wild with fright. They guided the horse past the yard to the pasture away from the barn. Kate followed with another two skittish horses, trying to calm one as it reared up. Both women were covered with soot. Kate had a bandana tied across her nose. When the horses were settled, Roxie and Gen hurried to their side.

"What the hell were you doing? Are you hurt?" Roxie ran her hands over large holes burnt in the right arm of Kate's shirt. Kate's brother Nathan was soon at their side with another horse.

"I'm fine. A little burn on my arm." Kate took Roxie into her arms and gave her a tight hug.

Yancy was coughing. Gen sprinted to her with her medical bag. "Yancy!" She took her pulse, then put the stethoscope to her chest. Yancy sat wearily on the ground.

Medics from the emergency ambulance brought up a stretcher. Gen said, "She's got some smoke inhalation. Get her to the hospital."

They belted Yancy onto the stretcher.

"I'm fine." She struggled to get up amidst the coughing. "I don't need any damn hospital!"

"Let me see you." Gen walked to Kate and looked at the burns on her arm. "You need to get checked out at the hospital for treatment for some of those burns. Get in the ambulance with Yancy." She looked around and found Nathan behind her. "How are you, Nathan?"

He had his hat off, wiping sweat and soot from his face with a red handkerchief, panting from the exertion. "Just a little winded. We got all the horses, that's the main thing."

Gen shook her head. "You may have saved the horses, but we've got two medical casualties. Let me check you out." She looked him over and checked his heart rate and lung sounds with her stethoscope. "You seem to be all right."

One medic walked with Kate and assisted her to sit in the ambulance. Two others trundled Yancy's stretcher into the back of the ambulance. One of them climbed into the driver's seat. Gen could hear Yancy still cursing from the back of the ambulance.

"I'll follow with my car. Gen, you can come with us." Roxie ran to her Prius and started it.

Nathan climbed into the passenger seat. "The fire's under control. The rain will keep things from flaring up. Nothing more I can do for the barn, but we lost all our expensive hay. At least the horses are all okay," he said with an exhausted sigh.

❧❧❧❧

By the time Roxie had pulled into Babcock County Hospital on the far southeastern end of the county, the ambulance had disgorged its passengers. Roxie, Nathan, and Gen scurried into the waiting area of the emergency department and were told in which exam rooms to find Kate and Yancy.

They located Kate sitting on the exam table, a physician assistant treating the burns on her right arm. The PA looked up when they entered the room, and then turned back to her ministrations on Kate's arm. "She has some second- and third-degree burns. I'll have her ready to be released in an hour or so."

"Oh, my God, Kate." Roxie sat heavily in a chair in the corner of the exam room. Nathan looked on from the doorway as the PA finished up the treatment. Roxie's face was strained, then more relaxed when Kate flashed her a grin.

Gen saw Yancy's exam was taking some time. The emergency room doctor had called in a consult, teleconferencing with a white-coated man via a video link in the room. "I'm Dr. Gen Lambert," she introduced herself to the on-call doctor, a medium-build, African-American man.

He nodded to her. "Dr. Lambert, I remember you from the barbecue. I'm Brandon Tyler. The guy on screen is Dr. Raphael Gonzalez, a pulmonologist from the U. Medical Center, giving me some points on treating smoke inhalation. I'm about to do a bronchoscopy to see if any particles are in the bronchioles, and he will be watching via telemetry. You're welcome to suit up and assist."

"Yes, I'd like that." Gen glanced down at Yancy, who seemed to be sedated but still awake. "We're going to look at your lungs. It's very important that no solid particles have gotten in. That would be big trouble down the road."

Yancy nodded. Her eyes drooped.

After the bronchoscopy, they wheeled Yancy into a patient room on the main medical floor of the hospital. Gen, Nathan, Kate, and Roxie waited outside while the nurse got her into the bed, arranged the IV pole, provided water on the bedside table, and walked out, motioning that it was okay for them to come on in.

Kate entered first, her arm bandaged. Her clothes were smudged with black, the right shirt sleeve cut off, her short hair in disarray, and her cheeks still sooty. As she came up to Yancy's bedside, she said quietly, "Hey, buddy. How's it going?"

Yancy croaked in gasps, "I'm fine, they say my lungs look good...but they want to keep me...overnight observation."

Roxie hung on Kate's left arm, and was bleary-eyed. She stroked Kate's back with her hand, then leaned in and gave Yancy a kiss on the cheek, but her look was fierce. "I could kill you both."

Yancy gave Kate a look of puzzlement. "The horses."

"She knows about the horses. How we love them more than anything." Kate looked sheepishly at Roxie.

Roxie glanced from Kate back to Yancy. "You both are cut from the same damn cloth. I swear if you—"

Gen finished her sentence. "You won't have to do anything, Roxie. I will beat you to it, and they won't like what I will do to them both." Her face scowled, her arms were crossed over her chest.

"Hey, Doc," Yancy quietly greeted her.

Gen squinted at her silently.

Kate looked at Roxie. "Maybe it's time for us to skedaddle."

"We hear you'll be released tomorrow, barring any problems. We'll be back to get you then." Roxie touched Yancy's arm, leaned down, and kissed her.

"See you, buddy." Kate made a little wave in the doorway.

Nathan said, "Take care."

As they left, Gen moved to the side of the bed, her arms still crossed at her chest. She looked expectantly at Yancy.

Yancy smiled widely, trying to hold back another cough but not being successful. She wheezed out. "Now, I can see that you are pissed...but I have some good news for you, Gen."

Gen squinted her eyes, "Oh, really. What, pray tell, might that be?" She breathed in and out audibly. "Did you win the Roy Rogers Hero Award?"

"Hey, that's funny." She inhaled a huge raspy breath. "At least I wasn't singing like Dale Evans."

"No, not at all."

"No." Yancy inhaled again, sending her into another fit of coughing. "Sorry." She got control over her breathing. "I got my physical exam the other day...I thought you would be proud of me." She looked at Gen with her best winning smile.

Gen put her hand over her mouth, containing a grin. "I'm so glad for you," she said flatly.

"You know...squeezing boobs...spreading the legs...stick in the arm."

Gen merely nodded.

"Geez, can't you give me a small reward or something?"

Gen pretended to think deeply, then shook her head. "You are one exasperating person." Her hands rattled Yancy's bed frame. "Why should I give you a reward for something you should be doing anyway? What about running into a burning barn, you and Kate together? Where is your sense of survival, Yancy?" Tears welled in her eyes.

"Please, don't cry." Yancy pulled herself up in the bed to a sitting position and reached out for Gen. Gen collapsed into her arms, shaking with emotion. Yancy stroked her back tenderly.

After a minute or two, Gen pulled back, sniffling, and reached over to the bedside table for a tissue. "Damn you. You could have been killed."

Yancy swallowed hard. "I'm a screwup, Gen." Her eyes found Gen's. "I'm so sorry. I never want to cause you pain."

Gen drilled her eyes back into Yancy's. "I don't know if I'm strong enough for you."

"What?" Yancy paled.

Gen backed away from the bed, turning to the wall. "I'm not sure we are cut out to be together."

Yancy attempted to get up from the bed, beginning to let down the bed rail.

Gen caught her. "No way. Get back in that bed." She pushed Yancy's chest back down.

Yancy grasped her hand and held it tightly. "Gen, please. Look at me."

"I can't."

The room was silent for several beats.

Very quietly, Yancy asked, "What are you scared

of?"

Gen looked up at Yancy, her eyes wide with surprise, and held Yancy's gaze steadily. Finally, she said, "God help me, I'm afraid of losing you. I can't lose you yet, I barely have you." Gen covered her face and let out more sobs.

Yancy grabbed both of Gen's hands and brought them to her mouth, kissing the palms lightly and stroking them. Gen looked at Yancy, afraid she would break from the contact.

"Gen. Gen, you have me."

# Chapter Eighteen

On Sunday afternoon, Yancy was released from the hospital. Roxie had come to take her home while Kate and Gen were at the ranch. Because it was Connie's day off, Kate prepared to grill steaks and chicken. Gen made side dishes and Yancy's favorite Oreo ice cream dessert. Yancy was released from the pulmonologist's care, but he cautioned her to be careful of the potential for lung infection.

Roxie and Yancy entered the great room, Roxie holding onto Yancy's arm.

"The conquering hero has arrived," Roxie announced as she got Yancy ensconced on the couch.

Gen came around the kitchen island wiping her hands on a dish towel, scrutinizing Yancy's face. She walked to the couch, leaned down, and planted a chaste kiss on her lips. Roxie went out the patio door to find Kate at the grill.

"You look good," Yancy whispered in Gen's ear.

"How are you feeling? No bullshit."

"I'm doing pretty well, Doc." Yancy winked. "I'm a little tired still. A lot's happened."

"Okay, I'll believe you." Gen squinted her eyes in her best professional manner. "But stay on this couch until supper is served. We should eat in a few minutes." She retreated to the kitchen, and returned in a minute to Yancy with a glass of juice.

"No beer, I guess," Yancy said matter-of-factly.

"You have a habit of being refused beer."

Later, Kate walked in the patio door with a platter of meat from the grill, followed by Roxie carrying grilled squash. They gathered at the large dining table in the far corner of the great room.

Yancy looked at Kate. "What's the score on your arm?"

Kate flexed her arm, shrugging her shoulders. "Getting checked later this week. Hurts like hell. But seems to be doing all right."

They tucked into the food.

"I'm starving," Yancy declared as she cut up her steak and took large bites.

Yancy looked up and found she was being gawked at. "What? Hell, a woman can't eat her steak?"

They all chuckled.

"Geez, it's the most I've seen you eat in months." Roxie's eyes were wide.

"Guess what's for dessert?" Gen smirked.

Yancy watched her through squinting eyes for a moment, then smiled widely. "Don't tell me. Oreos and ice cream?"

They finished their meal, talking about how well the riding therapy program was progressing, and the kids they had worked with the day before. This led to discussing the barn fire. No horses had been harmed. Kate and her brothers were going to have to see about their insurance and get a contractor out to begin replacing the structure before the end of fall. The next few weeks would keep the Martins harried.

"I will help out when I can," Yancy offered. "I will be gone for a weekend in October. Gen and I have the rural health conference in Phoenix." Yancy felt her cell phone vibrating in her back pocket. She brought it out to check the screen. "It's Mom. Sorry." She answered the phone and went to the couch to take the call. "Yes," Yancy said. "No, Mom. No one was hurt...Kate got a burn on her arm...They looked me over at Babcock General overnight...No. I'm fine now—Mom..." She sighed deeply. "See you then. Bye."

Yancy moaned as she returned to the table to finish her Oreo dessert.

Roxie looked at her expectantly. "Is your mommy coming down to the ranch to take care of you?"

Yancy jerked her head up. "No." She spooned more ice cream into her mouth and swallowed. "Hell, I don't know. She's coming down tomorrow morning. She heard the rasp in my voice and thought she wanted to see me."

Roxie smirked. "Smart lady. Doesn't trust you either."

Yancy shot Roxie a glare and stuck out her tongue.

Gen laughed. "Oh, boy. That's so mature. You two are like ten-year-olds!"

"You don't know the half of it." Kate shook her head.

After the dishes and kitchen were all squared away, Kate and Roxie begged off, with Kate still recovering and needing rest, and Yancy needing sleep as well.

When the door shut behind them, Gen found Yancy's hand and squeezed it. As they stood in the great room, she closed in on Yancy. Yancy's breath caught in her throat. She readied for the kiss, leaning in, took her lips tenderly, then more roughly, with passion. Gen threaded her fingers through Yancy's hair, stroking her neck. Every time with Gen was becoming more impassioned, more urgent with need, more compelling and physical in a way she didn't know if she could control any longer. Yancy pulled Gen into her hips as her hands ran over the sides of her breasts, then came to cup them through Gen's blouse. Heat radiated throughout her body, settling in her lower stomach, causing her to thrum with growing arousal. Her mind and body both gravitated toward Gen as if by magnetic pull. She willed it, and inexplicably, at the same time, could not control the pull.

Gen breathed heavily, grinding into Yancy's thigh. Pushing her over to the couch, Yancy lay down on top of her, positioned her thigh between Gen's legs to meet Gen's hot center, and thrust with gentle pushes. Gen found Yancy's shirt and pulled it up, stroking her back.

For a moment, Yancy knew she could stop. But she also knew her heart had been captured. Her body had succumbed. She whispered in Gen's ear, "My God, I want you. What do you want, Gen?"

Gen panted and pulled back. "I want you, too. What are we going to do? We're not moving very slowly are we?" Her eyes were dark with need.

With a mighty exertion of self-control, Yancy pulled herself from Gen's entangling legs. Her heart beat painfully, her soul soared. She felt like singing, so high was her spirit. She could announce her love to all the world. Yancy stroked Gen's cheek. "You are so damn beautiful, I feel I've won some sort of prize."

Gen chuckled. "Not the Roy Rogers prize, I hope?"

"No, the Gen Lambert prize," she said, putting feather kisses all along Gen's neck. *How do I show her I love her? Do I know what to do?*

Gen took Yancy's face in her hands and kissed

her hard, then lightly, then brushed her lips with her tongue. "I have a proposition."

"Oh?" Yancy grinned, her eyes glinting with mischief. *Her wish may be coming true.*

Gen slapped her butt playfully, her smile gentle. "Not that. No, I want to help us slow down, but still have some idea of where we're headed."

Yancy sat all the way up, pulling Gen beside her.

"I want us to be together in Phoenix. I want us to wait until then." Gen stopped. "Can we do that?"

Yancy yanked at her hair, scrunching up her face. Slowly, she said, "Geez, Gen, that's a long time." She kissed Gen hungrily and fully on the lips, lingering to taste her and remember her. "Only if we continue to date, right?" *Please, please. I can hardly hold on any longer.*

"Date, yes. But, no hanky-panky."

Yancy laughed aloud. "What, are you in the nineteenth century? Hanky-panky?"

Gen punched her lightly. "You know what I mean, dork."

Yancy held her at arms' length. "Wait a damn minute. Only my closest friends can call me dork!" She kissed Gen, pushing her back onto the couch. "You must be one of them."

"Off of me, tiger." Gen pushed her away gently. "I need to get home. You need to get to bed."

Yancy waggled her eyebrows and chuckled. "Oh, Doctor, don't you want to tuck me in? I may need medical assistance."

Gen stood and took Yancy's hand to pull her off the couch. "You're on your own."

They kissed lingeringly. Gen then dropped her hands, reached for her purse, and walked to the door.

Yancy followed her to her car.

"Call you tomorrow?"

"I'm at the clinic till six. Talk to you then." Gen stroked Yancy's cheek, kissed her lightly, then got into the driver's seat.

"Want to come for supper?" Yancy asked, leaning down into the open window.

Gen giggled. "Oh boy. I wonder who's going to cook?"

Yancy smugly smiled. "Connie. See you then."

Yancy stood at the front porch steps, watching the red car disappear down the road. She breathed the night air deeply into her hurting lungs, hardly noticing the pain. Her heart felt like skipping. While she was exhausted from the last two days' craziness, she didn't know if she could relax, so excited she was.

≈≈≈≈≈

As Yancy finished dressing the next morning, her mother called from downstairs, "I'm here, darling!"

When she made it down the stairs, Nina was sipping coffee with Connie at one end of the old oak table. Nina met Yancy at the kitchen island, grabbed her with her arms wide, and hugged her tightly. She then pulled back to scrutinize her face. "You look rested. Will wonders never cease?" She laughed lightly.

Yancy shook her head and quirked a lopsided smile at her mother.

Nina took her hand to lead her to the table. "Let me get your coffee. I brought some of that wonderful homemade coffee cake that Maria makes. Connie, will you get us some plates and cut pieces for Yancy and me? Please get one for yourself."

Yancy and her mother ate coffee cake, not Yancy's favorite thing, but she finished most of her piece, even as she continued to cough intermittently.

Nina looked carefully at Yancy. "I don't like the sound of your lungs. But I believe you have gained some weight and your color seems less pale." She caressed Yancy's cheek. "What's going on?" she asked with a sly grin.

Yancy clasped Nina's hand from her cheek, brought it to the table and cupped it in both hands. "Mom, I'm doing really well. I did my physical exam. They found I'm anemic, but I'm being treated for it. The psychiatrist and I have decided that the depression meds have improved my appetite and mood in the last two months." She took a raspy breath, then released their hands. "I'm a damn poster girl for healthy behavior!"

Nina smiled warmly at her daughter. "What do you think has caused this change?"

She let go of Nina's hand and scrunched a napkin in a ball. She looked intently at her mother, and breathed deeply. "I'm in love, Mom."

Nina raised her eyebrows slightly. Not missing a beat, she intoned, "Dr. Lambert, I presume?"

Yancy jerked back a bit, then laughed. "Wow, geez, Mom."

Nina gave Yancy a cheeky grin, with a tilt of her head, "Mothers have their methods of intelligence gathering."

"Connie." Yancy slapped the table.

Connie turned to them from her dusting in the great room. Yancy gave her a frown.

Nina and Connie both smiled enigmatically.

꙰꙰꙰꙰

After her mother left, Yancy walked out to the barn to clean tack and rearrange the tack room. She spent the rest of the morning sweating in the heat of the barn, but came back into the kitchen feeling accomplished and pleasantly tired, her lungs still hurting a little. Connie had made a cold lunch, including some vegetables fresh from a farm a few miles away. Yancy ate hungrily, finishing a full plate.

In the heat of the afternoon, Yancy first did some financial work on the computer. She next saddled Marquette for a short ride to see how the Martin ranch was faring. Kate met her in the yard, and took her on a tour of the damage. The insurance claim was substantial. Kate felt that, because lightning was an act of God, it should be covered fully. But, the insurance adjustor had just left some minutes before, and the Martins wouldn't hear until later in the week about the insurance claim.

When Yancy returned to the Triple D, she cooled Marquette down, gave him a small portion of oats, and let him into the corral for the night.

She came inside, seeing Connie finish up the preparations for supper.

"I'm writing the instructions down." Connie told Yancy how long to bake the ham. She also showed her the potato salad and coleslaw that cooled in the fridge.

Yancy nodded, but didn't pay much attention. How much could it require?

Connie left at 4:15, so Yancy went up to shower and change out of the sweat-stained, dusty work clothes she had ridden in.

As she came downstairs, she couldn't smell ham

cooking. She checked the stove and found that the oven had not been turned on, then remembered to read Connie's note. She was to have turned the oven temperature to 300 degrees as soon as Connie left. Yancy berated herself, and quickly turned the oven to 450 degrees, thinking this should speed up the process.

Drinking iced tea and relaxing with the *Denver Post* on the back patio for the past ninety minutes, Yancy heard a car pull in. She ran around the house to meet Gen at the driver's side, right as Gen was getting out. They kissed lightly. Yancy hugged Gen. "How was your day, Doctor?"

Gen pulled out of the hug, kissing Yancy again. "Except for some kids' beginning-of-school-year colds this afternoon, things went pretty smoothly. How about you? How's your cough?" She looked closely at Yancy.

Yancy shrugged.

"I'm starving. I hope we're having something good for supper," Gen said as they walked with arms around each other's waists into the house.

They entered the great room, where a burned odor emanated from the kitchen. Yancy raced to the oven, opened it, and found the ham covered with a black crust and smoke flowing off it.

"Damn." Yancy pulled it out of the oven, immediately setting off the loud claxon of smoke alarms.

Gen ran in to see the commotion. She noted the burned ham, and covered her smile with her hands. "Oh, dear." She burst into laughter.

Yancy looked at her sheepishly, then joined her as they laughed heartily.

"I thought Connie was cooking?" Gen managed

to get out in between chuckles.

"Damn. All I had to do was turn on the oven. Oh, hell. How about we have peanut butter?"

Gen grabbed Yancy by the shoulder. "You are so adorkable!" She kissed her soundly on the lips.

Yancy, a little taken aback, took a moment to register that she was being kissed, then leaned in to return it.

Gen turned Yancy's shoulders toward the great room. "Please, get out of the kitchen. Let me salvage what I can. We will definitely *not* be having peanut butter!"

"But—"

Gen shoved her butt away from her. "Go. Watch Monday Night Football or something. I'll be a few minutes."

Later, along with the side dishes, they ate pieces of ham that Gen had cut away from burnt crust. They laughed again at Yancy's lack of skills in the kitchen. Then they talked about Kate's barn, the clinic's day, Yancy's ride that afternoon, and of course, her mother's visit. Yancy did not include her mother's confrontation about the cause of her healthy behavior. They had an enjoyable evening that ended by watching the last quarter of the football game on TV, cuddled together on the couch.

After they turned off the TV and rose from the couch, Gen stretched and yawned. Yancy drew Gen in for a deep kiss, and her hands wandered to Gen's ass.

"Hey." Gen swatted Yancy's hand. "Remember our agreement."

Yancy smirked. "No hanky-panky. Ooh." She cowered in mock fear. "Are you off this Wednesday?"

"Yes, and you're coming to my place for supper

that night."

"Oh, I guess I am." Yancy nuzzled Gen's neck and jaw.

"Now, let me get home. Long day tomorrow. I'll be on call tomorrow night."

They kissed all the way to Gen's car. Yancy smiled and sighed as Gen drove away into the night. When she got to her room, she pulled her phone out of her back pocket and texted Gen. *"Miss you. Have a good sleep. YD"* and a heart emoji.

After a few minutes, Yancy's phone beeped with a text: *"Sleep tight. GL"* and a heart emoji.

# Chapter Nineteen

The last couple of weeks of September were spent alternating between Yancy's and Gen's, three nights of the week, for supper. They read, or watched a movie or football on TV. On the weekends, Yancy had the riding therapy kids on Saturday, and she rode with Gen on Sunday. One Saturday evening, they drove to Denver to hear The California Guitar Trio. As hard as it was, Yancy did her best to not approach Gen with too much sexual heat. But as the date of their trip to Phoenix loomed, she had more and more difficulty keeping her hands to herself. At night, she was consumed with pleasant thoughts of making love to Gen, which offered a backdrop for pleasuring herself occasionally.

Even so, Yancy felt the stress of sexual tension when around Gen. She felt her heat rise every time Gen spoke lovingly, caressed her neck, or stroked her hair. She loved to laugh with her, to tell her stories of the ranch, and to joke about her own bad culinary skills, or Gen's excellent ones.

It wasn't just sexual, but a sense that she could not get enough of Gen, her laugh, her intelligence, her sweetness, her tenderness, even her smirks and teasing. Yancy had never felt what she was feeling, could not remember being so stricken with constant thoughts of another person. Her wanting consumed much of her waking time, and even populated her dreams.

On a Wednesday night at Gen's, after supper, they lay together on the couch snuggling under a light cover in the chill of the early autumn air. Gen was running her hands through Yancy's dark locks dreamily, when she spoke up. "I've been wanting to do something with you."

Yancy sat up. She put on her sexiest grin. "We've only got one week to go, we could start a little early." She grasped Gen's hand and placed it in the V between her legs.

Gen laughed and tugged her hand away. She lightly spanked Yancy once on her butt. "Stop it!" She sat farther away from Yancy on the couch. "Now keep away. I have something I want to ask you."

Yancy sat erect and frowned slightly. "Is this serious enough, Doc?"

"Dork." Gen shook her head, then she turned to face Yancy, and said, "I want to go to Spanky's this Friday."

Shock and dismay raced through Yancy's heart. She quickly schooled her expression. "Why? What's so...?" Yancy scrutinized Gen closely. "How the hell do you know about Spanky's?"

"You had mentioned that I wasn't a Spanky's gal, so I looked up on the internet 'Lesbian Bars in Denver.'" Gen smiled seductively. "I love to dance. You've never taken me dancing." Gen raised her eyebrows in excitement. "They do country dancing on Friday nights, according to their website."

"Yeah, they do. I'm not sure about...Do you like line dancing and two-stepping?" Yancy tried to smile but found it hard.

"Well, I haven't done much country, but I love to dance, so I thought we could try it. Please, will you take me?" Gen punctuated the question with a nuzzle of Yancy's neck.

Not able to withstand the hotness in Gen's kisses, Yancy mumbled, "Sure, Spanky's on Friday." Her chest pounded, but she steeled herself. She could do this.

Much later, at home, Yancy sat quietly in the great room with a fire in the gas fireplace to take the chill off the room. She felt surrounded by a whirlwind, her life so changed in the months since Gen had arrived. Her emotions were in better check, she felt more like her old self, but most exciting were the feelings of love she had whenever she thought of Gen. Everything about her was enticing. She drew her like a calf to its mother. Yancy felt out of control, yet totally in control—weird and wonderful. While she knew intellectually she could walk away from this romance, emotionally she knew she had fallen deeply. She had never felt so committed to someone, never been so wanting to please them, to show them how much she loved them. It was outside her realm of experience, certainly, but somehow it felt natural, like she was being her true self with Gen.

Never much of a praying person, Yancy surprised herself by thanking God that Gen was in her life. Gratitude filled her heart. Giddy with happiness, she smiled and turned off the fireplace.

❧❧❧❧

On Friday, Yancy picked Gen up in the Rover. She knocked on her door and smoothed down the new black jeans and then pulled at the cuffs of her favorite red Western shirt from under her coat sleeves. In the window of the door, she checked the coyote slide of her bolo tie.

As she opened the door, Gen ogled Yancy with a big grin, grabbed her around the waist, and pulled her inside. "Ooh, you look cute!"

Yancy took in Gen's outfit of a new pair of dark blue jeans and a flouncy blouse with dark blue flowers. "You, too." She kissed her and grabbed her ass. "Maybe we could stay here tonight."

"Oh, no you don't. Let's get going. I'm so excited."

As usual, the low bum-bum beat of the bass guitar could be heard a block down the sidewalk from Spanky's. Yancy's pulse quickened at what she might find inside. Or who, to be specific.

They entered hand in hand, and looked around the crowd of women, lined up two-deep at the bar. Every table was full. Yancy walked with Gen to the wall nearest the tables and spoke directly into her ear over the din. "I'll get some drinks and be right back."

Gen nodded.

Yancy pushed through the crowd to catch a tall bartender with short, spiky hair, then she ambled back with two bottles of beer.

Together they scanned the scene, feeling the atmosphere of women together.

"I haven't been to a lesbian bar since moving to Colorado. I have missed being able to openly hold hands or kiss a woman in public." Gen looked into Yancy's eyes, and smiled like a kid. "I'm so happy to be here. Let's go." She grabbed Yancy's beer, placed both bottles on a shelf on the wall, and snatched her hand to lead her onto the dance floor for a Texas two-step.

The dance floor began to crowd with women, and they soon bumped into other couples. The next dance was a slow waltz. They circled the floor, floating together, their bodies fitting naturally. Yancy weaved effortlessly through the steps in smooth moves, with grace and a bit of athleticism. They smiled into each other's eyes. Gen snuggled closer as they spun and dipped to the strains of the oldie, "The Tennessee Waltz." The next old song was Dolly Parton's "Here You Come Again."

"One of my favorites." Gen sang along with the band while they moved in rhythm to the romantic lyrics.

Yancy saw a familiar face close by, and suddenly felt a little panicked. She tried to steer Gen over to another side of the floor, but the couples were too packed to move much.

"Hey, lover." Cheyenne sidled up to Yancy, threw her arms behind Yancy's neck, and kissed her full on the mouth.

Yancy pushed her back quickly. "Hi, Cheyenne."

A six-foot-tall, bulky woman came up behind Cheyenne, turned her around, possessively put her arm around her, and gave Yancy a steely glance. "What's happening, baby? Is she bothering you?" Yancy thought she looked like a para-military captain, in her tight black T-shirt, camo cargo pants, and combat boots. Suddenly Cheyenne's girlfriend pushed in closer to Yancy, inspecting her aggressively.

Yancy held up her hands. "No problem. Cheyenne and I know each other. Uh…this is my girlfriend, Gen." She pointed to Gen, who was taking in the scene before her, slightly grinning.

Gen turned Yancy toward her to continue the dance, but Cheyenne stopped them by seizing Yancy's arm. "Hey, don't you want to apologize for last time? You kinda ran out on me," she said in a high, whiny voice.

Yancy, wanting nothing more than to fall through the floor because Gen was witness to this, carefully removed Cheyenne's hand off her arm. "Sorry, Cheyenne. I'm kind of busy right now. See you later." She then focused on Gen's face, giving her a look of apology.

The combat woman holding Cheyenne's waist moved into Yancy's personal space. "Hey, cowgirl. The lady said you need to apologize." Then she shoved Yancy, who lost her balance by tripping over her boot and crashing onto the floor amidst the crowd of feet. Others on the dance floor moved away from them, watching the action, while women screamed or gasped. Someone cheered, "Go get 'em, cowgirl!"

Yancy's face clouded with fury, and she bunched her fists as she came up from the floor like a small tornado. Gen reached out to stop her forward movement.

"Get away from me, creep," Yancy said with a low growl.

Cheyenne's girlfriend began moving into Yancy's personal space again. "Yeah, or what, you little wuss?"

Gen grabbed Yancy by her belt and pulled her off the dance floor. "Let's get out of here." The other dancers opened a wide path for them, peering at the couple.

Yancy let herself be tugged out the door and onto the sidewalk, still breathing fire. "That son of a…"

They hurried out the door into the night. Yancy paced the sidewalk, trying to catch her breath. "Hey." Gen slowed Yancy's pacing, and gently stroked Yancy's cheek with one hand. "Hey."

Yancy looked at Gen. Her shoulders relaxed. She breathed heavily for another minute, then broke out into a smirk. She and Gen both cackled uncontrollably. Yancy made sure Cheyenne's girlfriend was not coming out after them, then gathered Gen up in a tight embrace and passionate kiss.

"Mmm, mmm," Gen murmured, throwing her arms around Yancy's neck. "I should not reward you for bad behavior."

Yancy laughed again. "Let's get the hell out of here." She tugged Gen's hand and they scooted quickly to the Rover.

৯৲৯৲৯৲৯৲

They held hands all the way home. During most of the drive, they rehashed the excitement at Spanky's, of Yancy's near-punch of the bully. Yancy shut the engine down after she pulled up in front of Gen's house, unlatched her seatbelt, and reached across to kiss Gen tenderly.

Gen's libido sparked into hyper-drive. Her mind shut off and her body took over. "It's still a little early. Would you like to come in?" she whispered in between kisses.

Yancy's answer was to sprint out of the Rover and over to the passenger side before Gen could completely shrug out of the seat belt and gather her purse. They walked arm in arm to the door, Gen unlocked it, and Yancy held it while Gen entered.

Yancy's hands found Gen's face, cradling it softly, and she peppered it with light kisses. Gen grabbed Yancy's hand to lead her to the couch in front of the fireplace, then she pulled Yancy to lie on top of her, where Yancy's solidness covering her felt so right.

Yancy crouched over Gen and kissed her deeply,

their tongues playing a game with each other. Gen's core heated. Yancy leaned on her elbow to kiss her way across Gen's face and chin for some moments. Yancy then kissed Gen's neck and down her blouse front, opening buttons as she went. She pulled the blouse out of Gen's jeans, and pushed it off her shoulders.

"Oh, God, you are beautiful." She breathed heavily into Gen's neck and cleavage, her hands massaging Gen's breasts. Gen groaned and thrust her chest forward, grasping and caressing Yancy's nape to keep her close. Yancy found the bra closure and unsnapped it. Gen shrugged it off. Her skin felt like it was melting at Yancy's touch.

Gen loosened Yancy's bolo tie and tugged at it to remove it over Yancy's head. Yancy's pearl-snap buttons flew open to reveal her tight, small chest. Gen palmed each of Yancy's breasts while Yancy positioned her leg between Gen's thighs and rocked into her. The solid muscles of Yancy's body spurred Gen to caress her back and those defined abs.

The sound of rasping breaths and moans filled the living room. Their hands roamed all over each other's bodies, hot core pressed up against hot core. Gen lost her ability to think as lust propelled her, took her over.

Gen grabbed Yancy's hips and ground herself into her thigh with small thrusts as Yancy continued to suck and nibble Gen's full breasts, first the left, then the right. The touch made Gen's clit throb and her core dissolve with heat and wetness. She pressed into Yancy, rocking her into her knee. Then Yancy took over and kissed Gen lower and lower. Gen could smell their scents of desire rising. Gen's mind in a fog of want, she closed her eyes and operated entirely on touch, taste, scent, and sound.

Gen moaned, writhing beneath Yancy. Just as Yancy began to undo the button at the top of her jeans, Gen opened her eyes wide, suddenly coming out of the fog of lust to realize what was happening and grabbed Yancy's hand. "No, Yancy. Stop. We've got to stop." Inhaling deep breaths, she pulled herself to a partial sitting position with her head supported against the arm of the couch, her body tingling and throbbing.

Yancy ceased her movements immediately. She cast a concerned look into Gen's eyes and said, "Did I hurt you? What's wrong, Gen?"

"Nothing. Oh, darling." Gen continued to pant, her breath slowing somewhat, her eyes still filled with need.

"Did you just call me darling?" Yancy grinned, her face inches from Gen's.

Gen nodded and caught her breath, trying to get herself under control. "We need to stop. You don't know what you do to me." She exhaled.

"Oh, I might have an idea." Yancy grinned wickedly.

"You are so arrogant." Gen slapped the arm still wrapped around her waist.

Taking on a serious tone, Yancy looked at her and said, "No, darlin'. I know, because of what you do to me. I have to tell you, no one has touched me the way you do. I love how you stroke me, fondle my cheek. When you brush your hands through my hair, you set me on fire."

Yancy pulled Gen to sit up beside her. Gen regarded her closely, hoping Yancy spoke the truth.

"I…You are so perfect, so beautiful. I don't…" Yancy's eyes held a plea. "Oh, hell. I'm in love with you

you." Yancy leapt up off the couch and stood in front
of the fireplace with her hands deep in her pockets.
Her red shirt flapped wide open, revealing tight abs
and white skin between her breasts. Her eyes studied
her boots.

Gen rose and came to Yancy. She cupped her
cheek, tipping her face up so that she could peer
directly at her. Gen felt tenderness toward her as she
brought her lips to brush gently against Yancy's and
continued to stroke her jawline with long fingers.
"You." She shook her head. "You are so many things,
so many contradictions. You make me lose my brain
function. I've tried to tell myself this...That I can't
possibly feel what I've been feeling." Gen took a deep
breath in her trepidation at being so open with Yancy
about her feelings. She kissed Yancy and pulled back.
"God help me, Yancy, I love you, too."

Yancy blew out and hugged Gen tightly to her.

Gen snuggled into the warmth of Yancy's arms.
Her heart pounded with exhilaration at the idea that
they loved each other. Gen softly caressed Yancy's face.
She exhaled with a satisfied smile. Then, she looked
down at both of their torsos. She was nude from the
waist up, while Yancy's shirt was totally open.

Yancy's eyes followed Gen's and she began
laughing. "What does this mean for the banned hanky-
panky, Doc? Are we out of compliance? Or at least
about to be?"

Gen hugged Yancy tightly to her, laid her head on
her shoulder, and whispered, "Oh, God. I don't know."
She then gazed deeply into Yancy's eyes, her heart
about to beat out of her chest. "I want you so badly. But
I was hoping we could have something very special in
Phoenix. To be together where we aren't distracted by

patients, or mothers, or horses...or bully girlfriends."
She searched Yancy's face. "Do you understand what
I'm saying?"

Yancy stroked Gen's back for a moment, then
said quietly, "I know just what to do, darlin'. Leave
Phoenix to me." She kissed Gen lightly on her lips, her
eyebrows, her chin, and back to her lips. She winked.
"I think I have been barred from the house for the rest
of the night, wouldn't you say? Knowing there is next
weekend..."

Gen, excited about next weekend in Phoenix, also
feared what Yancy had planned. What would happen?
Could Gen let go of her fears and open herself fully to
a woman who she still needed to trust with all her soul?

About twenty minutes after Yancy left, Gen
received a text. *"I will be dreaming of you all night,
chèrie"* And a heart emoji.

❧❧❧❧

The next Tuesday, Marlene Edwards's BMW
crunched on the gravel into the Triple D fifteen
minutes early for her lesson. Victor and Yancy were
fixing a water pump in the corral as Marlene strutted
up to them. Yancy's shirt and jeans were streaked with
oil and grease, and both her boots and jeans were wet.
Marlene cast her a look of disgust. Yancy grunted.

"I'm here. I'd like a word with you before we get
started." Her severe face brooked no refusal.

Yancy apologized to Victor while she wiped her
greasy hands on a rag, and followed Marlene into the
barn some twenty feet away.

"What do you want, Marlene?"

Marlene came very close to Yancy. So close

Yancy could smell her expensive perfume and feel heat radiating off her breasts. "I want us to be like we used to be," she said petulantly. "What have I done?"

Yancy took off her hat to wipe perspiration from her forehead. She did not meet Marlene's stare. "Marlene, it was never right. It wasn't in the past and it isn't now. I can't do this anymore."

Marlene's face looked like the personification of "hell hath no fury like a woman scorned," so Yancy backed up a step.

"If you think this is the end of us, you are sadly mistaken. I will gladly tell my husband that you forced yourself on me. That you caught me in the barn, and that you coerced me to have sex with you. He will believe me in a heartbeat, don't think he won't. Your reputation will see to it that no one will stand up for you. You will be kicked off the board in an instant. Mommy or no mommy!"

Yancy gulped. "You wouldn't do this, Marlene."

"Just watch me." Marlene moved in and grabbed Yancy's shirt.

Just then, Victor entered the barn. "I don't think you have much to stand on, Mrs. Edwards. You don't remember that I have been around nearly every Tuesday afternoon, and I know what you've been doing. You have been the predator, not Yancy."

Marlene's head whipped around. "Who asked you? You're Yancy's hired hand. No one will believe you."

Victor smiled innocently and shrugged. "Maybe, maybe not, but do you really want to take that chance with your reputation, Mrs. Edwards?"

Yancy breathed in gasps, watching Marlene's face go from sneering bully to hateful bitch in the blink of an eye. She shot Yancy a look of disdain. "You don't know a good thing when you've got it. You are one small-time player." She turned on her heels, and said as she made her way out of the barn, "I guess lessons are over, kids."

Yancy looked at Victor gratefully, took off her hat, and said, "I think we barely escaped, my friend." She laughed. Quiet Victor could always be counted on. "Thanks so much. I am sorry you felt you needed to come to my rescue, but I am very glad you did."

Victor smiled at her, nodded his head, and turned back to the work on the paddock pump.

≈≈≈≈

The rest of the week couldn't go by fast enough for Yancy. Tuesday evening, she was on the phone for about an hour with the host hotel for the RHA convention in Phoenix. On Wednesday morning, she met with Jim, the administrator of Valley View, because she was scheduled to make a presentation on their rural clinics, with Gen's assistance. Jim and she updated an existing series of PowerPoint slides with the latest information on the clinic's facilities, clients, staffing, and funding. Gen would then end the presentation with case studies of two clients. Because she had represented the board many times with various clinic funders, Yancy could do Valley View's standard dog and pony show by heart. On Saturday, Gen would present the case studies without slides, in a more narrative form. They were ready for the business of the Phoenix conference.

# Chapter Twenty

Gen heard a knock on her door Friday at 5:32 a.m., according to her cell phone. She had just put on a pair of light sweats after coming out of the shower, and was still toweling her wet hair, wondering who in the world would be showing up at her door in the dark of barely morning. She hurried to spy through the front picture window curtain. They weren't scheduled to fly to Phoenix until much later that morning, yet here Yancy was, patiently standing on her small front porch.

"What in God's name are you doing here at this hour?" she asked more curtly than she had meant, as she wrapped the towel around her head.

Yancy, grinning like the Cheshire cat, held up a brown bag. "Breakfast," she declared as she breezed past Gen to the kitchen. Gen followed.

"I thought you weren't a morning person?" she demanded, hands on her hips, the towel thrown across the back of a chair.

Yancy closed in and kissed her. "Good morning to you, too."

"You are crazy." Gen laughed.

"Darlin', this is just the beginning of the day. Get ready for some fun."

Gen pulled herself out of Yancy's arms and peeked into the bag. "What do you have? Ooh, my favorite, scones." She inhaled with pure joy. "Where did you get these?" She looked up at Yancy. "Don't tell me. Connie, right?"

Yancy smirked. "Got any coffee? I'm desperate."

"Coffee comes on in"—Gen glanced at the coffee-maker's clock—"six minutes. You have a seat, I'll get some clothes on and be right back. I'm all packed and ready to go after we eat." Gen turned around after two steps. "And thank you for breakfast. You're spoiling me." She surrounded Yancy's neck with her arms and kissed her soundly, then spun back on the way to her bedroom, smiling brightly.

While she dressed, Gen wondered what Yancy had planned for them in Phoenix. While she was excited to be going to RHA with her, she still retained her doubts about them as a couple. She had hoped that going slowly would curb their pure attraction, to give them time to really know each other. So far, Yancy had been attentive, even tender and loving toward her. Was this permanent? Could Yancy be real with her? Did she know Yancy well enough now to make a commitment...assuming Yancy wanted one?

☙ ☙ ☙ ☙ ☙

During their flight, Gen read a medical journal while Yancy dreamed of Saturday night. Excitement, eagerness, exhilaration, apprehension, trepidation—all had overcome Yancy this week at some time, while her plans for Phoenix gelled. An off-the-charts romantic evening would hopefully fulfill both her and Gen's dreams of showing their love to each other. She couldn't wait to see Gen's face tomorrow night, could hardly imagine getting through today's meetings and Saturday morning's presentation so she could put into place her surprise for Gen.

ℒℒℒℒ

At the Phoenix hotel, after they checked into their rooms, Yancy and Gen picked up their badges and program schedules at the convention registration desk.

Gen looked over the schedule. "I have a meeting of medical directors at three. You have your development board at three thirty. Why don't we meet here around five thirty for a drink before the big banquet tonight?" Gen asked as Yancy waved a greeting to someone she knew across the hall.

"Sounds good."

From behind her, a familiar woman's voice cried, "Gen!" Gen spun around and into the arms of Stacy Philpott, her husband Dan trailing behind and looking on with a wide smile.

"Oh, my God. It's so good to see you!" They hugged tightly. Then, Gen turned to Yancy. "You remember Mary Ann Delaney from Valley View?"

They all shook hands. Yancy briefly looked them over. "Great to see you again." Yancy smiled politely. "Gee, Gen, don't you want to catch up with your friends? We can forgo the drink."

"Are you sure?" Gen saw hesitancy from Yancy. *And was that a jealous look?*

"I'll meet you in the banquet hall with the tickets." Yancy checked her phone. "Oops, have to get to my meeting." She waved to everyone, turned, and jogged away.

"That was brief." Stacy gave Gen a quirky smile and a slightly raised eyebrow. "That's her, isn't it?

Wow, I had forgotten, she really does look like that actress."

Gen came back to herself after contemplating Yancy's quick getaway. "Oh, yes, that's Yancy."

"Something wrong?"

"I don't know. She can be a little dorky sometimes, not good in social situations. I think it's all fine." She looked affectionately at Stacy. "But, let's get to our meeting. It's so great to see you all." She put her arm around each of their waists as they made their way down the hall to their meeting room.

❧❧❧❧

After their afternoon meeting, Gen and Stacy sat down in the lobby bar for white wine. Both bubbled over with information about Colorado and Kentucky. Stacy led her through the latest pictures of the children who had started back to school six weeks ago.

"Boy, Mary Ann Delaney is as sexy as I remember."

Gen felt warm at the thought of Yancy.

"What's going on? I saw the look she gave you. She adores you."

"I sort of adore her, too." Gen drank sips of her Chardonnay, smiling so much she thought she might burst.

"I'm so happy for you." Stacy grinned. "Is it serious, then?"

"Oh, Stace, it's early days. I'm not sure exactly where this is all leading. I'm shocked at myself for being in this relationship at all."

"Why? The playgirl thing?"

"Yancy has a reputation. A local player, evidently, since her partner died several years back. Nothing long term since then."

"I remember you told me when you slapped her."
A small giggle escaped Stacy. She took a deep sip of her
wine.

Gen exhaled. "Long story short, I laid down my
rules. We've been dating, but she has to abide by the
rules. So far, so good. No macho sexual stuff since
then."

"Impressive. Do you think she has really changed?
Or is she just putting on an act to get into your pants?"

Gen stroked the perspiration from her glass.
"That's what I'm afraid of, but I certainly hope not.
I'm hooked on her pretty badly."

༄ ༄ ༄ ༄

Yancy loved the rural health meetings, which
were held in fun places around the country to entice
underpaid, isolated rural medical staff to get out and
enjoy themselves. Everyone was laid back and the food
was always pretty decent. An added bonus was she
could dress the way she wanted. She finished the last
touches of her Western shirt and pants for the banquet,
complete with lizard-skin boots. All the rural health
friends she knew expected her to be decked out in good
Colorado ranch gear, and she loved it.

At 6:20 she stood in the hall outside the banquet
room, watching for Gen. Soon a woman sauntered
before her, familiar green eyes shining, light auburn
hair swept up in a fancy clip. Gen looked smart in a
beige pantsuit, sporting a beige and green silk scarf,
and soft, light green shell.

Gen reached her, leaned in for a quick kiss, and
whispered, "Hi, good looking."

"Hi, yourself." Yancy gave her a close perusal. "I love your hair. Can we leave now?"

Gen shook her head, took Yancy's arm, and they entered the large hall to find their seats. They were assigned to the table with other development committee members, who were primary funders of clinics in their home states as well as being major donors to the RHA. Yancy endured the banquet meal by conversing with others at the table. She, however, had her mind elsewhere. She could not stop glancing at Gen as she chatted with Harvey Whitehead, a major financial backer of a rural center in Oklahoma. She felt a little jealous every time Gen laughed at something the distinguished man in his late sixties said. Once, Gen put her hand lightly on his arm, and Yancy inhaled sharply.

She quickly looked to her other side, noticing that Mrs. Nelson from downstate Illinois was engaged in a heated discussion with the new guy, whose name she couldn't remember, from Florida. Yancy was beginning to hate this banquet, feeling sorry for herself. She rubbed a headache that had begun behind her left temple.

"You okay?" Gen said softly, gazing at her intently.

"Sure, fine." Yancy tried to smile, and bumped her shoulder against Gen's.

"I thought we could have breakfast with Stacy and Dan tomorrow if that's okay with you. Our presentation on Valley View is not till ten, and they have to leave tomorrow afternoon to get back to their kids. They've been here since Thursday morning."

"Oh, sorry they have to leave." Yancy tried to be convincing, but was secretly glad not to have to share Gen's time with any of her professional friends.

She hated feeling this way, as if she were a child not wanting to share a new toy, but she couldn't seem to rid herself of the sense that she needed Gen all to herself. She'd never wanted anyone as much as she wanted this gorgeous, vibrant woman seated next to her.

"Breakfast sounds good." She leaned in to whisper to Gen as the speaker was being introduced. "By the way, this is for you." She produced a small envelope from the back pocket of her jeans and slipped it into Gen's hand.

Gen opened it furtively in her lap with a questioning glance. Yancy knew the words printed on the off-white linen paper by heart:

> *Your presence is requested at Seven in the evening*
> *Saturday, October 11th*
> *Hotel Verde, Suite 9601*
> *For cocktails, dinner, and moonlight dancing.*
> *Semi-formal attire.*
>
> *RSVP avec un baiser.*
> *M.A. Delaney.*

Gen looked up from the invitation in her hand. Yancy watched her, a small smile quirking her lips. "What are you up to?" Gen leaned over to ask.

Yancy took Gen's hand and held it on her knee under the tablecloth, rubbing her palm with her thumb. "Aren't you going to RSVP?" She grinned lasciviously with raised eyebrows.

Gen bussed her on the cheek.

"Hey," Yancy whispered. "*Embrasse-moi!*"

Gen kissed her quickly on the mouth. Yancy noted that the others at the table were focused on the keynote speaker and not on their PDA.

As they left the banquet, both women greeted acquaintances, but refused invitations to any of the several parties going on in suites, primarily sponsored by pharmaco-medical conglomerates. They rode the elevator to Gen's floor in silence, holding hands. When it stopped with a small ding, Yancy followed Gen to her room.

Once in the room, Yancy took both of Gen's hands, held her out to examine her fully, then said softly, "I know I have told you, and you evidently think it's one of my lines, but you are stunning. I don't think you know how beautiful you are, or you would be flaunting it. You turn heads wherever you go." She brought Gen close to nuzzle her neck.

Her head nestled on Yancy's shoulder, Gen replied, "How can I tell if it's one of your lines or not? You have to admit you have a reputation to live down."

With a pained look, Yancy backed away. "You can believe what you want. I only know that I've been more patient with you than I thought was possible. But you're worth it. Every damn part of you. You are worth my sleepless nights, my crazy jealousy." Yancy looked down at her boots while rubbing her fingers along Gen's knuckles. She sighed. "I'm doing my damnedest to be the best person I can be, because you are worthy of a good person." Yancy chuckled and looked back up at Gen. "You're even worth a dance at Spanky's." Yancy tugged Gen to sit on the edge of the king-sized bed that took up most of the hotel room. "I have a confession."

Gen looked fondly into Yancy's eyes and raised her eyebrows. "Oh?"

"I was like a spooked horse the night I took you to Spanky's. I was embarrassed for you to see the women

I had been with there." She dragged her hand through her hair. "And sure enough, good old Cheyenne shook me in my boots." Yancy turned to face Gen squarely. "But the thing is, you didn't flinch. You didn't judge me for who I was, who I had been. I think I fell in love with you a little more that night." Her trembling hands grasped both of Gen's. "I am not that person anymore, you have to believe me."

"How can I be sure?" Gen whispered. "I want to believe you, God knows. I want you to do your best for yourself, not for me." She caressed Yancy's cheek and the hair on her neck.

"You can be sure, because I've tried to be the old Yancy, and I don't have it in me to be frivolous with anybody's heart anymore." She fingered the clip in Gen's hair, then slipped it off, and the shining, auburn tresses tumbled down. As she raked her hand through the sleek hair, she whispered, "I care about you, and I care about me, too. I care too much to ever let that person take over my life again."

Gen slid on the bed closer to Yancy and cupped her jaw, pressing her fingers lightly along her cheekbones. She bowed forward to kiss her lightly, grazing her lips over Yancy's, sucking on her lower lip. Yancy let her lips be caressed, then attended to Gen's, licking and gently sucking them into her mouth. She let out a small moan and backed away. Their foreheads rested together for a moment.

"I'd better get going. We've got a big day tomorrow, starting with breakfast at seven thirty, right?"

They rose from the bed slowly, encircling each other's waists with an arm.

At the door, Yancy kissed Gen deeply, exploring

with her tongue, finding Gen's mouth opening to her. She let out a small moan, and brushed her hand through Gen's hair, caressing her neck. Gen rubbed Yancy's back. "See you tomorrow, *ma chèrie.*"

When Yancy reached her room, she quickly changed into comfortable sleep wear, and went over in her head all the preparations she had made for Saturday night in the penthouse she had reserved. George, the hotel staffer who arranged everything for dinner, had left a message on her phone about all the details of her order. She could do nothing more, so she relaxed with a movie on TV before turning in. Still a little nervous about everything coming together tomorrow night, she sighed and gave up worrying.

❧ ❧ ❧ ❧

Yancy was already drinking coffee with a menu in her hands when Gen appeared at the hotel café on Saturday morning. Gen pecked her cheek lightly. "Morning," she whispered.

Yancy smiled up at Gen, and, after she scooted into the booth, rested her arm above Gen's back. The server appeared and they ordered. Yancy took in Gen's black pencil skirt and flowing rust-colored blouse. She breathed in. "You look amazing as always, Dr. Lambert."

"All ready for our presentation?" Gen looked at Yancy, a slightly serious expression clouding her eyes. "I have a small thing to ask you. I don't think it will be a problem, but I wanted to check with you."

Yancy gave Gen her full attention, a little afraid of what was coming next.

"As one of my case studies for the session this

morning, I would like to use your treatment for smoke inhalation. I want your permission before I do it."

Yancy's eyebrows came up slightly. "Mmm."

Gen quickly added, "I, of course, won't use your name, only your age and sex."

"You want to show how we used telemedicine for the pulmonary consult, right?"

Gen let out a breath. "Right. How do you feel about it?"

Without hesitation, Yancy answered. "Hey, it's a great case study. Dad would have been proud about the telemedicine facilities. I know Mom is."

"Thanks. I have other cases I can present if you would rather."

"Good morning, cuties." Stacy walked up to the booth, leaning in for hugs. "I'm starved."

They both returned the hugs. When Yancy hugged Stacy, she felt a warm reception.

"We were just talking about our session this morning," Gen told her.

They chatted with Stacy about the content of their presentation. Stacy explained that Dan had received an invitation for breakfast with a group of other Kentucky rural health people, so he wouldn't be joining them. The server filled Stacy's coffee cup. "Tell me about yourself, Yancy." She leaned over the table and smiled enthusiastically at her with pert lips and an eager lilt in her tone.

Yancy was a little taken aback by Stacy's invitation. Although she was Gen's best friend, she felt friendly affection emanating from her. Yancy talked about her background in international agriculture. They discussed their hopes for both the horse therapy program and Gen's new position at the clinic. "We're confident Gen can bring medical residents to us, who in turn will be more interested in serving rural patients. This is the main reason we were interested in her."

Stacy smiled at Gen. "Well you've got the right gal for the job. She's a winner."

Yancy smiled at Gen with tenderness. "Believe me, I know that."

"Okay, you two." Gen laughed. "Let's move on from the Gen Show." She grabbed Yancy's hand, which had begun to stroke her thigh under the table.

Stacy gave them both a knowing glance, then ordered her breakfast when the server appeared again. She gave the menu to him, then leaned back in the booth with a mischievous grin, looking at both women. "Well, inquiring minds want to know…what's happening with you two? I need to see what your intentions are, Ms. Delaney."

Yancy stiffened for a moment. She looked at Gen, then back at Stacy and cleared her throat. "Damn, I…"

Gen, grinning at Stacy, looked back at Yancy. "Yeah, exactly what are your intentions?"

"Um…Hell, I'm being ganged up on." Yancy squirmed. "What do you think?" She challenged Gen with her eyes. Then she looked at Stacy directly. "I love her," she stated simply. She waited a moment, then she squinted her eyes. "Dan didn't have a meeting, did he? Did you two plan this little confrontation?"

Stacy blushed furiously, while Gen glanced at her with a raised brow. Stacy chuckled.

"I know what Gen has probably told you about me, Stacy. Hell, a couple of months ago, I wouldn't have given you two plug nickels for me as relationship material." Yancy shredded her napkin, and her voice fell to a whisper. "I want something real in my life. Gen has captured me, heart and soul."

Stacy became serious. "You're telling the truth, aren't you?"

Yancy didn't answer, but looked at Gen then at Stacy with a lopsided grin.

The server arrived with three plates, and refilled their coffee cups. "Anything else, ladies?"

"We're fine," Yancy answered.

"Yes, we are." Gen gazed into Yancy's eyes.

Stacy smiled widely. The spell of the serious conversation was broken, and they began to share stories of their shared interests.

As they finished their last sips of coffee, Stacy sighed. "Dan and I will miss the gala dance tonight. What are you two wearing?"

Gen grinned slightly and took Yancy's hand. "We've got other plans."

As they got up to leave, Yancy and Gen both gave big hugs to Stacy. Yancy felt good that she had a share in Gen's friendship with Stacy. The connection made her feel closer to Gen, and Yancy was glad Gen had Stacy in her life.

ऄॣऄॣ

The turnout of conference-goers for Gen and Yancy's presentation filled the moderately sized meeting room. The slides were shown, and Gen's case studies, including the one of the pulmonary consult for Yancy as the patient, were motivating. They received hearty applause as it ended. A few stayed to ask questions of Gen or Yancy. Business cards were shared.

Gen sighed. "That went well," she said, while Yancy packed up the laptop. Yancy turned around and their eyes met. Gen said, "I did want to ask, what does semi-formal mean? Should I wear what I had intended to wear to the gala dance tonight?" Gen moved closer to Yancy.

Yancy felt the warmth rise in her whole body by Gen's nearness. "Sure," she said, trying to keep herself from kissing her right there in the meeting room, even though the audience had left them alone.

Gen licked her lips. "Well, I think our schedules are both kind of full till then. Have a good day, darling," she whispered as she closed in to give Yancy a full kiss. "See you later."

"Damn." Yancy held her, then let her go slowly, breathing deeply.

## Chapter Twenty-one

By 6:15 Saturday night, Yancy had finished her shower and dried her hair, which she decided to leave straight and fanning across her shoulders. She carefully unwrapped the outfit the hotel staff had delivered earlier after being pressed, a Western-style, royal-blue suit. She put on the contrasting, lighter blue, pleated-front shirt and got the black string tie to tie evenly. She finished off the ensemble with her best, freshly polished, silver-tipped, black boots. Looking in the mirror, Yancy straightened the tie, smoothed the jacket, and decided she would pass muster.

As she awaited Gen's arrival, Yancy roamed the penthouse suite. She checked the flowers. She smoothed the tablecloth and straightened cutlery. She refilled the bucket holding a sweating bottle of champagne with more ice. Flipping on the playlist of quiet jazz that wafted immediately from the Bose wireless speaker, she let the music try to relax her. Lastly, she called down to the kitchen to confirm the arrival time of the food.

Then she paced. Yancy repeatedly glanced at her watch. Her phone came into hands, then was placed back on the coffee table, as if it had a will of its own. The light faded in the room, so she switched on a bank of low spots. *Am I nervous about being with Gen for the first time? Maybe a little, if I am completely honest with myself. I know how to make a woman moan. I sure as hell can give sexual pleasure. Do I know how to make love? To let someone fully into my heart? I think I have; I pray I can. I don't want to mess it up. The future with Gen, my future, rides on how tonight goes. God help me.*

At precisely 7:00 p.m., the elevator arrived at the penthouse, and she hurriedly strode to meet it as the doors swished open.

Yancy couldn't take her eyes off the amethyst cocktail dress Gen wore, floating around her like a cloud when she gracefully emerged from the small elevator. Yancy was captivated by Gen's smile and also with the milky smooth mounds peeking out of the low cut of the dress.

Gen came into Yancy's arms. "Is this where a sexy rancher invited me to dinner?"

They held each other for some moments. Yancy relaxed into Gen's warm embrace, her previous nervousness melting away.

❧❧❧❧

Scenes of the Phoenix skyline, backed by the black shadow of mountains, were framed in the floor-to-ceiling windows from which Gen took in the beauty of the night. Nat King Cole's voice softly crooned "Chances Are" in the background. She smelled the vase of red roses, and was enfolded in the warmth of low spotlighting around the walls. Candlelight spilled onto accent tables beside a couch. On another wall, glass doors led to a small balcony lit with sconces rising at intervals from the wrought iron balustrade. Gen looked at Yancy. "How did you…This is lovely."

Yancy grinned. She took Gen's hand and led her out through the sliding door to the balcony, where a warm Phoenix night enfolded them. The chilled bottle made a pop as the top exploded off, and wine gently fizzed into the crystal flutes Yancy produced. "To this night," Yancy said softly, clinking glasses.

Gen sipped the champagne. "My God, this is Roederer Cristal." She glanced at the bottle in the bucket. "You can't get that at the supermarket!"

Yancy grinned and shrugged. When a Miles Davis instrumental began to play, she put her flute down, and offered her hand. "May I have this dance?"

Yancy's eyes sparkled in the candlelight on the balcony. Guiding them expertly to the music, her hands ran down Gen's bare back.

Gen drew back a bit to gaze into smiling eyes. "You look very striking in this suit." She fingered the black tie and ran her hand down the pleated shirt front.

"And you, wow!" Yancy exclaimed, eyeing Gen from head to foot. "I'm glad I didn't have to share you with anyone else on a public dance floor tonight."

The elevator dinged at the entrance to the suite. Yancy pulled herself away to usher in a waiter in a black tux, pushing two linen-covered carts. He left the smaller cart in front of the doors to the balcony, and trundled the other cart behind a half wall to the galley kitchen, where he placed covered dishes in a small oven, and others in the apartment-sized refrigerator.

"Thanks, George," Yancy said as she signed for the food. She spoke in low tones to him briefly. He nodded, then disappeared down the elevator.

Gen, after witnessing the tuxedoed man's actions, was taking in the view of the Phoenix lights on the balcony when shortly Yancy stepped out carrying two small plates.

"This looks wonderful." She took the plate of

pâté and crusty bread from Yancy, while Yancy topped off their champagne.

Nibbling at the food, they gazed intently at each other. Gen felt her passion rising, and she hoped she would be able to make it through dinner. Right now, all she could think of was undressing Yancy, and making love with her where they stood on the balcony.

After finishing the pâté, they danced some more, feeling the air begin to chill slightly as the evening darkened, but at the same time, their skin warming as the champagne began to take effect.

"What are you thinking about?" Gen asked softly.

"How lucky I am to be dancing with the sexiest, most alluring doctor in the world." Yancy kissed Gen's neck as she slid them around the balcony to the gentle jazz.

"Funny, I was thinking I was the lucky one, dancing with Angie Harmon's twin." Gen giggled as Yancy squeezed her tightly.

They danced through several more jazz sets.

"Are you hungry?"

Gen, nuzzling Yancy's neck, hummed her answer. "Mmm."

Yancy clasped her hand and led her into the suite, to the china- and crystal-laden table. She pushed a button on the wall, and George entered from the kitchen area, lit the candelabra, and then began to serve them from the dishes as he retrieved them from the oven and refrigerator.

Amazed, Gen watched as first a Caesar salad was impeccably served, followed by an entrée of filet mignon in a light sauce. After George poured them each a glass of full-bodied French Beaune wine and left, they lifted their glasses again in a toast.

Yancy smiled winningly as Gen picked up her fork and ate. Gen shook her head. "Do you want to tell me—"

"No. This is for you, darlin'. Don't look a gift horse...well, you know."

"You are a devil, Mary Ann Delaney."

"I think more like an angel, tonight. Because there is certainly a heavenly creature sitting with me."

"As I said, smooth-talking devil." Gen continued to eat her meal, glorying in the tastes, while they looked longingly into each other's eyes. Their conversation recapped the day's events.

After they finished, George quietly cleared the plates and brought an assortment of cheeses, a pear compote, and fresh grapes to the table, then disappeared again. Gen marveled at the quality of the wines and the food that Yancy had ordered. She was touched and a little overwhelmed by the assault on all her senses and the beauty of Yancy's dark hair and eyes, sparkling in candlelight across the table from her.

A few minutes later George returned with a carafe of coffee. "Do you wish to have your coffee in here or on the balcony, ladies?"

"On the balcony, please." Yancy rose and took Gen's hand to lead her to the balcony. "Thank you, George. That's all we'll need this evening."

George dipped his head in a small bow, leaving with a swish of the doors.

Yancy sipped her coffee, watching Gen, where they both sat on lounge chairs looking at the evening sky. Yancy stood and asked for Gen's hand, then pulled her close to dance to the quiet tones of "Isn't It Romantic."

Gen's head was on Yancy's shoulder. "I'm feeling

pretty mellow," she murmured into Yancy's ear.

Yancy brought her body into Gen's and pushed her thigh into the rustling flounces of the dress. They swayed to a rhythm of their own. Gen's body heated from the contact with Yancy's body. She moaned softly, nuzzling and then kissing Yancy's ear, then farther down her neck. She wanted to get closer and closer. "Darling," she sighed.

Yancy groaned slightly. "We could take this into the bedroom."

"I thought you'd never ask." Gen leaned back and nipped her lip quickly, then grabbed Yancy's hand.

⊰⊱⊰⊱

The bedroom was lit with spots over two paintings of the desert, the duvet picking up the reds and ochres of the oils. Gen grinned at Yancy as they met face-to-face. She pulled Yancy's suit jacket down her arms, then began to slowly untie her tie and take out the studs on her pleated shirt, all the while meeting her eyes with a smoldering look. Yancy returned the gaze with half-closed lids.

This was the moment Yancy had planned, now, the culmination of her proclamation of love for Gen. So far, the evening had gone perfectly, but her pounding heart told her she felt new at this game of true love. Yet she reached back to her time with Trisha, groping for muscle memory in making love, not just having sex.

Turning slightly, Yancy's hand found the zipper of Gen's dress, carefully lowering it. She cupped both of Gen's breasts through the sheer fabric, groaning with the lovely fullness of the flesh filling her hands.

Gen's dress floated down, shimmering like a

waterfall. Gen reached to pull off Yancy's shirt. Gen stepped out of her dress pooled on the floor, to reveal matching bra and bikinis in black lace. Yancy leaned in, inhaling sharply of her scent, reaching and fumbling for the clasp of the bra, all the while guiding Gen with her toward the bed.

They collapsed on the duvet, Gen's bra hit the floor, and her bikinis followed quickly after. Yancy's shirt had also been pulled away. "Lovely," Gen intoned as she reached for the button of Yancy's trousers and pulled at the zipper. Yancy helped her remove them by lifting herself off of Gen and pulling them down, to toss them off the bed.

Before Gen could reach for the waistband of her silky boy briefs, Yancy kissed her neck and down between her breasts and began a frenzied exploration with her tongue and teeth. Yancy breathed heavily with excitement.

Gen hissed and pulled Yancy to her, her head rearing back and her eyes closed. "Yancy," she cried as she sought Yancy's thigh with her legs, and pushed her hips to rest there. "God, yes."

Yancy's heart pounded. She kissed down Gen's front, from between her breasts to her stomach, to the soft, tufted mound, and back up again. Thrusting her hips, both of them rocked into a cadence that mimicked the buildup of wetness and heated skin. Emotions swirled when Yancy reveled in the velvetiness of Gen's skin. Equal parts impatience and slow adoration swept over her.

Not believing her great fortune in finding Gen, Yancy worshipped the body beneath her. Gen's softness, her silky skin, her beautiful mouth, her sensuous breasts, all bombarded Yancy's senses, overwhelming her with love.

"I'm going to savor you slowly," Yancy murmured into Gen's ear. She then began a very deliberate feathery touch along Gen's back and buttocks, the side of her hip, and the top of her thighs. She caressed Gen, feeling as if she were adoring a piece of art, her fingers outlining, barely brushing up against breasts and the hills of her hips. Over and over, Yancy relished the downy pillows of her butt, the planes of her back, the curves of her breasts. Reverence and peace infused Yancy as she breathed a sigh.

"I need you," Gen breathed. "Yancy, please."

Yancy herself was mad with arousal. Even so, she tamped down her emotions to retain the slow caresses, but moved them lower to Gen's inner thighs, just brushing across the skin, merely a hint of a touch.

Gen's hips rose, her legs opened to Yancy. She pulled Yancy's hand to her opening. Yancy began a sweet assault on Gen, cupping Gen's mound, then using one finger to explore her wet, silky folds. "Yes," Gen cried.

"God, you are soaking." Using the moisture to coat her fingers, Yancy began a measured circling of her clitoris. Her strokes were fairy-light. "What do you want, darlin'?" she whispered.

"I want you. All of you."

Yancy moved her mouth along Gen's white stomach, tasting the sweet skin. She reached the curly mound, stroking it softly with her tongue, then placed delicate kisses on Gen's inner thighs. Gen bucked slightly, moaning and humming. Yancy traced the folds of Gen's pussy with her tongue. When her tongue found Gen's clitoris, Gen jumped. "Yes, darling. Yes."

Her fingers and tongue searched the length of

Gen's folds, nearly imperceptibly kissing and licking, while Yancy groaned with her own building need. The taste of Gen was exquisitely complex, changing as she felt Gen's orgasm building. Her touch increased in rhythm and intensity.

Gen moved her hips to meet Yancy's mouth, pushing closer, grasping Yancy's head and guiding her. Her moans grew louder, her body began to gyrate around the rhythm of the kisses along her inner lips. Yancy entered two fingers into her.

Crying out, Gen raised her hips in a spasm. Her body shook, her hands clenched Yancy's head. She stroked and grabbed at her hair. "Oh, God, Yancy!" She groaned and shivered with orgasm.

Yancy watched Gen's climax ripple through her in a series of moans and gasps. As soon as one orgasm had finished, Yancy began a ritual of kissing that brought yet another, and another. Gen's chest rose violently with deep breaths. Her voice was gravelly. "Darling."

Finally, stilling and relaxing, Gen pulled Yancy up to her. She wrapped her arms around her tightly. "I need you close. Don't leave me."

"I'll never leave you. I love you, darlin'."

Gen's movements subsided, gently lowering her into her surroundings. She looked at Yancy's grinning face and smiled languidly. "Satisfied with yourself, eh?"

Yancy put her elbow on the bed and leaned her head, looking at Gen. "I will never be satisfied." She smiled shyly and kissed Gen deeply, running her hands over Gen's arms and hips.

Gen cradled Yancy in her arms, stroking her cheek, then she kissed her breasts, while dipping her hand under Yancy's silky briefs into her moisture.

"I'm nearly there," Yancy said breathlessly.

Gen stroked the length of Yancy's engorged wetness and around her swollen clitoris, her own breath coming faster now. Yancy rested her hand on Gen's, guiding her toward the most sensitive spot, and cried out with a shuddering of her whole body, writhing, panting, and groaning in Gen's arms.

"I...I don't usually..." she stammered, looking at Gen in affection and awe. She breathed in rasps until she got her breath under control.

Gen gentled her by caressing her, from stomach to neck, with a long sweep across her breasts.

The night had only begun. While the soft refrain of jazz played in the suite, Yancy and Gen were in each other's arms, stroking, caressing, fondling, kissing, coming to heights of pleasure again and again.

Sometime later, they lay spent in the bed. "You," Gen said, smiling, holding Yancy's face in her hands, stroking along her jaw and through her hair.

Yancy smiled in return. "This has been my dream come true. And more. I love you, Gen."

"Oh, darling, I love you, too." Gen kissed Yancy gently, then more passionately.

Finally, exhausted, they drew each other into a spooning snuggle. Yancy pulled Gen's butt toward her, wrapped her arms around her waist, cuddled, and softly rubbed against her breasts, as their words were lost in sleep and rest.

Except, as tired as she was, Yancy could not drift into sleep. Doubts started pounding into her thoughts, making her brain kick into double-time. This was her first time since Trisha to give completely of herself to another person. *What would Trisha say? Would she see this as betrayal of what we had together? Will I be able to let Trisha go and open fully to Gen? What will happen now? How will Gen want to be in my life? Can I let her in fully?*

❧❧❧❧

The bedside clock read 3:27 in yellow numbers. Gen stirred, noting that she was in the bed by herself, and wondered where Yancy had gone. She listened for movement, but heard nothing. For a brief moment, the worst-case scenario dwelt in her mind, making Gen's heart beat rapidly. Images of Yancy's skittishness toward their budding relationship reared their ugly heads. She slowly brought her feet onto the floor, grabbed Yancy's discarded blue shirt as a cover-up, and went to the bathroom. She splashed water on her face and took in the fragrance that was uniquely Yancy, and smiled. She tiptoed around the rest of the suite, seeking Yancy.

When she didn't find her in the living room or the kitchenette, her heart took a small, painful plunge. But then she turned and caught sight of Yancy's shadow on the balcony, sitting in one of the patio chairs. She couldn't tell if she was sleeping, so she crept to the balcony doors and peered through them.

Gen slowly opened the doors, and, as she did, Yancy's head turned to look at her. Her eyes were unreadable in the low light, but her body was turned into itself. Gen made her way over to the chair and sat on the arm, placing a light kiss on Yancy's temple, and stroking her shoulder. "Hey."

"Hi there." Yancy gazed up at Gen, cupped her chin, and brought her lips down for a kiss.

Noting that she wore only a sleep shirt in the

cool night air, Gen asked, "You okay? What are you doing out here?"

Yancy's eyes had a sadness underneath a slight smile. "I'm good."

"Why don't I believe you?" A wave of tenderness swept over Gen.

"Cause you're an overprotective type?" Yancy took Gen's hand in hers and kissed the knuckles softly.

"Not getting out of it that easily, Delaney. Want to come clean?"

Yancy stood up and brought Gen to her in a strong hug. Gen regarded her intensely, the hint of sadness more apparent in the light from the hallway spilling out onto the balcony. "I...I'm fine. Just mulling things over a little."

"Contemplating running away?"

Yancy grinned, looking down at her bare feet. "You know me too well, or at least my reputation, Doctor. No, I wasn't thinking of running, but if I were truthful, I would confess to some hints of fear and a little guilt on top of that."

"Guilt?"

"I didn't expect to feel a little like I was betraying Trisha. While I was trying to get to sleep, I couldn't get her face out of my mind. Then I thought, you are the first person I have loved since her, if I did really love her. I don't know. Anyway." While Yancy's words faded away, her face rose to study Gen. She stroked Gen's shoulder and upper back.

Gen studied Yancy in turn. She pushed hair from Yancy's face tenderly, caressing. "Oh, darling. I don't imagine anyone or anything can totally erase Trisha from your mind, and I don't want it to. She was your first long-term relationship. We can't snap our fingers to make our past disappear. If you hadn't loved Trisha then, perhaps you wouldn't be able to love me now." Gen continued to gently caress Yancy's face. She shivered. "Let's go in. You feel cold, and I'm getting chilled."

Yancy let herself be brought back into the bedroom and gently pulled down onto the bed. Gen nestled close, laying her head on her shoulder. "Why do you love me?" Yancy asked plaintively.

Gen raised her head off Yancy's shoulder and gazed tenderly at her lover. "Go to sleep. You haven't had enough rest, and it's too damn early in the morning to be having these conversations."

Yancy chuckled, pulled Gen's head back to her shoulder, and was asleep within minutes.

In the morning, they awoke to come into each other's arms and continue the dance of love that they had started the night before. Finally, in late morning, Gen, her body totally satiated but sore, turned to Yancy and said, "It's time for some food, rancher. I'll order some things up, okay?"

"Mmm," Yancy murmured, and stretched in her state of sleepy, post-coital bliss.

Gen rose from the bed, and found that all her clothes from her hotel room were hanging in the closet. "When did my stuff get here?"

Yancy turned in the bed and yawned. "George or one of the hotel staff packed and cleared you out of your room, then brought it up while we were dancing before dinner."

Gen shook her head. "Okay, one more thing to give me pause about this whole weekend."

"Glad I could give you pause, Doc." Yancy grinned.

"You're not the jolly rancher, you're the jolly roger, a devil." Gen came back to the bed and launched herself on top of Yancy with an oof. She started tickling her. "You are too much."

"Stop it! I'm very ticklish. Get off me."

They laughed as Gen continued to torment Yancy until Yancy cried, "Uncle. Please, stop!"

The bed looked like a windstorm had hit it. They both giggled. Gen got up again, slapping Yancy's butt. "Going for a shower."

"Need a friend to wash your back?" Yancy drawled.

"You stay right there, I don't trust you."

"Ha, payback's a bitch, Gen."

⁂

After they ate a late breakfast, they packed their bags and arrived back in Denver Sunday midafternoon. The trip from the airport was fairly quiet, each woman caught up in her own reverie, holding hands. However, as the day wore on, Yancy began to be plagued by a raspy voice and slight cough. Her lungs began to feel congested. Both she and Gen dismissed it as the beginnings of a cold.

Yancy dropped Gen off at her house, helping with her luggage. She placed the bag in Gen's bedroom, and turned to find her gazing at her with love.

"Thank you for a wonderful time. It will go down as the most romantic night of my life." Gen took Yancy in her arms, kissing her lightly. "When will I see you?"

Yancy hesitated a little. God, this was hard, harder than when Trisha moved in, because she knew Gen would be in her life far more deeply. "How about you come over for supper tonight with Kate and Roxie, then a more private supper here tomorrow?" Yancy paused. "I've been thinking."

Gen continued to nestle in Yancy's neck. "Mmm?"

"I need to talk to you."

Gen pulled back, her arms around Yancy's neck. "What is it?"

Yancy squirmed out of Gen's hold, and put her hands in her pockets. "I, well. I wondered. Do you think you would…" She started for the front door, then turned back. "Would you consider moving to the ranch with me?"

Gen blinked, then slowly her face changed into a smile of total bliss. She took large strides to Yancy. "Oh, yes." She kissed her with passion.

Yancy beamed. "Great. Kate and Roxie are coming over tonight, so let's talk about it more tomorrow at supper. I'll see you in a little bit at my place."

# Chapter Twenty-two

Anybody home?" Roxie yelled from downstairs.
"Up here, Rox." In her bedroom, Yancy
pulled on her boots, then clomped down the stairs.
"Just headed to check the horses." Her voice rasped
with the cough that continued to increase in frequency.

Roxie met her in the kitchen. "Don't like the
sound of that cough. You okay?" She put her hand on
Yancy's forehead. Yancy swatted it away. "Kate will be
here for supper after she stops at the ranch."

"It's just the start of a cold. I'm okay. Haven't
gotten much sleep the last week." Yancy looked her
friend over, in her Birkenstocks with multi-color socks
she had knitted herself, comfortable, worn jeans, and a
red, blue, and purple variegated cardigan over a purple
mock turtleneck. Roxie looked as colorful outside as
Yancy knew she was inside, and she smiled.

"When's Gen getting here?"

"In about half an hour, I think. She wanted to
unpack first."

Roxie came up to Yancy and bumped her with her
shoulder, her smile widening with mischievousness.
"Come on. How was Phoenix, baby cakes?" Roxie's eyes
widened when Yancy's face heated. "Oh, that good?"

"Stop it." Yancy pushed her arms into her canvas
barn jacket and headed for the back door.

"Wait, I'll help you." Roxie ran to catch up with
Yancy.

As Yancy raked the stable aisle, she pointed to a shovel and to an open stall door. "Clean that stall, will you? And try not to step in anything in those sandals of yours."

"Not until you tell me how your trip went."

"Geez, nosey." Yancy leaned on her rake and rolled her eyes at Roxie. She felt suddenly shy. "It was...very nice. It was great."

Roxie lunged at Yancy to grab her into a bear hug. "Get off me!"

"Let me celebrate with you, baby cakes. This is wonderful news."

"You might as well be the first to know. We, uh—"

Roxie shook Yancy's shoulder. "Come on!"

Yancy picked up her rake and turned to her task. "She's moving in."

"Holy. Mother. Of. God." Roxie swept the rake from Yancy's hands and jumped up and down, swinging her in a circle.

Yancy swatted at Roxie's arms. "Damn it. Get off me, jackass."

Roxie was giggling like a teenager. She ran her hands down Yancy's arms, cupped her face, and gave her a big smooch on the lips. "Let me get a little wild, dorkhead. It's not every day that Mary Ann Delaney falls in love." She embraced her again in a bear hug. She calmed down, whispering in Yancy's ear, "I'm so happy for you, baby."

"Hey, what's happening? I went to the house, but didn't see anyone." Kate strode into the stable, catching the grins on Yancy and Roxie. "Is it good news?"

Roxie glanced toward Kate. "It's the best news ever. Gen and Yancy are an official couple." Yancy took up raking again. "Gen's moving in," she squealed, launching herself at Kate and hugging her.

Kate took the brunt of the collision with Roxie, stepping back and laughing at her wife's antics. "Well, I can see there is joy in the stable," she said drolly. "Congratulations, buddy."

Yancy smiled enigmatically, got caught up in a wracking cough, then continued to rake.

"Here you all are. I was beginning to wonder if I was feeding a nonexistent group." Gen stepped into the stable aisle, taking in the scene. "What is it?"

Roxie hurled herself at Gen, kissed her on the cheek, then ferociously grasped her in her arms. "I'm so happy for you two."

Gen beamed. "Thanks, Roxie. I'm pretty happy myself."

Yancy put the rake away and walked to Gen. "Hey, Roxass, this is my girlfriend. Go hug your own." She took Gen into her arms and kissed her soundly.

Gen kissed her back, then pulled away with effort, warmly smiling at Yancy, then looking at her with concern. "Are you still coughing?" She, like Roxie, put her hand to Yancy's forehead. Yancy shrugged it off. Gen then turned to the group and said, "I've got food. Who's hungry?"

They all went to the house for supper, Gen talking about the romantic night before in Phoenix. Roxie hung on every word, leaning forward and grinning like an idiot.

At one point in the supper, Kate leaned over to Yancy. "Hey, buddy, you just spoiled it for me. Am I going to have to buy big-ticket champagne now?" She punched Yancy's arm.

Yancy punched her back. "I can't help it if you

don't have a romantic bone in your body. Your idea of romance is a beer and a football game on TV."

Roxie chimed in. "Boy, have you got that right. I'm the romantic one at our house. She never wants to watch the Hallmark channel. I love all that lovey-dovey stuff."

Kate shrugged. "Sorry. If you want a good horse, call me. If you want horses, champagne, and moonlight mush, call Yancy."

※.※※.※

Gen had not heard from Yancy after their Sunday supper. She texted her twice on Monday, in the morning and in the afternoon, then tried to phone her when the evening news came on. Pictures of Yancy backing away from their new relationship whirled through her brain. Around 6:45 p.m., she called Roxie. "I'm trying to reach Yancy. Do you know what's going on? I was supposed to have dinner with her at six thirty."

There was a pause. "Didn't she call you? I brought her phone to her. That dorkhead!"

"What do you mean?" Gen's anxiety level rose considerably.

"She told me she was going to call you. Damn it." Roxie breathed in. "I'm sorry. I took her to the hospital this morning, early. She was having trouble breathing. They said it was aftereffects of the smoke inhalation. Damn it, you can't trust her. Why didn't she at least return your calls and texts?"

Gen's heart was in her throat. "I don't know. How is she doing?" She looked at her watch. "I'm going over to the hospital right now."

In the lobby of the small rural hospital, Gen

asked for Yancy's room number and headed to the elevator. She found room 208, knocked lightly on the half-closed door, and peered in. Yancy was sitting in a bedside chair hooked up to an oxygen cannula, half asleep. When she saw Gen, she raised up a little from the chair, rasped slightly, and sat back down with a thud.

"Gen," she murmured.

Gen came to the chair, knelt beside it, and grasped Yancy's hand. "Why?"

Yancy gulped. She inhaled and exhaled several times with an audible wheeze. "I'm sorry, Gen. I didn't..." Tears welled up in her eyes. "Damn it, I don't know that I'm any good at this relationship stuff."

"Just tell me why you didn't let me know you weren't feeling well." Gen was hurt.

"I don't know exactly. You're always taking care of me. I wanted to let you off the hook for a change," Yancy said, her pallid face blushing.

"Off the hook? What hook?" Gen stood, looking down at Yancy. Her muscles tightened. Her hands fisted. "Let's make some things clear." She walked away from the bed to put some distance between them. "We are not yoked up together like oxen, but we are a couple who takes care of each other. We care about what happens to the other person, we support them, and in turn they support us. You took care of me totally when I first got here. You took me for trail rides. You introduced me to the movers and shakers in Babcock County. And Saturday night, my God, that was totally you." Gen strode back to Yancy's chair and knelt again, tears coursing down her cheeks. "How could you shut me out, after what we had this weekend? What about you and me is still scaring you, my love?"

Stillness. The whir of the oxygen concentrator filled the room.

Yancy's tears welled up. She looked at Gen, then down at her hands in her lap. "I am so sorry." Her eyes met Gen's, imploring. "Do you think you still want to be with me? Am I a lost cause?"

"Oh, darling." Gen wrapped Yancy in her arms, kissing her temple, her hair. "You are a dork, but I still love you." She laughed tearfully. "Don't ever withhold information from me again, though. If you are hurt or sick or feeling badly, darling, I need to know. What if it had been me who had been hospitalized? How would you feel?"

"I would feel shut out of your life, like I didn't matter," Yancy confessed, then had a fit of coughing.

"Oh, sweetheart." Gen caressed her hair. "I'm going to see if I can find your doctor. I can probably do this bronchial therapy for you at home. If the physician agrees, I'll stay at the ranch tonight and tomorrow. I'll teach Connie what to do, so she can take care of you while I'm at the clinic." Gen rose and kissed Yancy on the top of her head, then left to find her doctor.

❧❧❧❧

By ten that night, Yancy was ensconced in her own bed, the equipment for her treatment set up at her bedside. Her lungs were still congested, but the first stages of pneumonia were under control, and her doctor at the hospital said it should be subsiding shortly. That evening, Gen had stopped at her own house to get a few things before coming out to the ranch.

When Gen arrived, she went upstairs to make sure Yancy was tucked in. After bringing Yancy a light bedtime snack on a tray, Gen kissed her and turned to leave the room.

"Hey, where're you going?" Yancy's surprised look stopped Gen.

Still at the door, Gen replied, "I can't sleep with you. You're all tied up with oxygen and breathing equipment. I'll just be next door in the guest room."

Yancy pouted. "Man, what good is it if this knockout of a doctor is at my house for a sleepover, and she's not sleeping with me?"

Gen came back to the bed, laughing. "Okay, girlfriend, it's been a long day. Get some sleep. I'll see you in the morning. We'll get Connie on board with the treatments before I leave. Don't make me come in here to keep you in line." She kissed her hair.

ᘏᘏᘏᘏ

By the end of the week, Yancy was doing much better, due to the bronchial treatments to which her lungs responded well. Gen had stayed overnight all week, while during the day Connie had supported the therapies Yancy required at home.

Early on Friday evening, Gen walked into the house carrying a large suitcase. She tiptoed to the couch, leaned down, and, finding a sleeping Yancy, took her suitcase upstairs. She came back down into the kitchen and located Connie's supper instructions on the countertop. After sliding a casserole into the oven from the refrigerator, she poured a glass from the open bottle of Merlot sitting on the counter. She took her wine into the great room to relax in a club chair with today's paper.

After several minutes, brown eyes opened

slightly. Yancy yawned. "Hey, what's up, Doc?"

"Funny, Bugs Bunny." Gen sipped her wine. "It's about time for some food."

"I'm not very hungry."

"You don't have your appetite back yet?"

"If you come over here and kiss me, I might feel better." She grinned lasciviously.

Gen put her wineglass down and scooted onto the couch next to Yancy, taking her in her arms and kissing her. "We need to talk. Are you up to it?"

"I know, and no." Yancy scrunched her face in distaste.

"Not your favorite thing, talking about emotional stuff."

"No, you've got it wrong, darlin'. I don't mind talking, as long as you lead the discussion. And do most of the talking." Yancy laughed at her own joke.

Gen playfully swatted her, shaking her head.

Yancy huffed. "We need to talk about my bad behavior." Yancy squared herself to look directly at Gen. "I was a jerk. I was thinking for both of us, like Dr. Foster says I do. I decided that you were going to be upset that I was in the hospital. That I hadn't taken care of myself or something. I got scared, so didn't call you. Then I ignored your calls, because I couldn't figure how to explain it all to you. I really screwed up, I'm really, really sorry."

"Now you've got it all wrong. There was nothing you could do to prevent the aftereffects of inhaling smoke. It is what it is."

"Really?" Yancy pondered Gen's words. "I didn't screw up?"

"The effects of inhaling any foreign substance can wipe out your lungs' ability to fight off bacteria or viruses. I don't think you screwed up, at least not about this." She tickled Yancy's ribs. "Unless you damaged your lungs by smoking tobacco or weed."

"Hey, no tickling." Yancy squirmed. "I should never have told you I was ticklish." She looked at Gen seriously, then. "I should have called you instead of Roxie, shouldn't I?"

"You and Roxie have been friends forever, and I would never get in the way of that. But, yes. As soon as you were headed to the hospital, I should have known, too. Other than not wanting me to be upset, was there some other reason that you shut me out?"

Yancy took Gen's hand and stroked it. "I thought you might think I was too much trouble. That I was being irresponsible again. That you would tell me you couldn't do it again."

"Do what?"

"Be with someone who couldn't take care of themselves."

"Oh, sweetheart," Gen said tenderly. "You can't take care of yourself."

"Hey! I think I've come a long way. I'm doing much better." Yancy squinted her eyes at Gen. "And since when are you the poster girl for self-care? You work awful hours, you eat stuff out of the vending machine. Yes. I've seen those wrappers in your office waste basket." Yancy nudged her shoulder. "So, don't go high and mighty on me."

They both laughed.

"Let's eat," Gen said, nuzzling Yancy's neck, then pulled her up to help get supper on the table.

# Chapter Twenty-three

The twelve-foot tree twinkled with matching red lights and bows. Spruce aroma, from the tree and two wreathes above the mantel, graced the air, while quiet Christmas music floated around the group gathered in the large living room where Nina had assembled her family. Aside from Philip and his family, and Yancy and Gen, Paul and Juliette Lambert also were there, having flown in from Kentucky the day before. They were to spend Christmas Eve with Yancy's family in Denver, then drive with Yancy and Gen back to the ranch early Christmas Day.

A crackling fire warmed the room, in front of which the adults sat on overstuffed chairs and a leather couch, conversing lightly and sipping hot drinks. In this after-dinner moment, Phil's two children, aged four and seven, shook wrapped boxes under the tree, hardly able to contain themselves in anticipation of opening gifts.

Gen sat next to Yancy, one hand languidly stroking the hand resting in Gen's lap, and drank her spicy mulled wine.

Paul Lambert was not a big man, but he was a good six feet tall, with a slight belly and thinning gray hair. He drank the warming spiced liquid with obvious pleasure, then addressed Yancy. "I understand from Gen you have built a very successful rural health center. You must be proud of that."

"My dad and mom were the instigators of it all, after my brother Ryan's death. My dad especially felt the community needed some primary care presence, so he created a board to raise funds. It opened nearly twenty years ago."

"Mary Ann has been at the board helm for three years now. She's overseen several new grants and brought in another foundation's funding." Nina gazed lovingly at her daughter.

"You have two separate clinics, right?"

Both Yancy and Gen nodded.

"And do you have training in health policy?" Juliette asked Yancy sweetly. Her auburn hair had several gray streaks, her green eyes letting Yancy know without doubt who her daughter was. She was remarkably fit, her black trousers closely hugged her slim hips, and her breasts filled out a blue, wool turtleneck. Her eyes glittered in the light of the fire. Yancy could see the younger Gen reflected there.

"I have business training and picked up the health side over the years. Dad insisted that if I was to help with the clinic, I should get involved in the rural health association. It's been a good training ground for me." Yancy was relaxed with Gen's parents, liking their easy way, their friendly manner. Even though they had lived all over the world, they fit effortlessly into Nina's house with the Delaney clan.

After the children had opened their presents, Phil and his wife Megan said their good-byes, citing Santa Claus's impending arrival and overtired kids. Nina led them to the door, and, when she returned, announced that it was time to get ready to go to Christmas Eve at St. John's Cathedral. "All of you are invited, but don't feel you have to join me," she graciously said.

After dressing up for midnight mass, they all piled into Yancy's Rover. Yancy had not been to the Episcopal Cathedral since her teens. When they arrived and took their seats in a pew together, Yancy was moved by how the lights and smells of Christmas brought back all the memories of going to midnight mass as a family. She remembered her and her brothers being very tired when they returned home in crisp air, the moon glinting off snow sprinkled along the road.

Hearing the hymns during the service that had given her such pleasure in her youth encouraged her to carry out her plan for Christmas Day. Gen stood next to her, singing the verses of "O, Come, All Ye Faithful." Yancy gave her a wink and loving smile.

When they got home around 1:30 a.m., the familiar Christmas service fresh in their minds and its musical strains of "Silent Night" and "Joy to the World" still reverberating in their ears, everyone trudged up to bed. As she mindlessly stroked Gen's arm in the dark, Yancy quietly hummed Christmas carols. "Do you think you might like the Episcopal church?"

"Huh?" Gen answered sleepily. "Yeah, it's a nice change from Holy Family. The priest said some good things, I thought, about peace and loving our neighbors. About being in the world as if God was love, not judgment. I like that Episcopalians ordain women and gay people, too. I noticed the diversity of the priests serving at the altar tonight."

"Do you think you would want to go back?"

Gen yawned. "Where is all this coming from?"

"Nothing. I would like to have a place to practice my faith. It struck me all of a sudden, remembering my childhood there. There's a comfort, or something, that I've been missing." Yancy snuggled against Gen.

ॐॐॐॐ

Nina served a light brunch the next morning. Yancy drank a mimosa, and ate fruit and a scone, washing it down with two cups of coffee. After they finished, Gen, her parents, and Yancy loaded the car to zip home to the ranch.

"You can bunk up here." Yancy led Paul and Juliette up to the blue guest room.

"This is a beautiful house and setting," Juliette remarked as they climbed the stairs behind Yancy. "You're so lucky to have this lovely home and the breathtaking views of the mountains."

Yancy smiled in gratitude for Juliette's comments. "You get settled, then we can meet downstairs to unwrap presents. Gen has a light snack for us around noon, but we'll have our main Christmas dinner at four."

Juliette took Yancy's hand before she turned back down the hallway. Those green shimmering Lambert eyes held Yancy in thrall. "I hope you know how very happy Paul and I are that you are in Gen's life."

Yancy stuffed her free hand in her pocket. "I'm glad she's in my life. In fact, she kind of saved my life."

"Oh?" Juliette raised her brow.

"Yeah," Yancy continued. "I was in a funk for a couple of years, and not doing so well when Gen arrived. We got off to a bad start. But, well…"

"Mm, hmm."

"Anyway." Yancy was flustered with the attention from Gen's mom. "She definitely is a wonderful woman. I feel like I'm the lucky one to have her in my life." Yancy exhaled, happy to have been able to spit out her sentiments.

Paul walked out of the guest bedroom, into the hall, to his wife and Yancy. Both Paul and Juliette took Yancy up in their arms, in a small group hug. Yancy squirmed a little.

Just then Gen arrived at the top of the stairs and caught them, giggling. Yancy looked over Juliette's shoulder, her eyes pleading.

"Okay, let's break up this love fest," Gen announced. Her parents turned to her, released Yancy, and laughed good-naturedly.

≈≈≈≈≈

Christmas Day sped by in a warm Christmas spirit. Presents were ripped open, a savory goose with all the trimmings and some glasses of Burgundy were consumed, and scintillating conversation kept them happily occupied. Yancy gave and received loving looks from Gen all day, which she was sure Gen's parents had noticed.

Yancy felt comfortable and relaxed. After a long day, they sat before the fire with coffee and Connie's pumpkin pie, chatting about Kentucky.

"Gen tells us you spent some time in Europe when you were younger." Paul and Juliette focused on Yancy.

The story of Yancy's internship in France was relayed and the conversation turned to their joint fondness of France.

"Would you ever want to return to live there?" Juliette asked.

Gen and Yancy looked at each other. "I don't know. I've been tied to Colorado for most of my adult life, it never occurred to me. My French is not nearly as fluent as it once was. What do you think, Gen? Would you want to live in France?"

"I don't think it's the place for me. I am pretty tied to Colorado, too, wouldn't you say?" They grinned at each other like the lovers they were.

Juliette asked Gen, "Do you think you will stay in Colorado for a while?"

"I want to," Gen answered, glancing at Yancy. "If the board approves my next pay raise, especially." She grinned.

Yancy chuckled. She put a finger on her chin in mock seriousness. "I don't know. I hear the medical director is sleeping with the board president. Sounds like a conflict of interest to me."

"You've got a point there." Paul raised his brows and smirked.

"Mom, will you come look at my recipe for tomorrow's dinner? I've never made this tartine before." Gen and Juliette left for the kitchen.

Yancy frowned at Paul. "I have thought about this conflict of interest thing, too. But I have some ideas about how to take care of it."

"I hope you can without disturbing your board or your relationship," he answered. Paul yawned, then, and called out to his wife that he was going upstairs. Gen and she came from the kitchen, and Gen's parents said their good nights.

❧❧❧❧

Yancy looked into Gen's face expectantly. She hopped up, and began to turn off lamps around the great room, leaving only the fire and Christmas tree to light the room, then lit several votive candles and punched two buttons to bring up Christmas jazz from her wireless speaker.

From the comfort of the couch, Gen watched her scurry around the room. "Come back here. What are you up to?"

Yancy grinned charmingly. "Just one more thing." She bounded up the stairs and was gone for some minutes, leaving Gen to relax in the warmth of the fireplace. When she came back down, Yancy wore a Santa hat, a white tuxedo shirt with a red bow tie, and her black jeans.

Gen laughed to see her. "You look pretty cute, my rancher-elf."

Yancy went to her on the couch, but instead of sitting, she took both of Gen's hands, tugging her up to dance. She held Gen close, swaying to the quiet strains of music in the flickering firelight and muted light of the Christmas tree. She kissed Gen's neck, while Gen's arms surrounded her shoulders and pulled them closer together.

When the song finished, she pressed Gen away smoothly and looked her in the eye, then dropped down on one knee. Gen's eyes got wide. *My god!*

Yancy cleared her throat. "Gen, darlin', I uh." She cleared her throat again slightly, then took a big cleansing breath. Gen looked on, amused, but not wanting to make things easier on her lover.

"I have something." Yancy dug into her jeans pocket and brought out a small box. She looked at Gen with tears. She opened the box containing a sparkling ring and presented it to Gen. "I would be honored if you...I mean...Would spend the rest of your life with me? I love you so much."

Gen's eyes welled up in love. Tenderness gathered in her heart as she gazed at Yancy, swallowing her tears.

"Don't tell me that you're speechless, for once?" Yancy interrupted the serious moment. They both laughed a little giddily.

Yancy slid the gold band set with a single emerald onto the tip of Gen's ring finger. By this time both Gen and Yancy had tears coursing down their cheeks. Gen pulled Yancy up from her knee, embraced her, then caressed her cheek softly, whispering, "Yes, my love. Yes."

Yancy continued to hold Gen's hand and settled the ring completely on her finger. They danced, smiling like idiots, until they could no longer hold in their passion.

After a night of sweet coming together, they spent the next morning announcing their engagement to one and all. First were Gen's parents, who were very pleased, and much hugging ensued. Then they phoned all of Yancy's people who needed to be informed.

Yancy's mother cried. "My darling girl. I'm so happy for you. You've got the love of a wonderful woman in Gen."

Roxie whooped into the phone, making Yancy pull back to protect her ears. "It's about time, Studly!" she hollered. "Kate, come quick. I've got something to tell you." After a moment, she was back. "Have you set a date? Where is it going to be?"

"Hold on. For Christ's...for Pete's sake we've been engaged for only twelve hours. Back off."

"Well I want to be the first one you let in on the arrangements. Oh, man, will we have some fun!"

Kate's voice sounded into the phone. "Congratulations, buddy!"

"Love you guys." Yancy ended the call.

After Yancy's final call, to Phil, Gen sidled up next to her. "You've got me now. Does that mean you will quit doubting yourself, get yourself into gear, and take care of yourself?"

With an evil grin, Yancy took Gen in her arms, "No way, babe. That's your job!"

Gen shook her head and playfully slapped her arm. They kissed deeply.

*I think I have my life back, and then some,* Yancy thought, wearing the biggest smile she could manage.

# *About the Author*

JB "Joey" Marsden wrote her first short story at age ten, but, needing to make a living, spent many years writing academic tomes that no one enjoyed reading. Now, having finished her first published novel, she has realized her childhood dream.

JB lives on her family farm in rural Illinois, where she grew up, after living in urban areas in upstate New York, Michigan, and Kentucky. Her wife and sisters surround her with loving support and compete with her in rousing card games. Aside from writing, JB enjoys reading, outdoor sports and activities, and classic movies. Even though she can be found most often basking in the quiet of rural living, she travels for work and fun both in the U.S. and abroad.

Contact info:
Facebook: facebook.com/joeybmarsden
Instagram: joeybmarsden

CPSIA information can be obtained
at www.ICGtesting.com
Printed in the USA
LVOW10s2022200218

567274LV00004B/799/P

9 781948 232043